S

S

Over 100
Great Novels
of
Erotic Domination

If you like one you will probably like the rest

New Titles Every Month

If you want to be on our confidential mailing list for our Readers' Club Magazine (with extracts from past and forthcoming titles) write to:

SILVER MOON READER SERVICES

The Shadowline Building
6 Wembley Street
Gainsborough
DN21 2AJ
United Kingdom
or
sales@babash.com

or telephone
01427 816710
(UK office hours only)

NEW AUTHORS WELCOME

Please send submissions to
Silver Moon Books Ltd.
PO Box 5663
Nottingham
NG3 6PJ
or
editor@babash.com

SLAVEWORLD

BY

STEPHEN DOUGLAS

ALSO BY STEPHEN DOUGLAS
ROYAL SLAVE
SLAVE SCHOOL
SLAVEWORLD EMBASSY

ONE
ROYAL HUNTING PRESERVE
(SOUTHERN ENGLAND)

THE ROYAL HUNTING PRESERVE, mile after mile of gently rolling grassland dotted with ornamental lakes and small strategically placed copses for cover, was criss-crossed with paved paths. Harnessed and bridled slaves pulling their owners in lightweight two-wheeled pony-traps could manage a decent off-road sprint if well whipped, and could walk on grass forever, but for that easy long-distance ground-eating trot, you needed tarmac under your wheels. Prey would not be found on the edges of the preserve.

The Prince of Wales flicked his whip over his ponies' rolling buttocks, toned hard muscle flexing and flowing under dark whip-marked flesh and in pumping thighs. Both Nubian pony-boys were breathing hard, a nice sheen of sweat gleaming on muscular bodies but they were keeping the pace he set them easily. Possibly if asked, neither would have described their pace as easy, but which owner worthy of the name would ever consider asking? A good owner could judge his or her slave's limits for themselves, and push the slave beyond them.

The pair was a present from their country's King, beautifully trained, with excellent tongues and big heavy cocks. His father the King had returned the compliment with a team of four full-breasted blond pony-girls which the African monarch frequently drove in public. Both had been branded with a small crown high on the right thigh; a privilege of the purple. Other owners had to tattoo their marks on their property, the hot iron being reserved for royalty.

The blinkered pony-boys' harnesses jingled merrily as they trotted, both fitted with ass-stretching butt-plugs, tight cock and ball straps and with rings set through their navels and the heads of their cocks. Both had the tips of their erections chained to their bellies with short lengths of chain. It prevented

5

the heavy shafts waggling about untidily and tormented the desperately hard slaves to distraction.

Prince Samuel frowned, seeing a pony-trap pulled up onto the grass ahead. He vaguely recognised the heavy-breasted pony-girl and the Lady holding her bridle from the assembly area, but the field behind the tavern had been crowded and chaotic. How surprising! Not that a single pony-girl had matched his pair for distance; the slip of a girl driving probably weighed less than half his sixteen stone, but that the pampered looking pony-girl had been driven near two miles in such a short time.

It was a source of some regret to the Prince that the Royal hunts were becoming as much social events as debutante balls were. More and more eligible young Ladies, driving pampered toys that belonged in a dressage ring or on a hitching rail in front of a Swiss finishing school, were contriving to get invited to what had once been a serious hunt.

It was understandable of course. The hunt was where the eligible young men were, and any noble could put their name on the Chamberlain's unofficial rota and be invited in their turn. But it was irritating to a serious hunter nonetheless. Even his mother, normally one of the most placid of people, but an ardent hunter, had been moved to have a word with the Chamberlain.

Prince Samuel pulled his pair off the path and onto the grass opposite the naked pony-girl standing between the shafts of a black-lacquered and gold-leaf decorated dressage pony-trap and the Lady tending her. He'd seen the young looking Lady and her hack in the assembly area, but had dismissed her as one of the simpering husband hunters. Looking properly for the first time, he saw that the top-heavy pony, despite her ornate dressage tack and tits that belonged in a show-ring, was a big powerful girl. She'd been fitted with proper running slippers instead of a show-pony's 3" heels.

"Sir," the Lady acknowledged with an abbreviated curtsy as he holstered his whip and stepped out of his pony-trap.

He wasn't at all offended. The hunt wasn't the place for formality, and the Lady was busy. In fact she was quite intriguingly busy. She'd unbuckled her pony-girl's bit, now hanging from one side of her bridle, and was holding up a large plastic squeeze-bottle, about two pints, to her slave's lips.

The harnessed young slave, buttocks well striped and with her arms strapped behind her wrist to elbow, head up and ankles neatly together, was gulping frantically as a slimy, off-white gelatinous substance was squeezed and poured into her mouth. He could see her throat flexing against a too-tight bridle collar as she swallowed. Even more fascinating, her stomach actually seemed to bulge around the indentations caused by a corset-tight girth, a mere brutal eighteen inches, and a crotch-strap pulled up hard between her sex-lips digging into her belly.

"That's a nice animal you've got there," he said conversationally. "Is that real semen you're feeding her?"

"Yes Sir. Good protein. Walk her for fifteen minutes to settle her and she'll be ready to trot all day. It's Lady Isobell by the way. I was presented at Court four seasons back."

"Yes of course," he agreed.

A tactful reminder. He hadn't had a clue who she was. The young-looking Lady was short, delicately slender, the top of her head only just reaching her pony-girl's shoulder, looking very smart in a dark velvet riding jacket and cream jodhpurs, another reason he'd mistaken her for a husband hunter. Serious hunters tended to dress a little more casual on the Royal hunt; it showed you were in the know. She looked about twenty but could have been in her forties with rejuvenation treatments. Her lovely slave, sweat gleaming on her flanks, and not just sweat he saw; her juices were running down the insides of her thighs, was probably just the twenty or so she looked.

Lady Isobell capped the now empty bottle and tossed it into the seat of her pony-trap. The pony-girl quivered in pleasure when her over-large breasts were given an approving squeeze, and was perfectly docile as her young-looking owner re-fitted her with a vicious looking bit.

As well a chain running from her second set of reins to each pierced nipple down through the rings on either side of her bit; a good yank of the nipple-rings usually being enough to keep the most spirited girl on track, this slave's bit was combined with a tongue-clamp. It was a dressage device, so that a tug on the reins not only yanked the desired nipple and pulled the pony-slave's head to one side, but yanked her tongue to one side as well.

"I've never seen a clamp-bit with pins in it before," he said as the Lady pulled out the girl's tongue. The docile slave whined softly, a low keening wail of distress forced from her, as her Mistress screwed the clamp down tight on her tongue, and dozens of tiny pins sank into both sides of the thick muscle. Gingerly she closed even white teeth over what now looked like a perfectly normal clamp-bit.

"It's a special order," Lady Isobell explained, stepping back and looking over her helplessly harnessed charge with satisfaction. "Not for control you understand, she's very willing to please, quite docile; but I find I enjoy her more, and she responds better to pain rather than kindness."

"Of course," he agreed. "A natural?"

"Oh yes," the aristocrat replied with a faint cruel smile, her eyes on the rise and fall of her pony-girl's large breasts. "Not only does she love me, but of course I can keep her in an almost permanent state of arousal. So she was ridiculously easy to obedience-train. I've had her tell me, hooked to a lie-detector, that whatever I do to her is a privilege and deserved."

She must have caught the faint "So what?" look on his face. Once they'd been broken in, all slaves loved their servitude, begging and tears not unusual when it came time to release them.

"She was only just out of basic training then," the aristocrat said with a sly smile. "Do feel free to handle her if you wish."

Prince Samuel nodded his thanks, running his fingers

through a thick, dark, shiny ponytail with copper highlights pulled back by the slave's bridle. All slaves could be trained to a suitable level of subservience, and turning a girl into a bitch-on-heat, forcing her to sexual arousal, was just a case of aphrodisiacs surgically implanted in the body. But a natural submissive, a masochist, was a rare prize. The girl shivered just the tiniest little bit when he stroked her marked buttocks, his free hand hefting a deliciously heavy breast. Show-ponies were top-heavy with wasp-waists, dressage rules requiring a bust measurement twice the girth size, but he realised that this slave, while superbly proportioned and edibly sexy, would never get a winner's rosette pinned to her breast in a show-ring. She was too tall, too big, to compete with those dainty toys; over 5'10" he guessed. The ideal dressage-slave was a cute little thing of 5 foot, never more than 5'2". A pity. She deserved an audience.

Clearly quality merchandise; the placid brunette's flesh was flawless, warm, soft velvet in his palm. He nodded appreciation to the lovely toy's owner. The power and stamina of a hunting-hack combined with the looks, sex-appeal and meticulous training of a show-pony wasn't a new idea, but was a hard one to bring off. Lady Isobell seemed to have managed though, if her impressive-looking mount could last the hunt. Funny, only yesterday he'd been agreeing with his mother that a pony-girl with tits this big had no place on a hunt.

"So I was ordering our village harness-maker to run up some pin-lined tit-straps," Lady Isobell continued, "And I suddenly thought to myself, why not the bit as well?"

"Ingenious," the Prince of Wales agreed.

The golden-skinned pony-girl's large heavy breasts were of course tightly bound. He noticed now what he'd taken for a double row of decorative studs on the outside of the thick straps buckled around the base of each full globe, were pin-bases; though there were none in the thinner criss-crossed supporting straps of her harness. Lady Isobell stroked the bulging tightly-strapped melons with evident pleasure, and then let her fingernails trail down either side of the crotch-strap digging deep into her tit-tortured plaything's belly.

"I've got pins lining the inside of her crotch-strap as well," the aristocrat confided, clearly proud of her pony-slave, and delighted at his interest. "Almost up to the clitoris."

"But not on it," Prince Samuel agreed.

They exchanged knowing smiles. The trick was as old as pony-girls. A tight crotch-strap provided a light pressure against the slave's clitoris as she trotted, but lubricated by sweat and the slave's own juices, very little friction. Frustrating stimulation without release, but necessary of course. A hot and wet slave-girl took the whip better and was far more eager to please than a pony-girl who'd been allowed an orgasm.

"And from the way her juices are running I'd hazard a nice big dildo?" he guessed.

"Not that big, but it's got flexible spines, and a fat plug up her ass," the aristocrat agreed happily. She patted her pony-girl's dildo-stuffed belly, the lovely slave quite defenceless in the tight straps and locks of her tack, hitched to the little two-wheeled carriage until her owner decided otherwise. "Nicely filled, but not as stretched as some of the poles I've mounted her on. Isn't that right, Treasure?'

The naked pony-girl whinnied obediently around her stretched and clamped tongue and was rewarded with another breast-squeeze. Her eyes, an attractive light hazel, wide and innocent, were glazed with lust.

"Poor little Treasure," she teased. "You're dripping wet aren't you? Desperate to come? And you know I can prance you around all day without letting you don't you?"

The tall, velvet-skinned slave groaned in forced lust, the sound a mixture of helpless despair and longing; and a plea for mercy, when her petite owner squeezed her bound breasts harder. The Prince of Wales quite understood the glee in Lady Isobell's voice. He loved sex himself, passionately, urgently, didn't think he'd ever get enough, so controlling the sex-lives

10

of others was a singular pleasure. Property was not only used and enjoyed when, where and how the owner wished, but could be forced to arousal or could be denied the pleasure it craved and begged for. Masturbation was forbidden, orgasm a privilege that the slave was never allowed to refuse.

"Sensors?" he asked.

Lady Isobell nodded agreement. There were of course no visible scars, vets catering to the slave-trade were highly skilled or they were back in the hovel they came from, treating peasants, but the coin-shaped surgically implanted devices would have been attached to the brunette's skull at the temples. Set to measure a specific brainwave pattern, any orgasm would be detected and recorded on the owner's personal computer.

"She's never once tried to masturbate without permission," the aristocrat said, brushing the pony-slave's long fringe out of her eyes, "But she loves sex so much she did used to sometimes come spontaneously when I first started working her. I've mostly trained her out of that now. Obedient sex-toys only have orgasms when they're told to. Don't they, Treasure?"

The hazel-eyed slave-girl, placidly enduring being intimately handled by a complete stranger as well as her owner, gave another obedient whinny.

"You've got her nicely broken in," he complimented. "I must admit when I first saw her I thought she was a show-pony. You know, top-heavy, a wasp-waist, the nipple-bar, the dressage tack?"

The nipple-bar was just that. A metal rod with a screw-down clamp at each end that linked the pony-girl's nipples. It was a dressage device, used to make neater the performances of top-heavy show-ponies whose big breasts tended to swing and bounce untidily when compared to the average racing-pony, hunting-hack or carriage-slave. Simply, it was a device to make tits swing neatly together, though he'd never seen one on a hunter before. It was also, he knew, having trained a show-pony or two himself in his time, a quite severe nipple-

11

torture for a heavy breasted girl.

"They are quite huge aren't they?" Lady Isobell agreed happily hefting her pony's spectacular breasts. The bound globes, trailing reins from nipple-rings and with the fat tortured nubs linked by the nipple-bar, looked like footballs in her small hands. "She was a bit small up top before she was collared and tattoo-branded. Waist was much too thick as well, and I had to have her legs stretched a bit. Her face was okay; I just had to lighten the colour of her eyes a little. She actually belonged to my stepmother originally, but she left me to do the body-sculpting. And to be honest, I've always liked tits! I was just ordering the vet to make a pillow-slave really, though she obviously had a pony-girl in her. But the first time I saw her in harness, being carriage-trained, I just knew I was looking at a superb hunting-hack."

The aristocrat idly stroked her pony-girl between the legs, toying with the base of the dildo that impaled her. Blinkered eyes half-closed in pleasure.

"And people, mostly old people, keep telling me she's not suitable to hunt! Some people are just so set in their ways! Of course you can't hunt a show-pony; they haven't got the stamina, but that doesn't mean you can't hunt any big-titted pony. Now I've got her trained, she's a superb hack, and once people stop disapproving and start looking, they usually end up asking to buy her. You'd be surprised at how many offers I've had."

The Prince thought he might not be. The long-legged pony-slave, powerfully built but beautifully proportioned, was on closer examination a magnificent beast; quite gorgeous standing proudly tamed in her bonds. He imagined her spread-eagled across his own bed with taut chains. Some rides you just knew were going to be especially satisfying.

"As for her waist? Well, the same reason as a show-pony. A wasp-waist looks good, which is far more important than Treasure's comfort. Isn't it pet?" The dildo-impaled, tongue-clamped pony-girl, prompted by her owner giving her abused breasts another squeeze, whinnied obedient agreement. "She was a bit breathless to start with of course, but a few hours on a treadmill in full harness every day for the last couple of months has improved her lung capacity no end. Hasn't it, Treasure?"

Lady Isobell planted a light kiss on each of her mount's straining breasts. Prince Samuel smiled indulgently. The petite aristocrat was obviously not husband hunting, here to hunt and proudly show off her property. Besides, it was nice to see somebody so unselfconsciously enjoying a slave; himself, he worried about becoming jaded. Happily for the smartly dressed aristocrat her top-heavy brunette looked like she'd be able to endure a lot of being enjoyed.

"Oh, sorry Sir, I'm prattling on," she belatedly realised.

"Not at all, you've got her trained nicely. I'd be happy to own her." He admired the lush young slave's harnessed curves, her pretty bridle-framed face, her long, long legs and the raised welts criss-crossing the firm swell of her buttocks. "Would you care to hunt with me?"

"Oh, thank you. I mean, yes, of course."

They set off at a walk into the grasslands with occasional trots to keep the ponies limber. Prince Samuel found it very restful to be in the company of an attractive young woman who obviously wasn't angling, except maybe in daydreams, to be the next Queen of England. Just sharing a perfect day.

And more and more as the day went by, he found himself admiring the straps digging into her mount's large heavy breasts, the way the placid pony-slave's broad girth nipped her waist tight and emphasised the flare of her hips; and the delicious roll of her whip-marked buttocks as she pranced, bisected by another tight strap pulled up between them. Lady Isobell was using her whip and reins more than necessary, amusing herself teasing and tormenting the helpless and helplessly aroused pony-girl. Despite which the bridled girl wasn't at all twitchy, placidly leaning into her harness, she barely flinched and made no attempt to shy away when a whip-stroke, warning or teasing, hissed through the air. Only when her legal owner's lash actually landed on her perfect haunches did she gasp, the hands buckled behind her clench into fists. He did like a girl that took good whip!

A hunter crested a gentle ridge far to their left, and politely angled away. Hunter's etiquette. You didn't crowd another sportsman unless invited or responding to a hunting-horn. In the brief glimpse he got he thought he recognised his aunt's considerable bulk and her familiar team of four matched blondes. She'd let him use two of the four sexually the night before last, but they'd just been flesh. Today he wouldn't be able to pick them out of a pack.

He let his eyes stray back to the much more rewarding sight of Lady Isobell's ride's swaying hips, remembering again the pleasing weight of breast in his hand, the velvet-soft of her belly. Slaves were strange creatures. You could use one, and then another, a dozen, and feel no emotional attachment whatsoever. Just a couple of hour's strenuous physical pleasure, the girl forgotten before your semen was even dry on her body. And then, just when you thought you really were getting jaded, one like this came along. And you wanted to know her name, lick every inch of her body and train her to adore you!

Prince Samuel smiled dreamily. His favourite method of enjoying a female slave was doggie-style, the girl hooded and controlled with a choke-chain. He had a breast-clamp with attached wrist-cuffs, which having been designed for top-heavy pillow-slaves he'd never imagined using on a hunter, but which would fit the impressive brunette a treat.

"Have you considered training her to wrestle?" he asked. "She's got the size and weight. The European Mud Wrestling Championships are being held in Londinium this year. I'm the patron."

Lady Isobell gave an apologetic smile. "I'm afraid I've never been very interested in sports. Except for racing," she shrugged.

14

"How much did you pay for her?" he started to ask, but the aristocrat's suddenly urgent voice cut him off.

"There! Movement in that wood!"

It was about mid-day. They'd heard a couple of hunting-horns in the distance, but too far away to bother with. Suddenly he saw a flash of pale skin between the trees.

"Go right!" he called, raising his horn.

Lady Isobell's pony-girl squealed in pain at a vicious double lash across her hindquarters, and lunged forward against the burden of pony-trap and Mistress. The top-heavy pony fairly flew up the gentle slope, squeaking in high-pitched yelps each time her driver's whip caught her, her owner not just lashing her haunches, but skilfully curling the long carriage-whip around her body to bite into the soft flesh of her belly and between her legs.

Prince Samuel nodded approvingly to himself. The lovely slave's agonised cries would send chills down the prey-slaves spines. You just couldn't get that desperate high-pitched yelp out of a pony-boy. He whipped his own pair into a gentle trot, stalking, now that Lady Isobell was placed to cut off the open ground to the right, the nearest cover a small forest over a hundred yards away. In the shallow valley in front of him were scattered a dozen small but dense copses, some with no more than twenty yards between them. An answering hunting-horn echoed from somewhere ahead.

The first instinct of the slaves they hunted was to hide in thick cover, but prey knew in the open they had the pace and endurance to outstrip their hunter's burdened ponies. The trick was to cut them off from open ground or flush them into another hunter's gun. Reinforcements pounded in from the left, the yelps and cries of well-whipped pony-slaves and the crack of leather on flesh announcing their approach. The Prince of Wales waved acknowledgement, recognising an experienced hunter. The German ambassador's wife was driving a muscular blond pony-boy. Her son on his first hunt was driving a pair of svelte racing pony-girls. Another horn sounded and he replied.

"Tally ho!"

Realising he was being surrounded, a slave-boy made a desperate dash for open ground. The young German Count didn't even pull up his ponies, just angled them to one side, firing at the gallop. He dropped the slave-boy in his tracks before he'd gone a dozen yards. Nice shooting! Though his mother had been better placed to take the shot, she'd let her son have the slave, he saw.

A full-breasted blonde, puppy-fat plump, breasts swinging and bouncing prettily, broke cover in a frantic dash. The naked slave had her wrists fastened behind her to prevent tree-climbing and a mesh visor, like wrap-around sunglasses, buckled into place to protect her eyes. Prince Samuel pulled his rifle from its scabbard. She wasn't nearly as well endowed as Lady Isobell's spectacular pony, but still a very nice little handful. She was going to be a pleasant screw when the successful hunters gathered at the evening's hunt-orgy. It was always satisfying to enjoy a slave you'd hunted.

He pulled up his ponies, sighting carefully. The tranquilliser dart-gun had a range of near two-hundred yards, but even in expert hands was only accurate below a hundred, most hunters preferring a fifty yard shot. The prey-slaves were aware of this. As well as the ability to outrun their hunters, it gave them an additional sporting chance. Only one or two slaves a decade evaded ten hunts and won their freedom, but the knowledge that it was possible made them run all the harder. And of course provided greater sport for the hunters.

About a hundred and twenty yards! He squeezed off two bursts of three darts. The blonde shrieked in panic, stumbled, and came up running.

"Tally ho!"

Prince Samuel looked up from his sights. Damn! The ambassador's wife and her son, both dismounted to hog-tie the Count's prize, were firing at long range at another pair. It was of course beneath their dignity to give chase on foot. He slammed his rifle back into its scabbard and lashed his black ponies into a sprint, both responding with pleasing gasps of pain, leaving the blonde for Lady Isobell. This pair would have to slow, climbing the steeper bank to the valley's left. Bringing them into range for just long enough?

He brought the girl down with a nice single shot to the left buttock, but the male slave with her wasn't so elegant. Just as he was about to disappear over the ridgeline, the Prince emptied his magazine in a long burst, and got lucky. He looked back, but couldn't see through the trees, hoping Lady Isobell had brought down the blonde. He chuckled, the thought occurring that the short Lady did seem to be getting all the best tits to enjoy.

***

Heart pounding fit to burst, tears and snot streaming down her face and trying desperately hard not to sob or pant too loudly, Sally rolled and squirmed into damp soil, the dirt camouflage sticking to sweat on her shamefully naked body. She wriggled under a large fallen branch with some leaves still on it, some ferns providing additional cover.

She thought she'd left behind all but one of her hunters, a Lady driving a single pony-girl, in her mad dash for safety across open fields. The poor slave's shrill cries of pain as she'd been whipped into an exhausting sprint in pursuit of Sally, still echoed inside her head and wouldn't go away. Only bad girls were whipped! Sally was a good girl. But twigs and sharp stones pushed uncomfortably into her breasts flattened under her and her wrists pulled behind her back were bruised from the unyielding handcuffs. They'd taken away her robes and veil!

Sally had worn head to toe clothing all her life, but she knew only too well what a naked body looked like. Her Lord always trotted a pair of pony-girls through the village, leaving them hitched outside the courtroom, when he came to sit in judgement. She'd seen her own cousin, naked, on a lead, a pet for her Lord's daughter. And while the ex-slaves, her own father amongst them, rarely talked; traders, soldiers and those who worked at the big-house, were always ready to tell a curious teenager lurid tales of what went on.

She'd known it could never happen to her though. She was always polite, respectful, would never dream of going with a boy or touching herself; and slaves were all dirty, disobedient girls. Up until the barn fire, she'd known it would never be her. The Provost said the fire, a whole season's hay, was arson, village children playing with fire. Her Lord's judgement was that the village had to hand over 10 girls and 4 boys in reparations. She'd nearly escaped, only eighteen by two days when judgement was passed, but those two were two days too many. The Lady of the House had kept Sally's sister for her own use, the rest going to auction.

Sally froze when she heard a harsh panting, looking up through her visor, muddied hair and undergrowth. There was a jingling rattle of metal on metal, silence a moment, then a slapping noise. Slowly the pony-girl pulling her little two-wheeled carriage moved into view, a bare 25 yards away! The Lady driving the panting girl was working her way slowly and cautiously between the trees, sitting up on the back of the pony-trap's seat for a better view, rifle held upright, its butt resting in the crook of her arm.

She pulled her pony-girl to a halt with a tug of the reins in her left hand, the gasping slave's large breasts bobbing as her ringed nipples were yanked. The rattling noise Sally had heard was the chains linking the reins the Lady held to her property's nipple-rings, running through the rings on the ends of her bit. The aristocrat's eyes flicked over Sally's hiding place; and passed on! She slapped the leather reins against the harnessed slave's back; a signal to walk on.

Closer, Sally didn't dare breathe, but the Lady's attention was beyond her. She thought she'd already looked underfoot. The hunter was young, her sculptured face quite beautiful, but with a haughtily proud look a serf could only ever find

18

cruel and cold. Her neatly braided hair, crisp, clean clothing and unruffled appearance were staggeringly unfair, not even one bead of sweat dotted her perfect brow.

She pulled her panting, sweat-lathered pony to another halt; Sally was close enough to see how the hard-worked slave's nipples stretched cruelly when her reins were yanked again. The harnessed and bridled girl was drooling, slavering helplessly, as she gasped around her bit; saliva running down her chin and in rivulets over the bulging mounds of her tightly strapped breasts. The enormous globes, nipples joined with a bar, were purpling slightly, the straps so tight.

Sally had seen several pony-girls in her life, not just the Lord of the Manor's favourite pair. The Lady of the House and their only-child daughter could both frequently be seen exercising favourite hunting-hacks and racing-slaves in the fields and on the paths around the village. And any visitors wishing to explore had the use of the team of four big-breasted, dildo-stuffed pony-girls who pulled the larger four-wheeled carriage the family used to visit chapel on Sundays. Not only did the Lords and Ladies enjoy the use of their legal property, only using limousines for long distances, but it was a practical demonstration of what any serf who stepped out of line could expect. But she'd never seen a slave as hard used as this one.

The sweat-sheened pony-girl's girth looked like it was cutting her in two. Vicious whip-strokes had left welts curling around her hips and across the soft flesh of her belly, and Sally knew that the crotch-strap pulled up tight between her legs would be holding a fat dildo in place. Old Jake, the retired soldier who ran the village tavern, was fond of recounting the days when tacking up pony-slaves had been a part of his duties. Sally, at the time amused, now horrified, was only too well aware of what went into a pony-girl to give her the correct mental attitude. The poor thing had to really hate the cold, cruel woman who owned her.

Suddenly Sally realised the harnessed girl was looking directly into her eyes, the pony-girl's blinkered eyes widening in surprise as she realised what she was seeing. The Lady flicked her reins across her mount's shoulders again, but the slave harnessed to her carriage didn't move.

"Come on Treasure. Walk on!"

Another flick, but the pony-girl didn't move.

"Treasure! Walk on!" she was ordered.

Sally watched with sick horror, unable to comprehend why the abused slave was betraying her. With a sigh the Lady exchanged her rifle for a whip, and gave the helpless slave-girl a cruel slash across the buttocks.

The crack of leather on flesh was shockingly loud in the quiet forest clearing. For just a fraction of a second after the whip landed the pony-girl was still; then her eyes went wide, her nostrils flared and she squeaked in pain, lunging forward against her harness, teeth tight around her strange-looking bit. Then incredibly she held her head up again and put her ankles neatly together, tightly bound breasts heaving.

"Don't try me bitch!" the aristocrat warned menacingly. "Just because I've turned down a couple of offers to buy you, doesn't make you special. I'll decide when you've had enough!"

The harnessed girl cried out again as a vicious double-lash drove her forward three paces. Then sobbing helplessly, tears splashing onto her large heavy breasts to mingle with the saliva and sweat that already coated the strap-supported globes, she put her ankles together again. Sally remembered Jake the innkeeper slyly telling her and a group of breathless friends that the Lords and Ladies liked to see slave-girls sobbing. It made their tits wobble.

"Oh Treasure, you do love me. Good girl!"

Sally dragged her gaze away from the tortured slave, and straight into the eyes of her tormentor. The rifle was already coming up as she bolted out of cover, branches lashing her naked body. She felt a sting on her right buttock, and then the world span away. In a dreamy haze as she was hog-tied and radio-tagged for collection, her thoughts in cotton-wool, Sally was still bemused at her betrayal. By another slave!

***

Lungs on fire, gasping around her bit, legs like lead; lathered in and half-blinded by sweat, Treasure was trotted back up beside the two black pony-boys again, and with a painful tug to her nipples and tongue, was pulled back to a walk. Lost in a haze of lust, pain and exhaustion, she was incapable of rational thought, but her prime emotions were relief and satisfaction.

Mistress was pleased! Nothing else mattered, though it was nice to not have to trot for just a moment.

After she'd been walked a while—ten minutes, twenty, an hour? —her breathing was merely heavy. The dancing spots had faded from her vision, and the roaring from her ears, enough for her to hear her beloved Mistress chatting animatedly with her new friend. After a blow-by-blow account of the blonde's capture, her legal owner, having belatedly noticed his interest, was offering him her pony-girl's sexual use.

She didn't really mind heavy breathing, ever since her owner had once remarked casually in passing, that she liked seeing bound tits heaving. As for being lent to the hunter driving the black pair, well of course she'd have rather been reserved entirely for Lady Isobell's personal sexual use, but it wouldn't be an unusual or new experience. A sort of compliment in fact. Only well trained, subservient and sexually accomplished slave-girls were passed around. Inexperienced toys were likely to disgrace their owners. Once again Treasure reflected that knowing she'd been brainwashed didn't really help her in the slightest; she still couldn't help or prevent herself from loving her owner and wanting to please her. Leaning into her harness, the pressure against the straps constricting her body a familiar sensation, she savoured the weight of her beloved sat in the comfort of the pony-trap she pulled.

Treasure was dressage harnessed, too much of the weight

21

of the pony-trap she was hitched to on her nipped waist and crotch-strap; instead of spread to shoulders, hips and with hands cuffed to the shafts like a carriage or racing-pony. But her owner thought she looked sexy, and also liked a clean whip-swing, so she placidly accepted and endured the extra exertion and pain required. Pride was punished, frequently and painfully, but she knew her heavily enlarged breasts, tortured nipples, wasp-waist and the juices that so often ran down her thighs turned more heads than the average hack. And Treasure also knew, even when the love of her life was attaching sharp-jawed electrodes to her nipples and clitoris as a punishment for making a public spectacle of herself, that Lady Isobell really liked nothing better than to have her mount noticed.

She gasped as the aristocrat's whip licked lightly across her throbbing, burning-hot buttocks; just a light sting to keep her harnessed plaything alert and focused, Treasure not actually doing anything wrong. The tug on her reins to prevent her breaking into a trot was almost as painful. She yelped helplessly again, her legal owner flicking the whip across her hindquarters, simply because she could, and enjoyed it.

Treasure lived to be enjoyed! It was her whole purpose in life; the reason for her existence. Legally of course a slave existed for precisely that reason; to be used for the pleasure of her owners, but her own devotion went well beyond lip-service to the law. To Treasure, lip-service was being allowed the privilege of bringing her beloved to orgasm orally. She loved it when she was patted, stroked and praised and was quite content in her nudity and almost permanent physical restraints, because that was how the love of her life liked to enjoy her. She knew it was necessary that she suffer pain and humiliation, because that gave her owner pleasure, and had been told, and been trained to believe, that her most important function in life was to be used and enjoyed, helplessly bound, in cruel sexual games.

Another flick of the whip made her moan in mingled

pleasure and pain, her love reminding her sweat-sheened, panting toy of her instructions that morning, Treasure realised. She hoped the aristocrat's whip-arm wasn't too tired. Lady Isobell had been quite adamant she didn't want to have to exert herself on the hunt. Treasure squeaked as the lash was flicked up between her legs, braided leather biting into the soft sensitive flesh of her pussy, sex-lips plump around the strap that bisected them, and held in place the dildo and plug that were driving her mad!

In her wildest, wettest imaginings, before she'd become collared property, over two years ago now, she'd never dreamed, couldn't have imagined, that it was possible to be this hot, this aroused. So powerful was her all-consuming lust, she thought it might actually be possible to die of pleasure. But her mind was as well trained as her body now, and the implanted sensors at her temples always watched! No matter how desperate she became, she didn't think she was even capable of an orgasm in harness without her beloved's touch or permission any more. That realisation had pleased her owner no end; proof that Treasure had surrendered herself totally.

The really cruel bit was that no matter how intense, how shattering, how powerful the all-consuming orgasms she was made to experience now were, she was never really satisfied. There was never a sense of release. True satisfaction. The aphrodisiac implanted in her body, slowly dissolving into her bloodstream, kept her almost permanently on heat; a squeezed breast, a slap on the behind, even a barked command, and her nipples would obediently rise, her breasts would swell with lust, her juices would flow and the spark that never really went away would be fanned to a raging heat in her belly. From an owner's point of view, very convenient, because the slave was always ready to be used sexually, addicted to sex, and like any addict was further in the power of her supplier. But also like any addict, no matter how often she was made to come, it was never enough. Treasure always wanted more, and knew that only through obedience and subservience would she be allowed more of the sex she'd been made to crave.

And to think she'd once wondered at how docile slaves were! If she didn't so desperately love Lady Isobell, Treasure thought she might have gone quite mad. At least when she was bound, naked, and being made to cry out in pain or moan in pleasure, in public, she was submitting to her love, not just being used, like so many of the other toys. Treasure was intelligent, had once been highly educated, and was only too sadly, terrifyingly aware that the woman she adored was at best fond of her. At worst she was an interesting diversion, who would be sold when boredom set in. It made her strive harder every second of every day to be just that little bit more pleasing, subservient, sexy, obedient and the best sexual plaything the aristocrat had ever owned.

Both Mistress and slave understood the situation and were aware of the irony. Unrequited love in a sex-slave only made the slave more devoted. There was no need for Lady Isobell to return her sexual-plaything's love. An incentive not to in fact.

For the moment she was unworried, knowing the proud aristocrat thoroughly enjoyed using and owning her. But for the distant threat of the auction-block, she thought she might have even been content. Except at night, when the dreams came with memories, and sometimes she sobbed quietly, remembering a girl who had never been made to cry out in ecstasy, hooded, gagged and three-in-a-bed with her nipple-rings chained to the headboard. A girl who didn't think having her behind caned or her boobs slapped was gentle foreplay. Who had never licked her own juices off a dildo, and wouldn't have taken pride in performing live sex on a stage, tit-strapped and handcuffed, penetrated fore, aft and with a third slave-boy's cock in her mouth, while four dozen elegant, beautifully dressed aristocrats, looked on.

Fortunately she had a considerate Mistress who ensured she mostly went to sleep too tired to dream. A combination pet, hot-water-bottle and cuddly toy. Lady Isobell liked the naked bed-warmer with wrists chained to the headboard she habitually slept snuggled up to, to lie still and silent. And she felt disloyal, guilty even, just imagining the possibility, the faint possibility that if she'd done something different, there might not be a bar-code and serial number tattooed on the underside of her left breast, devices implanted in her body and a bill of sale with her name on it in her love's bureau.

Mistress's lash flicking up between her legs brought her mind back to where it should be. She realised that the next time she was given permission to speak she would have to confess her moment of inattention and disloyalty. Mistress Isobell always enjoyed the challenge of thinking up a new punishment or humiliation, and Treasure, who couldn't help herself, lived only to please.

***

The hunt-orgy was warming up into a nice party, the last few hunters just straggling into the Huntsman tavern, the traditional starting point and climax to all Royal Hunts. It was still a long way from the slave sex-feast the evening promised, but the easy convivial atmosphere held the promise of an excellent night. The buffet was superb, the Chamberlain had found an excellent Chablis, the hidden musicians were of course first-rate, and all around, hanging naked from their wrists, were the evening's entertainment. Young, attractive, ball-gagged slaves, brought down on the day's hunt, waiting, trembling, to be enjoyed by those who had hunted them.

A balcony ran all around the tavern's central dining-hall providing access to first-floor bedrooms, and it was from this balcony's railing that the naked slaves had been hung, a pair of male house-slaves on hand to hang up or lower the prey-slaves as needed. Archways led to ground-floor playrooms, the bedrooms being for those who preferred to enjoy their slaves in comfort. Lords and Ladies strolled along the line, admiring the day's catch.

The hunt-orgy didn't only rely on prey for its sexual

entertainment though, a Lord or Lady just had to have caught one to gain admittance. It wasn't unusual to bring along a more experienced pet or hunting-pony to add a little spice; especially to be used for oral sex. Most prey were inexperienced, being hunted their first taste of slavery and they wouldn't have their ball-gags removed. The implanted aphrodisiacs wouldn't have kicked in fully yet and virgin slaves, begging, pleading, screeching, or worse, offering insults, did nothing for an orgy's ambience. Gag-muffled moans and gasps of pain or pleasure, and gentle sobs, made for a much more pleasant atmosphere.

And of course the experienced sex-toys could not only be counted on to know not to speak without permission, but also to moan and gasp in eager, delighted, pained pleasure. On cue, Lady Isobell arrived, with her pony-girl, Treasure, naked, bound and docilely following the lead clipped to her collar.

Prince Samuel allowed himself an appreciative nod. Some efficient groom had been hard at work, the heavy-breasted toy, last seen sweat-lathered and trembling with exhaustion, now looking quite edibly sexy. Her hair had been washed and brushed into a shining dark wave, her body piercings had been polished, and when her owner led her closer, softly scented soap and shampoo wafted over him. Unlike when he'd handled her on the hunt, eyes glazed with lust, more than a prisoner of just her bonds, Treasure was focused now, alert, looking around the party with bright-eyed interest. She was still being made to drool on her impressive tits though— obviously an effect her owner liked—thanks to a large ball-gag buckled into her mouth.

The docile brunette was perched on her toes in 5" stiletto heels, the footwear of a favoured pet, polished steel bands padlocked around shapely ankles linked with the short chain of a hobble. He had briefly wondered on the hunt if the top-heavy plaything had been trained for polite company, considering how natural she'd seemed in harness and bridle, and the ease with which Lady Isobell had controlled her. But at a glance it was obvious now the lovely slave was equally at home in heels and hobbled.

The large orange ball buckled into Treasure's mouth was held in place with a tightly buckled chin-strap as well as the strap buckled behind her neck; purely decorative, but why not? The lead clipped to her collar was chain, with a leather handle looped around Lady Isobell's wrist. The collar itself was broad, black leather, a padlock hanging at the naked slave's throat, the thick band snug enough to firmly hold her head up. Polished metal bands, matching the ankle-cuffs, locked the big-breasted girl's arms together at wrist and above the elbows behind her, thrusting the nipple-pierced globes into even greater prominence.

Prince Samuel had to admit the petite aristocrat really did have an eye for how to display her property to best effect. In a very neat finishing touch, a chain ran up under her toy from her wrist-cuffs, pulled up hard between her sex-lips, secured to a ring set through her navel; ensuring the girl's arms stayed neatly down her back.

He thought the chain digging lightly into the swell of Treasure's belly a particularly attractive effect, especially the way the polished silver links pulled between her pussy-lips actually looked like they were disappearing up inside her. In fact Treasure made an even more delectable party-treat than she did a hunter, and she was the nicest little filly he'd seen between the shafts of a pony-trap in several seasons. Even with all the other succulent, chained, flesh on display, she turned heads. The slave-slut just oozed sex-appeal! There was clearly something fresh about Treasure, something exotic, but for the life of him he couldn't quite identify it. It did make a thoughtful man wonder whether there were any more like her at home though.

She had a pretty face, well suited to a ball-gag, and a wonderful body, but that didn't make her anything special when owners routinely controlled slaves' exercise and diet; and when cosmetic surgery was simple, commonplace, and limited only by the owner's budget. She did have a very pleasant personality, docile, trusting and subservient, which made her more valuable; and she loved sex even more than most slaves, which raised her auction value more still, but none of that should make her unique. He wondered how large a sum it would really take to get Lady Isobell to part with her?

Even without the spice of chained nudity, watching Lady Isobell's pet led across the room towards him was quite delightful foreplay in itself, as erotic a display as any one of a hundred live sexual performances he'd witnessed. All slaves were deportment-trained, but even with her hobble and heels forcing her to take small, neat, steps, the sway in the chained brunette's stride and the way her large, heavy, tits quivered and wobbled as she walked, just had to be a result of conscious effort as well as long hours being trained on a treadmill. She might as well have had a sign hung around her neck saying PLEASE FUCK ME. The gorgeous creature walked like she had a dildo up her, even when she didn't.

Lady Isobell bobbed a curtsy, and to the intense interest of the Royal-watchers present, handed over her slave's lead without apparent concern.

"If you want to give her a treat, she loves having her tits squeezed when she's being shafted," the aristocrat said in a low tone with a sly grin. "Oh... almost forgot."

She turned back, handing over the key to Treasure's bonds, the key worn on a bracelet like a charm. The slave's ringed nipples were already swollen rigid, her full breasts rising and falling noticeably faster as she saw the key to her restraints being handed over. Prince Samuel couldn't help noticing, with each swell of her stomach as she breathed faster, the way the chain linking the lovely slave's handcuffs to her pierced navel was digging deeper into her belly. He wondered how much work it had taken to train her not to pull back on the chain through her crotch with her wrist-cuffs and make it dig even deeper. Most slaves, driven wild with lust by their surgically implanted aphrodisiacs, would be hard pressed to resist in her position, no matter what their orders.

He slipped the bracelet over his own wrist, meeting the bound sex-toy's eyes. Both of them knowing her bonds wouldn't so much be removed this night, as variously replaced. In private it was rumoured some owners chose to indulge themselves sexually without restraints on their property, as was their legal right, though the Prince found the idea mildly distasteful. But certainly it would never happen at a public orgy!

Arms firmly chained down her back, Treasure submissively lowered her eyes when he looped the handle of her lead over his wrist with the key bracelet, sighing happily when he reached up to heft her lust-swollen breasts. The firm melons filled his hands, and he couldn't help the feeling that the warm, heavy, silken flesh settling into his palms belonged there.

"Pant!" he ordered. "Let's see those tits quiver."

Treasure's compliance was instant. He shifted his grip, rubbing his thumbs over erect nipples, the heavy mounds wobbling in his hands. Another droplet of saliva splashed down onto her flesh. The drooling sexual-plaything's eyes were quite placid, calm; obviously this was familiar territory for her. No doubt she was intelligent enough to have worked out owners considered her breasts her best feature long ago.

She moaned delightedly when he squeezed, and gasped in pleasure when he slapped her tits, which were almost big enough to leave a complete handprint on. Heavy flesh bounced and swung under his blows, his palms leaving red splotches all across her flesh, but the top-heavy toy's head remained up throughout, standing straight, ankles neatly together. Looking closely he could see rows of little dots on her flesh, where the tiny pins of her harness's tit-straps had been.

His finger through a nipple-ring, the Prince lifted one heavy breast, lightly touching his lips to a cruelly stretched nipple in an approving kiss. His plaything's wide eyes closed in pleasure when his free hand followed her crotch-chain down between plump sex-lips, his probing fingers finding the bound girl very wet.

"You want to please your Mistress don't you, Treasure?" he asked.

She nodded quite emphatically, another droplet of saliva from the rivulet running down her chin, dripping down onto a large breast. Holding his prize in place with ringed pink nipples, the Prince bent forward and rubbed his cheek against a burning hot, scarlet, well-slapped breast.

"And as your Mistress has given you to me for the night, I expect you really want me to enjoy using you?" he probed.

Another nod.

"You know, I think I might," he allowed.

Without a backward glance he turned and walked over to where his two captives from the day's hunt hung, Treasure placidly following on her lead. A small silver metal disc hung from a short length of chain, attached with sharp-jawed metal clamps to each girl's clitoris, and each boy's scrotum, the name of the hunter who had brought down that prey-slave engraved on it. The tag not only identified who had shot which slave, but gave that hunter first sexual choice. After a moment's thought he removed his tags from the pair leaving them available to anyone. He had a different slave to screw.

The plump, full-breasted blonde hanging beside his pair had Lady Isobell's name engraved on the metal disc hanging from her clitoris, his first good look at the girl he'd almost caught. Nice! The pain, terror and fear in her eyes gave way to a look of momentary venom as she recognised the pony-girl whose actions had helped in her capture. With a grin he strolled on, admiring and occasionally handling the rest of the day's catch.

A couple of slaves had already been taken down by the more eager—younger—hunters, a girl strapped down astride a bench squeaking loudly around her gag as a kneeling young Lord thrust into her pussy from behind. By the bar a slave-boy was being whipped, another had his head between a Lady's thighs.

For the less urgently energetic, those without the fire of youth, there were the traditional party-games; to ease the hunters into that orgy sort of mood. Mud-wrestling and curling.

"Hello Samuel. Fancy a match?"

He turned, responding politely. "Countess."

Kattrena was another of the would-be fiancés he was constantly tripping over. Though to be fair it was his own parents who mostly kept pushing her into his orbit. She had a slender, quite lovely, blonde girl on a lead.

"What do you say? Your carthorse against my little pet here?"

He didn't bother to argue her description of Treasure. Possibly she was being provocative, but possibly not. Some women seemed to have a quite large blind-spot when trying to judge what attracted men; never quite believing sex-appeal could ever come before beauty. Her own pet was strikingly beautiful, a testament to the cosmetic-surgeon's art. That was another of the things about Treasure, he realised. Even though she'd had some work done on her in a clinic, her appeal was still natural somehow.

More to the point, Kattrena clearly thought she was going to win. If he accepted that Treasure had been worked hard all day, he had no idea when she'd last been allowed to come, or even how well she responded to pain. She'd already been aroused when he'd seen her take the whip earlier. Thinking, he idly stroked Treasure's haunches.

Kattrena surely knew her own toy's abilities, the blonde had the usual slave's air of subservience about her, but did she have his plaything's measure? Treasure seemed almost frisky!

"Odds?" he asked.

"Two to one," Kattrena offered.

"Five to one," he responded. "For all I know she's never done this before."

Interestingly, Lady Isobell who could have answered that question seemed to have momentarily faded away. He could have asked the chained girl, a ball-gag didn't stop her nodding or shaking her head, but the uncertainty added spice. They settled on four thousand crowns to his one. Four to one seemed about right to the audience too, until Lady Isobell reappeared and put ten thousand on her property. After that, Kattrena's blonde could only get two to one.

They played in the centre of the hall. Both naked slaves were chained standing, spread-eagled, facing each other about ten feet apart. Ankles were secured to ringbolts set in the floor, chains with wrist-cuffs lowered from above by electric winch. And then the dildo-poles were slowly cranked up, fat, ribbed shafts sliding slowly into defenceless pussies. Treasure moaned in delight as she was penetrated, groaning softly as the blunt prong stretched her wide.

On a hunch Prince Samuel left his naked victim wearing her 5" heels and her gag in place, using the winch to pull her body taut. Kattrena's blonde wasn't gagged, her bare feet touched the ground and she was loosely chained; the easier to breathe, and squirm around on her dildo as she was whipped. Already Treasure's firm thighs were trembling with the strain of standing with her ankles chained wide.

Seeing how firmly the big-breasted brunette was secured sparked a new flurry of bets, as the audience realised he was planning to rely on pain to force Treasure to orgasm, not movement on her dildo. His collared slave's impressive tits rose and fell faster still in her excitement, and Lady Isobell taking more bets reassured him he'd called it right.

A neutral judge was quickly agreed on. Both slaves had sensors surgically implanted under the skin at their temples to measure brainwaves; and orgasms would be recorded on the judge's comp'. It was the work of a moment to scan the pair for the correct frequencies, Treasure's tattooed bar-code on the underside of her left breast, Kattrena's blonde, on the inner thigh.

"Contestants. Select your whips!"

He chose a small, thin whip. Thin for maximum pain, but

short to ensure accurate strokes. Kattrena laid her selection lightly across the rump of her dildo-mounted blonde, the traditional signal she was ready to begin. After a moment's thought Prince Samuel let his whip rest on his girl's flesh just above her pubic hair. The golden-skinned toy already had her haunches well marked from the hunt, but only a few stripes had curled around her hips to her belly, and he preferred to work on this relatively unmarked flesh. Not only did he not want to risk damaging her, but whipping on top of another whipping, it was hard to know exactly how much pain you were applying.

The tautly spread, chained girl he was just about to whip met his eyes for a second, shivering her eyelashes, almost as if she was agreeing with his decision to rest his crop on her belly! Could she be? God, this was one superb slave!

"Begin!" the judge called.

The dildo-mounted toy jerked at his first stroke with a gasp of pain, the crack of leather on her flesh quite delightful, a perfect horizontal line left across her belly. She squeaked at the next stroke, just above the first, crying out helplessly at each blow after that. Prince Samuel spared a glance back. Kattrena's whip was making her girl squirm and twist on her dildo.

"First orgasm. The Countess," the judge announced.

That didn't matter; the girl could have been in a chastity-belt for a month for all he knew, but some of the audience groaned. It was the second and third times that counted! Any slave with the usual aphrodisiac implanted in her could be whipped to one orgasm.

He settled to his task and with every lash he landed on Lady Isobell's lovely hunter, the girl's eyes met his bright with tears now as she soaked up the anguished pain of the burning sting of each crack And loved it!

Each lash was forcing a pitiful yelp from her, he could see muscles clench in her thighs and stomach. She was bearing down on the dildo filling her sex, obediently clenching internal muscles around the shaft in time with his strokes.

"Good girl. Go! Yes! That's my slave-slut!" He whispered to her.

Treasure could swivel her hips slightly as she was lashed, screwing herself down on the dildo, but nowhere near the wild gyrations Kattrena's whip was forcing her blonde to. She was forced to clench the shaft inside her, obediently allowing Prince Samuel's whip to control her rhythm. He saw her eyes go wide, and let his lash lick across the tops of her thighs, right across her stuffed pussy. His toy threw her head back, squealing in mingled ecstasy and anguish behind her gag.

"First orgasm to Prince Samuel."

He gave the girl a couple more cuts across the belly and thighs to get her back into her rhythm on the dildo, and then began to work on her tits. Treasure's flesh danced in a most attractive manner as she jerked and sobbed under the lash, but clearly the large, heavy globes weren't being moved by such a light whip. There was none of the swing and bounce of a slap, just a quiver, a ripple running across each heaving melon when his strokes landed. Tears flowing freely now, her squeaks and yelps much higher pitched as raised welts were left all across her breasts, the top-heavy toy still obediently thrust and clenched herself onto the shaft impaling her, in time with his whip.

"Second orgasm to Countess Kattrena," the judge announced, followed with rising excitement only seconds later by, "second orgasm to the Prince of Wales!" Treasure put her head back and shrieked her delight at the way the Prince's whip tormented the copious mounds of her breasts, striping them again and again.

The breathless crowd pushed closer, excitement rising as it became obvious that the tit-whipped brunette was catching up. Kattrena lashed her blonde in a frenzy, her girl screeching and begging in a fog of lust and pain, but Prince Samuel continued his slow, methodical breast-whipping. Juices running down the dildo-pole, the chained girl's squeaks of pained delight at each stroke were now almost wails of ecstasy, tears, sweat and saliva glistening on the large sob-quivering, pant-heaving mounds he was torturing. Before the night was out, he would have to add semen he knew, to complete the set.

Again he saw the moment she started to come. Her eyes went wide, lips pulled back to reveal even white teeth clenched hard into the orange ball filling her mouth, and he gave her one last savage cut across her pussy. Shudders wracking her bound, dildo-impaled body, Treasure's squeal as she came was quite deafening. The judge's announcement was somewhat redundant.

"The winner. Prince Samuel!"

"Useless bitch," Kattrena snarled petulantly, giving her blonde one last vicious cut across the hindquarters.

Friends and winners clustered about offering congratulations, curious hands exploring Lady Isobell's gasping hunter, still standing spread-eagled in her chains. Her whip-marked tits were hefted, eager fingers probed between her legs seeking a taste of her juices, and one young-looking Lord lifted the shattered slave's head with a handful of hair to look into her lust-glazed hazel eyes.

"Is she for sale?" an older man asked.

"Not mine I'm afraid. You want the Lady over there."

Taking a moment to secure Treasure, a length of chain padlocking her ring-set clitoris to the base of the dildo would ensure no one took her off the pole to fuck in his absence, he left the panting toy in her circle of new admirers, and wandered off to find a well deserved drink. Whipping slaves to orgasm was surprisingly hard work!

The party was hotting up now, more of the hanging slaves caught during the day having been taken down for humiliating physical inspections, a prelude to sex or punishment. He had to step around another young Lord thrusting energetically into a girl he had on her back, her legs spread, wrists chained to ankles, on the carpet. The luxuriant dark-blue pile was thick and soft for that very reason. The collared and gagged plaything he was on top of had her breasts tightly roped and was pushing her hips up to meet her hunter's thrusts with squeaks of pleasure. By the buffet another inexperienced toy was just earning herself a whipping, having balked at the task of licking chocolate spread off a male slave's erection.

He made a slight detour on the way back from the bar to watch the first couple of mud-wrestling matches. The standard was well below competition level, the girls amateurs, first-timers in some cases, but still stimulating and fun to watch. They didn't actually use mud any more; the thick, clear, viscous oil lining the bottom of the pit having replaced the traditional slime over a century earlier. Oil was not only just as slippy, but clinging to bare skin, added an attractive gleam to the contestants' naked flesh.

Two girls fitted with strap-on-dildos, harnesses buckled tight around waists and under crotches, slipped, slid and squirmed against each other in the pit. Ball-gags prevented biting, punches were not allowed and scratching wasn't a problem as slaves weren't permitted long nails anyway. But otherwise, it was anything goes. The winner was the first to successfully penetrate her opponent anally. Prince Samuel clapped politely with the rest when somebody's pony-girl easily tripped an inexperienced prey-slave, and thrust her dildo into the girl's ass. The oil sheened toy, controlled with one arm twisted up behind her back and a handful of hair, squealed in protest.

The bonds Treasure had arrived in seemed to have disappeared when he wandered back to take her off the dildo-pole, no doubt being worn by another girl now, only the brunette's collar, ball-gag and heels remaining. With a shrug he clipped the lead to her collar, and just had her follow him around on hands and knees, heavy, whip-marked breasts, swaying under her. She was quite cute on all fours.

The roll of her equally well whip-marked buttocks as she crawled must have been even more enticing than he'd suspected. Ten or so minutes later while chatting to an acquaintance, on hearing a gasp of pleasure, he looked down to find her being taken doggie-style by one of the guests. The German ambassador's son, obviously thoroughly enjoying his first hunt, grinned up at him companionably. Treasure gasped each time he drove his cock into her, his pelvis slamming up against her buttocks with each deep, hard, thrust.

"Give her tits a squeeze," he advised the young Count. "I'm told she likes it."

Treasure responded with a gag-muffled wail of delight as fingers sank into the full, firm, weight of her breasts, her groans each time the flesh shaft thrust into her more urgent now; louder. Hiding mild irritation, knowing it was his own fault not the young Count's, Prince Samuel resumed his conversation. Orgy etiquette dictated that you clipped a tag to your slave's clitoris if you didn't want her shafted until you'd enjoyed her first. He'd forgotten. There were 'exclusivity tags' on the buffet table and by the front door. They were similar to the silver tags with names engraved on them that adorned the displayed prey hanging from the banisters, but these discs were blank and red.

While waiting politely for the Count to finish, Prince Samuel had an untagged prey-slave from the collection on the balcony taken down. The lovely brunette still on the end of his lead was firmly braced on all fours, fingers deep in the carpet now, squeaking each time the young noble's cock was rammed into her. As the Count began to thrust faster, more urgently, his hands came off the girl's breasts, fingers sinking into the firm flesh of her hips instead, to yank her back harder and faster onto his thrusts. As he watched, Treasure, eyes unseeing, tossed her head and squealed ecstasy into her mouth-filling gag, her user's own orgasm only a few thrusts behind.

The German nobleman was still for a moment, exhaling with a long satisfied sigh; and then he pulled his shaft out of the girl, the heavy-titted toy still obediently maintaining her position. He wiped mingled semen and juices off his penis with one hand, absently wiping his hand dry on one of the collared girl's striped buttocks, gave her a careless pat, and then ambled off, unconcernedly naked, to see what other entertainments the hunt-orgy had to offer.

Prince Samuel had his borrowed prey-slave lick the come out of the kneeling girl while he snagged a red tag off the buffet table. Better late than never! Treasure was moaning happily, eyes closed, as the unseen slave-boy's tongue probed her sex. With a grin, he pushed the male slave over onto his side and off her with a careless foot.

"You! Sit and stay, until someone wants you!" he ordered the slave-boy, dropping down to one knee beside his naked plaything and giving her a slap on the backside. "Spread your thighs, Treasure," he ordered.

Lady Isobell's toy flinched at his first touch, but then held herself obediently still as he inspected her rings and probed between her plump sex-lips. She squeaked softly when she felt cold metal, the sound becoming a rising wail of distress as he slowly allowed the spring-loaded, sharp-jawed clamp, to close onto her clitoris under the shiny ring already set through her flesh. The red disc hanging from a short length of chain between firm thighs now marked her, most attractively, as unavailable.

"You're gorgeous. You know that, don't you?" he asked softly, reaching under her to stroke her breasts.

Treasure nodded without hesitation; trained out of false modesty, and more than smart enough to realise the effect she had on owners. Whether she actually wanted that effect or not was quite immaterial. Nature had placed in noble hands a mind and body that was sex personified, and it would be a waste not to enjoy her to the full.

He led his now safely tagged prize, still on her hands and knees, out to the back patio to watch the curling. The match in progress was just concluding, so he happily entered his borrowed slave in the next round.

The broad expanse of the patio was covered in a smooth

film of wet ice, a target of red concentric circles and a dot dyed into the course's far end. From inside the bar a flat-topped ice-covered ramp, starting waist-high, sloped down to the patio; and it was from this ramp that the contestants launched their hog-tied slaves onto the course. Little wheeled trolleys, matching the height of the top of the ramp, were used by contestants to move their prepared pieces up to the ramp.

Treasure had obviously been played with in this game before, and at his command, without surprise, hopped up astride his trolley and then bent forward to lie face-down. She lay placidly on her stomach while he tightly hog-tied her. With practised hands Prince Samuel finished by weaving a rope into her hair, and then tied it off to her ankles, both to hold her head up and keep it out of the way. Her roped ponytail pulled the brunette's head back hard, neck and spine arched. Only flesh, body-piercings and attached drags were allowed in contact with the ice. Some contestants were removing decorations and restraints; but he saw no reason to take off Treasure's ball-gag and heels. The collar had to remain so that the course-boys could hook her off the ice.

Curling was a very simple game; whichever contestant's hog-tied slave's crotch finished closest to the target circle's centre won that heat, eight or sixteen players starting. The skill lay in how you launched your game-piece down the ramp, your estimation of her weight, and the size of the drags—ice brakes—you attached to her nipples.

Prince Samuel got lucky, drawing the 3rd heat. It let him watch four slaves launched down the ramp before his own first match, giving him a chance to judge the course. A slightly fast game he decided, one girl sliding right off the ice and onto the grass, two others overshooting. A very warm evening, perhaps leaving a little more surface water than usual? His opponent seeing this, was attaching large drags to her girl's nipples.

The drags were cone-shaped with hooks at the base, or if

your game-piece didn't have pierced nipples, clamps; which would score through the ice, slowing down the naked, hog-tied girl as she slid across it. Sliding a hand under one of Treasure's large breasts, idly squeezing, Prince Samuel selected much smaller drags. The way her heavy tits were flattened under her by her own weight, would press down hard on the ice-brakes he hooked to her nipple-rings. He wasn't surprised to find the hazel-eyed sex-toy looked delectable in a hog-tie. A course-boy, naked and collared, reached out with a hooked pole, snagged the last girl's collar, and pulled her off the ice. She was lifted onto a waiting trolley. Two more slaves wheeled Prince Samuel's trolley forward, and with an arm and a leg each, lifted Treasure onto the top of the ramp. With a sharply indrawn breath, she was laid on the ice, lying on belly, breasts and thighs. She squealed when Prince Samuel thrust his thumb into her anus, groaning happily when his fingers penetrated her sex. The thought of lying on ice made him shiver, but for the big-titted slave, the chill on her recently whipped flesh was probably quite pleasant.

A one or two-handed grip was acceptable, women, who had smaller hands usually preferring their right hand's fingers in the game-piece's pussy, left thumb in the ass. He slid her back and forward a couple of times, testing his grip and gauging the ice, before gently easing the naked sex-toy forward onto the ramp. Treasure's breasts were fully on the ice-covered ramp before he felt her start to pull forward against his grip. He squeezed harder, Treasure groaning in pleasure again as his fingers gripped the small bridge of flesh between anus and pussy, making sure of his aim before releasing her. His borrowed slave spun to a perfect stop, crotch directly over the target's central dot.

He won the second heat as well, but in the final he misjudged his launch, his fingers slipping out of Treasure's dripping-wet pussy and his plaything slid right off the course onto the grass. With a rueful nod and smile to the winner, he went to retrieve his game-piece and re-attach her red tag. It wasn't really her fault she was hot and wet, she was supposed to be; but that didn't mean he couldn't punish her for the lost game. He found himself feeling quite stimulated!

Back inside the tavern things were hotting up. He opened the doors on two playrooms while Treasure crawled after him. The tavern was filled now with the sounds of orgasms, both forced and unforced, the new slaves discovering that they could climax in bondage and under whipping with a bemused enthusiasm.

There was room for one more in the third room he tried. Two older Ladies were chatting amiably on a sofa while handcuffed male sex-toys lapped between their thighs, watching a couple opposite attaching electrodes to a girl on a rack. Two younger Lords, more energetic, were sharing a full-breasted blond on one of the beds. The girl was on her back with arms bound behind her, her head hanging over the edge of the bed. That allowed the aristocrat standing to thrust into her mouth— possibly a latecomer to the action—the other, sitting astride her, tit-fucking his bound toy. Two other naked, gagged, slaves had been forgotten, or abandoned in favour of more succulent flesh. A slave-boy chained facedown on the second bed, and another blonde girl, bent forward from the waist, her head and wrists locked in wooden stocks. Crowding in behind him, a young Lady wearing only a tiara and a strap-on-dildo, led in a hooded, body-harnessed, girl by a nipple-ring and threw her onto a spare couch.

But the winch was free.

From the room's toy-box Prince Samuel selected leather cuffs which he buckled around Treasure's wrists, clipping them together behind her, and with the winch-chain attached, slowly cranked her arms up behind her until her body was bent deeply forward from the waist, hands pulled well above her head. A spreader-bar, locked around her ankles spread wide apart added to the strain on the brunette's shoulders and left her nicely helpless. As punishment for spoiling his curling game, he tied weights to her nipples, the ball-gagged plaything's

41

large breasts dragged down into tortured cones.

Lady Isobell's hunter was a wonderful screw, gasping and squeaking in pleasure no matter how hard he squeezed her tits or spanked her haunches, swaying back in her bonds to meet his thrusts each time he rammed his cock into her from behind, her cunt juicy but tight. He could see himself in a mirror, standing behind her, hips pumping; and it was suddenly obvious that the velvet-skinned slave, a red metal disc swaying on a chain from her clamped clitoris, perched on her toes in 5" heels, legs widely spread and almost hanging from her wrists pulled up behind her, could take all he had to give and more. He had to have her!

Watching his peers as they watched him, roping, fucking, tormenting and humiliating the collared sex-toys who existed only to be enjoyed, he thrust faster, sighing softly when he finally pumped his come into his lovely conquest. Again the girl seemed able to come as effortlessly as he did, taught that she could only come without permission when the person using her did, she squealed into her gag in delight. Lady Isobell had trained one hell of a slave!

Pulling his cock out of the still bent-forward plaything, he paused in thought a moment, stroking her hips, and then removed the tag clamped to her clitoris. She wasn't his property, and such a magnificent toy deserved to be shared.

Returning later with his wide-eyed personal vet, the man having been in easy reach, tending his black hunters, Prince Samuel found Lady Isobell's brunette still in the bonds he'd left her in, but now being enjoyed by a young couple. He waited politely until the pair had finished with her, the young Lord thrusting into her from behind while his wife licked the welts on Treasure's stretched tits, and then ordered his vet to give the bound toy a physical.

"But...but...Your Majesty," the man stammered, gawking at the mingled semen and juices running down Treasure's thighs—she'd been enjoyed by more than just these two in his absence—the weights swaying from her now purple nipples, the gleaming trails of semen and her wide open pussy all attested to that.

Prince Samuel laughed aloud at the look on the man's face, all he could see of Treasure was her well-used pussy and whip striped buttocks, vets didn't usually see slaves in action, just before and after.

"Just do it," he chuckled. "And I'd hurry if I were you. Somebody else'll probably want to use her soon."

Later, in the early hours of the morning when most hunters had sated their sexual lusts, the youngsters competing by whipping tug-of-war teams of slaves out on the floodlit lawn, he joined the more sedate port and sherry crowd by the oil pit, entering Lady Isobell's pony-girl in the mud-wrestling bouts.

Although graceful, Treasure was a powerful girl, and easily overpowered most of her opponents unless they'd had some wrestling training. But every time she managed to struggle astride another slippery, wriggling, dildo-wearing slave-girl, an arm or two twisted up behind her opponent's back, she would pause, looking up to him for approval before raping her conquest with her own dildo.

At the slightest shake of his head, the oil-gleaming brunette would obediently lose her grip or balance, or her opponent would somehow manage to twist away just as she was about to ram the dildo home. Within a minute she would be face-down in the slippy pool, her big, oiled, tits being brutally squeezed; groaning with pleasure behind her gag as a fat dildo was rammed painfully deep into her ass. Prince Samuel found he enjoyed watching Treasure lose far too much to allow the hard-used girl to win more than a couple of bouts.

* * *

The day after the Royal hunt, Lady Isobell Philippa St-John Franklin lay sprawled naked across a giant bed, drifting, dreamy content in post-orgasm lassitude. She did so love sex. Idly she reached out and handled the serving-slave's cock, the vein-throbbing purple shaft and his balls tightly buckled into an Arab-strap, twitching in her hand as she squeezed. The ball-gagged slave-boy with his wrists chained to his serving-tray, two dew-chilled champagne glasses waiting, moaned softly in frustrated despair. She was trying to decide whether to have him for seconds, or watch him give the ever-compliant Treasure a good shafting.

Her favourite toy knelt in the centre of the bed, wrists buckled together behind her back and pulled up above her to a winch set above the bed, forcing her to kneel with her head and upper-body down and her tail up. The heavy-breasted slave was blindfolded, lips still lightly touching her owner's sex-lips, and being taken from behind doggie-style, by Lord Percy, Isobell's fiancé.

It was a very pleasant sensation. Each time the naked toy gasped in delight as the surgically enhanced cock penetrating her plunged to the hilt, her breath caressed Isobell's pussy. With a sigh of contentment she sat up, took a little sip of chilled champagne, and slid her hands under the golden-skinned slave, scooping up her superb boobs. Treasure's flesh was warm, soft and silky, the ring-tipped globes, heavy but firm, wobbling in her palms as the girl's body rocked to her shafting. She'd spent many a happy hour playing with the big, deliciously squeezable, slapable, ropeable mounds and had never regretted having her property's udders enlarged more than was fashionable. Of course her plaything would, as well as a certain amount of awkwardness and discomfort, experience back troubles in later life, but Isobell was prepared to live with that. Owners paid the vets' bills after all, so it was their choice.

She stifled a sudden giggle; hiding it by leaning forward to smell Treasure's hair, copper highlights glinting in the shiny dark mane. She'd looked up and unexpectedly noticed that her fiancé, thrusting contentedly into the bound slave's sex, had a look of vacant, bucolic stupidity on his face. Gods, she hoped she didn't look like that when she was absorbed in enjoying a slave.

44

Lord Percy had also insisted on a tight waspie-corset and the tube of an inflatable butt-plug disappeared into Treasure's anus. She didn't mind, her pet looked great with an hourglass figure and a stuffed ass definitely made the top-heavy slave a more responsive screw; it was just that he didn't listen!

Unfortunately her fiancé was a total mummy's-boy. He'd never really broken in and trained a slave to his own standards; he just used the sex-toys his doting mother bought him. And he liked, as many men did, a nice tight sheath to pump into, hence the corset and plug. But Treasure had excellent control of her internal muscles, had been trained to hold heavily weighted dildos inside herself, and could have gripped him as tightly as he liked if he'd just tried her. It was every aristocrat's birthright to enjoy their slaves in the manner that most pleased them, no problem there. But his chauvinistic assumption that he knew his way around her property's lush body better than she did... now that was irritating!

The aristocrat groaned, fingers sinking deeper into the firm flesh of Treasure's hips, little ripples running across her flesh as he thrust faster, his pelvis slamming up against her. Head back, eyes closed, he sighed as he pumped his semen into the bound, blindfolded girl.

"That was a nice ride," he said, pulling his softening cock from the young slave and patting her marked backside. "Are you really going to sell her?"

Treasure's blindfolded head came up with a squeak of alarm. Lady Isobell sank her fingernails into the girl's breasts to settle her.

"If he wants her," she replied.

"I thought this one was your special pet?"

She shook her head sadly. Poor Percy. He was a kindly soul, just not too bright. Hadn't he realised by now she simply didn't get that emotional about property?

"I'll admit I hadn't planned to sell her just yet," she nodded, "She's got a gorgeous body, a lovely face, the sweetest personality and I've almost got her trained to perfection. I've thoroughly enjoyed owning her these last two years, but she's not unique. There'll be one or two just as good on the auction-block tomorrow. And it wasn't just that he offered me three times what she's worth. Some offers you really don't like to refuse."

"Does the Prince Royal really want her then?" Percy asked.

"He was very interested," she allowed. "I mean he didn't just give her a quick shafting and forget her like I expected. He wanted to know how old she was, if she'd had the youth treatment, and if she'd had any medical problems. He even had his vet give her a physical at the hunt-orgy!"

Tears were staining Treasure's blindfold, so she ordered the serving-slave to screw her. It would take the big-breasted toy's mind off the Royal brand that was soon going to adorn her pretty behind. Actually, now she thought about it, she'd seen the cutest little blonde for sale last week.

Treasure's distress was obviously genuine, and gratifying to an owner as a measure of her training, but fundamentally unimportant. After all it made little real difference to a sex-toy who owned her; the basic theme was still sex, bonds, nudity, humiliation, punishment and more sex.

To begin with Isobell had hoped the brunette might be that special one, the slave who became more than a toy. Some owners found pets they could love, became quite devoted to them and guarded them jealously, seeming to take greater pleasure in owning them. But though she'd taken pride in how well trained Treasure was, in owning and displaying such a magnificent body, in the end the lovely girl had never really meant more to her than great sex, though occasionally she had wished for more. As such, Treasure deserved to be sold.

And although the girl was upset at the moment, selling her was actually the kind thing to do. She might find love with a new owner. More important, with the decision to sell her favourite now forced on her, Lady Isobell was free to begin hunting anew for the perfect slave-girl for her. She was out there somewhere, she was sure.

46

Two
Aliens

Imagine a world, identical to your own Earth in every detail, the people, the history, your own double in the same place doing the same thing as you, with the exact same change in his pocket. The only difference, a blade of grass in Russia or Africa a centimetre longer.

Imagine another world, almost identical, but it's the next blade of grass over that's longer. Or shorter. Billions upon billions of realities with differences too small to detect. People slip between them all the time. Everyone's said at one time or another "Didn't that sign used to be green?" And as the realities curve away from each other, like images in two slightly offset mirrors, the differences between dimensions become gradually more significant, big enough for a traveller to observe. And you have worlds in which the First World War was never fought, a dimension where a South American Columbus discovered Europe and a reality where you don't, and never did, exist, because your great great grandfather was killed at the British defeat at Waterloo.

Theoretically travel between dimensions was quite possible, if a gate was opened from both sides at once. Unlikely? But if there were billions upon billions of possibilities, what were the odds of two sets of scientists tinkering at once?

***

In the centre of the lab, shimmering like a slab of mercury turned on its side and hanging in the air, bordered by a copper framework, the Gate rippled as a young man stepped through.

"My Lady," he acknowledged Professor Phillips-Webber, English strangely accented, but perfectly understandable. There was another England on the other side, though with a very different history.

"Sven. Back so soon?" the professor greeted him.

"He wants to see a big airport," Andrew told her. "I'm taking him and..... Where is, oh!" A second young man stepped through the Gate. "Him and George to Heathrow."

The two scientists from the alternative England were dressed almost passably casual, something not quite right about their gestures and haircuts, but not enough to attract more than a passing glance. The pair, both aristocrats in their world, gave a short bow to their lab-assistant counterparts, and deeper bows to the professor. Slightly more hesitantly, they gave Jenny an uncomfortable, half not-quite-noticing-her bow. They didn't really know quite how to treat her. In their England serf and merchant-class women wore veils. Only aristocrats, who the lower classes averted their gaze from, and bond-slaves, didn't cover their faces.

Jenny watched the two—aliens she supposed—led out with misgivings.

"Professor. Don't you think it's about time we went public?" she asked. "At least alerted the authorities? Or even tell the university?"

"Oh nonsense Jenny. The last thing we need is a bunch of suits closing us down for two years while they evaluate the situation. Or worse, some professionally paranoid intelligence agency burying the Gate in some underground lab and classifying even my laundry list top-secret."

"But we know practically nothing about them!"

"That's what we're learning now," she said with faint exasperation, heading for the Gate. "Coming?"

"But their system's feudal! They practice slavery!"

"Fascinating, isn't it?"

"Professor!" Jenny protested.

Professor Phillips-Webber was a stout tweed-wearing woman in her mid-fifties who looked at the world over half-moon spectacles. She was undoubtedly a brilliant mathematician and physicist, but her students generally figured she'd need to ask one of her computers to find out what day it was and would forget her own head if it wasn't screwed on. She really didn't seem to see the possibility that their gentle fishing might have caught a shark.

Her tutor gave Jenny a puzzled look, and with a shrug, stepped through the Gate. Jenny cursed under her breath and followed. It was her third cross-dimensional journey.

Academic Franklin was just rising from having kissed the professor's hand. The two seemed to have established a personal and scientific rapport of their own that owed nothing to either of their cultures. Certainly they were impressed with each other's scientific knowledge, technological advances not being equal on both worlds. And if Jenny didn't know better, she'd have said professor Phillips-Webber was infatuated.

An honorary aristocrat, the professor was allowed to remain bare-faced. Jenny, resigned, shrugged into a floor-length veil and robe with a mesh viewing-slit in front of her eyes, one of three hanging incongruously from a hat-stand beside the Gate. The garment was similar to those worn by Arab women, but came in a variety of colours, greens and blues through violet, with colour-coded wrist-cuffs, instead of just plain black.

In the Academic's study a topless slave-girl wearing a steel collar and with a steel belt holding up red translucent harem-pants, served tea. Jenny couldn't drink past her veil, underlings didn't eat in the presence of their Lords, and so had to just sit and watch. The slave-girl's metal belt, clipped together in a combination-lock in the small of her back, was digging deeply into the soft flesh of her stomach. Three rings set through both inner sex-lips and her clitoris, and whip-stripes across her buttocks, were visible through the see-through material of her harem-pants. Completing her humiliating decoration, a large perfect pearl hung from a smaller, fine ring set through the tip of each of the girl's nipples.

Academic Franklin gave the girl a totally unconscious pat on the behind when she'd finished. The displayed slave sank to her knees, head down, at his side. Out of the window Jenny could see a pair of young men, naked and in harness and bridles, pulling a garden roller across a perfect lawn.

It was no wonder the serf, merchant and artisan classes all

knew their places so well. One wrong word or action and you, or if too old to enjoy, your son or daughter, became a sexual plaything, a pet on a lead and would next be seen prancing naked in harness and bridle in front of an aristocrat's carriage. Only a tiny middle-class of priests, doctors and slave-dealers; and the families of soldiers, who of course helped maintain the status-quo, were exempt. They took care to raise dutiful, obedient children, especially the former slaves, the tattooed brands of their previous owners forever on their bodies.

"My Lord?" Jenny asked, interrupting an obviously fascinating discussion on the merits of commerce and war-driven scientific research as opposed to pure research; the alternative Earth having been well ahead technologically until the growth-spurt of two world-wars and one cold war. "How old is that girl?" Jenny asked.

The Academic looked irritated at this, probably unprecedented, interruption by an underling. He reached down and lifted the girl's head with a handful of hair, looking into her pretty face with puzzlement. The question had obviously never occurred to him. She wasn't a person, just a lovely possession. Possessions didn't have birthdays. Thinking, he hefted a full breast, rolling a pink pearl-tipped nipple between thumb and forefinger. The girl's arms stayed neatly folded behind her back.

Finally professor Phillips-Webber seemed to notice the almost naked young serving-slave, which had been Jenny's intention. 'Yes, go on, look! That's what these people are really like, never mind the 'noble scientist seeking truth for no reward routine,' she thought.

"Well she must be at least eighteen to have been sentenced," he mused. "She'll have a bar-code and serial number on her somewhere." He lifted both breasts by the nipple, looking at their undersides, pushed the girl to the floor to examine her whip-marked backside and checked the soles of her feet, not finding anything, he turned his attention to her head.

"Ah, here we are," he said triumphantly, pushing aside hair. The girl's tattoo was on the nape of her neck. "See the serial number under the bar-code? The first six numbers will be her date of birth. She's...let's see...nineteen."

"That's a strange looking tattoo," the professor said, to Jenny's dismay not appearing in the slightest horrified, shocked or disapproving at the young slave's demeaning treatment.

"Liquid metal. Doesn't fade like ink."

"I suppose she has a pedigree?" Phillips-Webber asked thoughtfully. "Owner? Bill of sale?"

"Previous owners, price at auction, height, weight, measurements, skills and medical history," he concluded.

"Name?" Jenny asked coldly.

"Tattooed on the underside of the tongue, but not terribly important to tell the truth," he replied unperturbed, flicking a nametag hanging from her collar. "Prized pets get pet-names. This is Perky for example, named after her personality as well as her nipples, but any slave knows to respond to 'Hey you!'"

"Is identification a problem at all?" Phillips-Webber asked. "A trade in stolen bond-slaves?" She grinned at Jenny. "Sold second hand with false tattoos and their ages put back?"

"She's not a toy!" Jenny snapped

"On this world, yes she is, and quite legally," the professor said mildly. "So lower your voice and stop being rude. We are guests here."

Jenny was glad the hated veil hid her stunned expression. She'd assumed it was just good old bumbling professor Phillips-Webber, who absent-mindedly hadn't actually noticed a real live slave under her nose, no more a person than a bug under a microscope. But it was worse, far worse. If owning human beings here was all perfectly legal and above board, then it seemed in her mind there was no reason to disapprove. Jenny couldn't believe her. A law didn't make something right!

Academic Franklin nodded approvingly as Jenny was put in her place.

"Valuable property must be readily identifiable," he continued, "And ownership readily transferable. For example I've won and lost girls at the card table before. As well as the bar-code, we take retinal scans and all slaves have an ID and satellite locator-tag surgically implanted in them. A personal computer can scan all three, and call up her pedigree in seconds."

"A satellite locator-tag?"

"Oh yes, at the touch of a button, I can satellite track the location of any of my slaves to within five yards anywhere on the face of the planet. A wonderful system. They can't escape if they wanted to."

"Clever," Phillips-Webber agreed. "We mostly use ours for communications and spying."

"It's usually implanted in the breast in girls. About the size of a pea, but you can feel it if you squeeze hard enough. Be my guest."

"Professor!" Jenny protested.

Two cold looks silenced her. At a command, the almost naked slave, breasts swinging under her, crawled on hands and knees to jolly, kindly, fussy old Professor Phillips-Webber's feet and sat up on her heels, arms folded behind her. Another command, and what Jenny had thought were ornamental metal bracelets, slid together with a click.

Jenny's tutor pushed her ridiculous half-moon glasses up her nose, and hesitantly held out cupped hands. They both watched breathless, Franklin indulgently, as the voluptuous slave-girl, now with her wrists locked behind her, leant forward and pushed her breasts into the waiting hands. The full mounds filled the professor's palms, her spread fingers sinking into the girl's flesh just from the weight she held.

"My, she is a big girl," Phillips-Webber breathed, sounding surprised and delighted.

The pink-tipped, pearl-decorated, melons she was supporting jiggled and wobbled as she shifted her grip. The nineteen-year-old plaything groaned softly in pleasure as her breasts were kneaded, pulled and squeezed together, nipples now standing out hard.

"Many slave-girls are top-heavy," the Academic agreed readily. "It's customary to alter your property's appearance to your own tastes."

"Surgical implants?"

He looked blank. Phillips-Webber explained.

"Oh no, no, no. What a lot of fuss and bother," he said, looking faintly revolted. "Just a simple injection to make them grow bigger. It's quite easy to fool the body, selective puberty, the same way contraceptives work by fooling the body into thinking it's already pregnant. And the bigger the dose, the bigger the breasts. Improves the toy's appearance, adds to her sex-appeal and does wonders for her state-of-mind."

"How elegant," Phillips-Webber agreed. The kneeling slave bit her lip as her nipples were rubbed together. "And this," she made the girl gasp, "represents your tastes?"

"She's a nice handful, but I'm not really exclusive to a type. I like variety. Plump, athletic, beautiful, cute, svelte or voluptuous; the auction-houses sell them all. Different strokes. My daughter for example thinks Perky's tits are too small, can you believe! But I'd say most girls are improved a little, with about a third large-titted.

The helpless slave-girl was now gasping and moaning softly as her humiliatingly enlarged breasts were twisted and squeezed harder. Jenny could take no more. She stood abruptly, ignoring Franklin and Phillips-Webber's surprised looks, and strode from the study. Throwing her veil aside in the lab, she practically dived through the Gate.

***

Later in the professor's study Jenny cradled a cup of tea between her hands, looking out of another window. In a perfectly ordinary university courtyard, a couple strolled with arms around each other's waists, the boy with his hand in the girl's jeans back pocket. Jenny could still see only too clearly two naked pony-boys leaning into their harnesses against the weight of a heavy garden roller, erections bobbing.

"They're more scared of us than we need to be of them," Andrew said. "They see an infection of social chaos, a moral crusade to free the slaves; not to mention an aristocrat's natural fear of democracy and a crime-rate a hundred times theirs. And our military, technologically and tactically, is light years ahead of theirs, and they know it. They couldn't stop us."

"Except by cutting off the Gate while they still control it," the professor agreed.

"But their technology's mostly ahead of ours," Sarah protested.

"Not in all areas," she disagreed. "Politically they're very unsophisticated. Militarily, as Andrew's already mentioned, and we're catching up fast. Explosively. They're only ahead because they never had a dark age. Slow, measured, but constant progress since Roman times, which is where they got their social order."

"Then we don't need them. We'll get it ourselves. We should have nothing to do with them," Jenny said firmly.

"Don't be foolish dear," Phillips-Webber said mildly.

"Foolish? It works both ways. They contaminate us with every contact. You all didn't see her today, actually enjoying one of those poor slave's humiliation. Why don't you try a whip next time?"

"If that's what it takes to be a polite guest," her tutor replied in a sharper tone than Jenny would have thought her capable of. "When in Rome! Disapproving of them will only make them more likely to cut us off. They have cures for cancer, rejuvenation treatments that can hold back twenty years and a broken back or neck is routine surgery. Not to mention centuries' worth of history, literature and arts. You want to be a scientist, and yet a whole new world to explore doesn't tempt you? Vote!"

Professor Phillips-Webber looked around the faces of her students. Karen, Afro-Caribbean and a would-be Olympic sprinter, pursed her lips and then nodded decisively, long legs stretched out in front of her.

"Charles. Sarah?"

The inseparable childhood sweethearts looked into each other's eyes, blond heads together, and nodded as one. As usual they were holding hands.

"Andrew?"

The unattainable object of Jenny's desires, dating yet another cute but brainless bimbo at the moment, brushed back his dark hair, gave Jenny a little shrug of apology, and nodded agreement. He was friendly enough, would look down her blouse if the opportunity presented, but was obviously not interested. The old story; too tall and too smart. But she still hoped.

"Jenny? Make it unanimous?"

"Oh alright. But when in Rome, I'm going to be disapproving."

Her friends and their teacher laughed at her reservation. Jenny forced herself to laugh back, but in her mind's eye she could still see a young slave-girl on her knees. It was all too easy to imagine herself in that poor girl's place, a lovely plaything on display, legally owned, wrists secured behind her, rings set in her flesh and a total stranger handling her breasts.

Jenny shivered, nipples rising in fear, her insides turning to jelly. Fear was strangely similar to sexual arousal she realised in confusion, pulling her cardigan closed and hoping no-one had noticed her erect nipples. She'd always been a little body-conscious, which was perhaps why she found the very public displays of sex and nudity in the slaveworld harder to take than her friends?

Her mind still on the alternative England instead of back in her own Britain, it was easy to imagine how the Lords and Ladies really saw her friends under their polite veneer. If you weren't one of them, you weren't a real person, and had none of the rights of one. Without the Academic's restraint because of the professor's perceived equality, how might a group of young explorers fare?

It was surprisingly easy to imagine. Long-legged, athletic, Karen would have undoubtedly become one of the racing pony-girls she'd seen on her second visit in a brief glimpse of a racetrack, while the Academic had channel-hopped, demonstrating his three-dimensional TV. She would be whipped to exhaustion pulling a professional driver in a little two-wheeled carriage, while pretty aristocrats cheered and laid down bets. She already knew dark skin had a rarity value.

The blond couple, Charles and Sarah, both attractive and so obviously a perfect pair, she could imagine as household pets. Pillow-slaves, Lord Sven had called them. She could almost see them, interchangeable in chains, performing oral sex with wrists locked behind them, or, Jenny folded her arms under her breasts gently squeezing herself, tied face down on a bed, mouths full of underwear, a thick owner's cock pumping between pale buttocks.

Jenny felt her breasts swell within her bra, a heat in her groin, panties damp. Until she'd met Andrew, she'd always had a bit of a thing for Charles, and as they so obviously came as a package, Sarah as well. She of course hadn't mentioned her secret fantasies, which were the reason the alternate England hit a little too close to home. Thinking about what the Lords and Ladies would do to the beautiful Andrew cooled her lust a little though. With his powerful rugby player's physique, they probably thought he'd make a suitable agricultural beast of burden.

The professor didn't see any danger Jenny realised. To her the other dimension was just something to be studied, not to get involved in. But she had the right technique. It would be important to go along with the slave owning rulers of the alternative Earth, not to spook them, certainly not to have them consider their visitors a danger. Because if she, or any of her friends, got stuck on the wrong side of a closed Gate, her daydreams might not be far wrong.

56

THREE
A PREDATOR'S EYES

EXPLORING THE ALTERNATIVE England proved to be much easier than Jenny had expected. None of them could pass for aristocrats; the Lords and Ladies were too much an in-crowd, sharing more than just accents, education and in-jokes. They also shared a common heritage, slave-owning lifestyle and all knew each other. Somebody was somebody's daughter-in-law, or somebody knew somebody else who was her uncle. It was one big interconnected clan!

Fortunately there was another way. While the serfs of the agricultural communities didn't travel much, commerce demanded the merchant and skilled classes did; with permission. But no soldier would dream of checking the papers of a driver or secretary accompanied by an aristocrat. Franklin didn't want 'the powers that were' interfering in his project any more than Phillips-Webber did for the moment. Mostly Andrew and Charles were given the guided tour as they were less conspicuous than veiled women, Karen, Sarah and Jenny being guides in their own world. Jenny preferred it that way, still spooked by the sight of honest to goodness slaves.

The professor had been right though. The little pile of medical text-books, a belt-carried personal computer about the size of a mobile phone but smart enough to understand and respond to verbal orders, and a small vial of a drug that gave the user a photographic memory for a week or so, all locked safely in her study desk, more than justified their contact. And Jenny found herself increasingly fascinated by the rejuvenation treatment, the alternative England's ruling aristocracy were all much older than they actually looked; their medical technology even more advanced than any of Phillips-Webber's team had suspected.

Unfortunately that treatment was a state-secret, known to the scientists of only a few countries, aristocrats from scientifically underdeveloped countries forced to pay through the nose for it, which was going to make it hard to get at. Jenny couldn't deny that she liked the idea of still looking 25 at 50, and she wasn't alone, but getting access was going to require Academic Franklin's assistance. A non-aristocrat couldn't just walk up to the door with a fistful of money and ask for the clock to be put back without answering some awkward questions. Like "Which noble did you steal that money off, girl?".

Worse, Phillips-Webber had been so right about not openly disapproving. More and more, even in their own environment, they were having to tip-toe around their visitors, words like Magna-Carta, Lincoln, Human-rights and Votes, all made them twitch. Worse still, because Jenny actually found herself having to be especially nice to the spoilt, haughty, stuck-up, plumy-voiced, arrogant Lady she'd been paired with. She'd got off on the wrong foot with Lady Isobell, and things were only a little improved a week later.

"You mean I actually have to associate with a serf as an equal?" she'd demanded when they first met.

Lady Isobell was Franklin's daughter and one of his research team, scientific study being one of the few areas of endeavour not beneath an aristocrat. It hadn't helped introductions that at the time the aristocrat had been leading a gorgeous naked girl by two lengths of rope secured around each full breast. Jenny had gaped in amazement at the two hangman's nooses sunk deep into the flesh of the girl's breasts, nipples forced to protrude, skin shiny-taut, the large globes squeezed out into almost perfect spheres. Jenny had fantasies about being led around naked in public with a collar and lead, but you couldn't pull a girl around or tie her to things by her breasts! You just couldn't! The lovely brunette had been perched on tall stilettos, her arms pulled up cruelly behind her back and secured to the back of her collar with a too-short length of chain, had had a large orange ball-gag buckled into her mouth and a bell hanging on a short length of chain from her pierced clitoris. She'd stood placidly in place under Jenny's, Sarah's, Charles's

58

and professor Phillips-Webber's disbelieving gazes, while the aristocrat tied her breast tethers to a wall-ring. Deliberately tying the rope off too short, so that her toy's big heavy breasts were dragged up.

Jenny had had enough. "I'm not a bloody serf!" she stormed.

Lady Isobell had raised one perfect eyebrow. "You look like one," she'd retorted mildly.

Jenny had snatched off her veil. "And now?"

"Now you look like a slave," the aristocrat had said amused. "Nice face if we hollow your cheeks out a little. Fuller lips and lighter and wider eyes I think. Body not bad; a little heavy around the hindquarters and not enough up top. But I might buy it."

Jenny had learnt not to argue with the young-looking Lady. She could tie her in knots. Partly it came from having been raised thinking that 99% of the world were her inferiors who should know their place; and partly it was experience. She may have looked about 20, but actually she was 37. Jenny thinking she was dealing with someone her own age had been caught out time and time again.

Lady Isobell watched impatiently while Jenny, juggling two carrier-bags full of Haynes car-manuals, their dimension being ahead in car design, unlocked her flat's door. It wasn't that the aristocrat was rude, she'd come to realise after getting to know her, it was just she'd never had to carry a bag in her entire life. The Lady stopped in front of the hall mirror holding out her collar, and grimaced in disgust.

"Gods, this city is filthy! Why is there so much grime?"

"Industry? Cars?" Jenny shrugged.

"Then perhaps we'd be better of without them."

In fact Jenny half-agreed. The alternative world was a much more pleasant environment. Clean air, an intact ozone layer and far fewer endangered habitats and species. The working-classes had medical care, running water and plumbing, but only the nobles had use for cruise-ships, aircraft; owned cars, more than two or three sets of clothing and had electricity in their homes; with all the gadgets that went with it. It made for a much smaller industrial base; less pollution, less concrete. A wonderful place to raise children, providing they were going to grow up to be owners, not owned.

Lady Isobell pulled her blouse over her head and dropped it on the floor, unbuttoning her skirt as she walked to the bathroom. She wore no bra, her breasts small and firm, not needing one; totally unselfconscious. As far as Jenny could tell the Lords and Ladies had no inhibitions about nudity. Jenny tried not to look too obviously as she turned on the shower, though she knew the other-Earth woman didn't care. Lady Isobell was tiny, maybe a fraction above five foot, her figure slender, almost girlish. Jenny easily stood a head taller and probably out-massed her by two stone.

Like a china doll with big wide eyes and a pixie haircut, she looked fragile, vulnerable. Naked now, almost sweetly helpless. And then Jenny remembered the casual, practised ease with which this woman had tied a slave to a wall-ring by her bound breasts and casually stroked her voluptuous curves while they talked. Like Jenny the full-breasted brunette had been much bigger and probably stronger, but even without her hands tied, she was suddenly sure Lady Isobell could have bent the girl to her will. There was, when you looked for it, something cruel and infinitely threatening about the aristocrat's smile.

"Scrub my back will you darling?"

"I...I...I'd rather not," Jenny stammered, embarrassed at being caught looking.

"Oh don't be shy. You people are so repressed."

Reluctantly (eagerly?) she rolled up her sleeves.

"No! Take it off. You'll get it wet," she was ordered.

Jenny looked into a predator's eyes, knowing she was at a crossroads. She could say no now and get away with it, but the offer might not come again. But obviously if she obeyed, she'd be agreeing to far more than taking off her blouse. Excitement building, Jenny let white cotton fall around her

60

ankles, finally admitting what she'd been trying to deny for days. Of course she didn't want to be a slave, but slave-owners, true dominants, not just people playing at it, fascinated her.

Lady Isobell reached out and hooked a finger under her bra, shaking her breasts. "That too!"

Naked from the waist up she stood still, displaying herself like one of this woman's slaves. One of her own dreams, of being coldly inspected, without kindness or sentiment, coming true. The aristocrat nodded approval; Jenny's nipples were suddenly hard, breasts swelling with lust. Lady Isobell turned her back, examining Jenny's now soaking bra.

"You can start with my legs. Feet first."

Jenny got down on her knees, excitement growing.

"You should kiss them first!"

Jenny looked up.

"A girl should never lay hands on me without permission. Kissing my feet is a way of asking my leave if I haven't given you permission to talk."

Slowly, Jenny leant forward, water running down her back, soaking into her jeans and plastering her hair around her face. All her submissive fantasies coming true, she lightly touched her lips to first one foot and then the other.

"You may continue."

Jenny was initially surprised to find the aristocrat didn't shave her legs or under her arms, as all the slave-girls she'd seen had been baby-smooth, some even without pubic hair. It made sense, she realised. While her playthings were expected to be softly, sexually feminine, witness all the stiletto heels, waist-length hair, big boobs and hour-glass figures, there was no such compulsion on her.

"What does 36C mean?"

"That's the size of the garment. My size,"

"Oh. Do my back now."

Jenny obeyed eagerly.

"I was wondering...?" she said hesitantly.

"Yes?"

"The girls.... the slaves," she corrected herself. "Some of them.... well quite a lot of them, seem to have quite large breasts and small waists. I was wondering....? Well, your father said something about an injection?"

Franklin had said about a third of slave-girls had large busts, but his idea of large and the traveller's seemed to differ slightly. There were some slender girls; it was every aristocrat's birthright to own the type of slave that pleased them most, but about two thirds seemed to be well endowed, a third of them hugely so; probably the toys Franklin had been referring to. Andrew and Charles had gleefully renamed the slaveworld, and were now referring to it as Tit-world.

And this was the woman who had the power to turn a person into a sex-toy! Jenny's soaped fingers traced the ridges of muscle on either side of the aristocrat's spine, slowly sliding up and then down, pausing with her hands just above the swell of the naked woman's buttocks. Under pale skin she was whipcord muscular, not at all the delicate Lady of first impressions. She'd never dreamed she might really get to touch a real Mistress like this.

"Yes, some owners like heavy tits to play with," Lady Isobell agreed. "It's a simple change to make, just an injection, and I for one have always thought a sex-object should first and foremost, look like one. Oh, that's good! Bit lower! An hourglass figure is more expensive, you have to send the girl to the clinic to have her waist nipped whereas tits you can do yourself, but there's no point in stinting on your pleasures. You only live once, so you have to enjoy your slaves to the full I say."

"But don't the girls get back problems? And it must be uncomfortable for them?"

"And?" she shrugged. "As for back trouble, our doctors can do spine-transplants. A little back-ache is easily fixed."

"But don't they droop?" Jenny blurted, darkly fascinated by the depths of humiliation one of Lady Isobell's sex-toys was expected to endure for her owner's pleasure.

"Not really, the treatment works naturally, building up fatty deposits in the breast, but we've improved slightly on nature to make them a little firmer. Not too much; still nicely squeezable and ropeable. Just enough to last a girl's sentence, 5 to 10 years most of them. Slaves on longer sentences can be given tiny doses. If you keep making the tits fractionally bigger, that keeps the girl's appearance satisfactory. And of course slaves on longer sentences get the rejuvenation treatment anyway."

Jenny froze in her soaping, Lady Isobell meeting her eyes across her shoulder. Her grin was that of a cat, and that only left one mouse.

"Thought that might get your attention. I was discussing it with Sybill and Father." Lady Sybill was Karen's guide. "We tend to assume the treatment's exclusive to the nobility, and forget about the exception. If you can pass as slaves, we can get you in no problem."

"A slave?" Jenny asked, suddenly cautious.

"All slaves' sentences assume time off for good behaviour, but if an owner has a favourite he wants to keep, then of course he wants to keep her young," the aristocrat said offhand. "It would not be unremarkable for my father to pay to have five young slaves treated."

Thinking on that, Jenny obediently stripped and washed herself while the strange young/old woman watched, and ordered her to squeeze her soaped breasts, shampoo her pubic hair and work the soap into her pussy. Could she trust a stranger who owned people? No, of course not, but for the moment she was incredibly horny. It was incredible! Somebody was actually watching her shower. Ordering her to masturbate with a bar of soap. In rising excitement, still under the shower she was made to shave her legs and under her arms, then brush her teeth, and was finally led still wet to her own bed by a firmly held handful of pubic hair. It was so deliciously easy to obey.

She was ordered to kneel on all fours, head up and thighs

spread while Lady Isobell handled her. The hands sliding over her wet slippery flesh weren't a lover's caress, Jenny suddenly realised. She was being evaluated, inspected, compared to the other merchandise the aristocrat had enjoyed, and might actually be rejected. The thought drove her wild, and it was all she could do to remain obediently in place.

"You'll do," the woman decided.

Jenny nearly came on the spot. Her lust-swollen breasts were squeezed, just short of painfully, her nipples were twisted, just short of painfully, a handprint left on each cheek of her backside, the sting making her gasp in pleasure. The slave-owner's touch was deft and sure, so unlike the uncertain fumblings of lovers her own age. Finally, the pain delectable, a pubic hair was plucked from either side of her pussy. Jenny cried out in ecstasy as fingers penetrated her sex while her clitoris was simultaneously squeezed, a wave of pleasure engulfing her body.

Long before she'd recovered her senses, Jenny had been flipped onto her back, arms above her head, Lady Isobell sitting astride her face facing down her body, her legs trapping Jenny's arms under her. For the first time in her life, Jenny tasted soap and woman, her nose filled with the scent of her.

Jenny was unfamiliar with lesbian or submissive sex, except in her fantasies, but was quickly and firmly introduced to the rules of the game. When her nipples were twisted she worked her lips over the sex-lips of the woman astride her, when her nipples were squeezed, she used her tongue. If her breasts were squeezed she had to plunge her tongue as deeply as she could into her controller's sex, tongue working in time with squeezes. Yanked pubic hair meant lick Mistress's clitoris, and slaps on her belly meant harder or faster.

She was being ridden! Jenny didn't consider herself promiscuous, but she'd had a boy-friend or two in her time, and at least knew the difference between making love, and being fucked. Half stifled, juices smearing her face and obeying the hand commands of the aristocrat riding her to a leisurely orgasm without hesitation, Jenny realised she was very definitely being fucked. It was wonderful!

Finally, when Lady Isobell was satisfied, Jenny having been ordered to lie across the top of her own bed so that the small of her back could be used as a pillow, she was allowed to cradle her abused breasts and pubes. Being dominated was darkly wondrous, but pity the poor slave girl who didn't have the right to set limits or say 'enough'.

"Do you know," the aristocrat said idly, "that's really the first time I've ever made love the old way? It was different. Strangely pleasant actually. I've never had to be that considerate or gentle before. You know, with property you just do what you like with her and expect her to enjoy it. You don't have to worry about her feelings. We'll do that again I think. But I want to use some rope on you next time."

The crotch-rope was driving her wild, the rough fibres dragging between her sex-lips and over her clitoris. She felt rubbed raw, and was terrified the crotch of her jeans, an old too-tight pair without panties that Lady Isobell had made her wear, were going to be damp.

"What's that shop over there?"

"Huh?"

"Pay attention, Jenny dear," the aristocrat said, patting her on the bottom. Two men passing by both grinned widely at the blatantly intimate touch. Jenny felt herself flushing with embarrassment and lust. "I said, what is that shop?"

"A chemist. A medicine shop."

Both men's eyes lingered on her breasts until they actually passed. Her Mistress had selected a tight tank-top to better display her breasts, and so that she could see at a glance if Jenny's nipples weren't erect.

***

Naked and tightly hog-tied, ropes tight around her breasts and gagged with her own underwear, Jenny lay on her own kitchen table while Lady Isobell ate a light lunch. A rope tight around her waist and woven into her hair held her head up, forcing her to meet her Mistress's eyes, neck and spine uncomfortably arched.

The sandwich hadn't really become popular in the alternative England, the aristocrat eating her bread with just butter, taking occasional licks of the patches of jams, patties, pastes and marmalade she'd dabbed on Jenny's straining breasts for flavour. Jenny was in heaven, even prepared to concede that perhaps her lover hadn't been that cruel tying that curvy brunette to that wall-ring by her boobs. She absolutely loved breast-bondage! The way her nipples protruded, the delicious constriction, the incredible sensation of a tongue or fingernail on sensitised, squeezed-taut flesh. And as for the lightest of squeezes!

Dildos penetrated both her pussy and back-passage, her virgin anus throbbing painfully from being stretched so wide, but it was bearable because her pussy was similarly stuffed. She'd been told she was being acclimatised, loosened up, for the strap-on-dildo Lady Isobell planned to use on her at some unspecified later date.

***

Jenny washed, blow-dried and brushed her hair, and carefully applied just the lightest touch of make-up that Mistress liked. She knelt down and snapped two padlocks closed, and then tightly buckled and padlocked into place a black leather collar. The broad polished band dug in uncomfortably under her chin if she didn't hold her head up high and still. Naked except for the collar and a pair of 4" stiletto heeled pumps with locking ankle-straps, that the aristocrat had brought back with her from her own world for Jenny to wear, she presented herself for inspection.

She walked slowly and carefully, used to platforms, but still a little unsure of her balance in her first pair of stilettos. Both sides of the Gate had independently developed almost identical designs for stiletto heeled shoes, though one side of the Gate went in for more in the way of built-in manacles and locking ankle-straps. She stood in the centre of her living-room, head forced up, feet set a neat eighteen inches apart, tummy in and hands folded back behind her neck, taking deep breaths to make more noticeable the rise and fall of her breasts.

Lady Isobell lounged on Jenny's sofa, wearing Jenny's robe, eating one of Jenny's apples, remote in hand, channel hopping. After about ten minutes or so she deigned to notice the naked girl awaiting her pleasure. Jenny caught her breath nervously when her lover's eyes finally turned to her. If she were found unsatisfactory, she would sleep alone tonight, the aristocrat returning to her own dimension to use one of her slaves. Jenny found herself resenting the slave-girls more and more. How was she supposed to compete with a real slave? Twice already she'd been found unsatisfactory, nipples not hard enough and pubic-hair not fluffy enough, having to sleep in collar and heels and wear them all through the next day, her Mistress of course not letting her have a key. Besides the frustration, she'd got some funny looks, wearing stiletto heels and a polo-neck jumper in summer.

"I think it's time you experienced nipple and pussy clamps," the aristocrat decided.

Jenny let out the breath she didn't realise she'd been holding in relief.

***

The rowing machine actually belonged to the athletic Karen, temporarily stored in her flat when her friend had moved house, and not yet collected. Blindfolded, hands and feet tied to the paddles and stirrups and the machine set for maximum effort, Jenny strained, rivulets of sweat running down her naked body. She bit down hard on the piece of cut-off broom-handle tied through her mouth like a bit, knowing she wouldn't be allowed any sex tonight unless she exhausted herself thoroughly.

One of Lady Isobell's pleasures was a pony-girl worked

until she dropped, lying exhausted in her bed. Tonight she'd decided she wanted a limp, pliant, spent body to play with. Jenny yelped as scalding candle-wax was dripped onto her breasts. She'd had to freely agree, knowing otherwise she couldn't compete with one of her lover's pony-girls. Those slaves had the whip to push them to the edge of exhaustion. In between tormenting her with the wax, the aristocrat kneaded, handled and stroked her body. She said she enjoyed the play of muscles under her skin as Jenny rowed.

"You know dear, you're quite a powerful animal," she said, one hand light on Jenny's stomach, the other gripping a thigh. "A little chunky, but bigger tits and a nipped waist would put you nicely in proportion." She picked some dried wax out of Jenny's pubic-hair. "I'd bet with some hard training I could make a half-decent pony-girl out of you."

She untied the rope holding the bit-gag between Jenny's teeth, removing her blindfold, Jenny seeing the faint smile on her face was unable to escape the feeling she was being tested, evaluated, somehow.

"Lick!" the aristocrat ordered, thrusting the strap-on-dildo she was now wearing buckled around her hips under Jenny's nose.

Jenny glanced up with a wordless, pleading, look of protest, the shiny plastic shaft looking clean enough now, but still one of the same ones that had been tied inside her pussy, or worse her back-passage, while she'd been hog-tied on the kitchen table the day before.

"I don't like to repeat orders," Lady Isobell said mildly. "And if you don't lubricate it properly, you'll wish you had when it goes up your ass!"

Hesitantly Jenny reached out and touched her tongue to the tip of the shaft, fortunately unable to taste anything, and then let her lips close over the black plastic. Closing her eyes to help fool herself it was Andrew's penis instead, and make easier the revolting task, Jenny sucked saliva into her mouth, obediently giving the dildo a coating of lubrication. With a slight chill of fear, she couldn't quite ignore how fat the shaft was, no matter how hard she pretended it was Andrew's flesh.

Jenny was brutally butt-fucked as she lay limp where she'd been thrown, panting, shattered and face-down on the floor. She squealed as she was penetrated, anus stretched wide, thinking surely flesh would tear, but the shaft just plunged deeper. The thin carpet was rough under her breasts and stomach as she was made to squirm under the weight of her rider and to writhe in response to the aristocrat's thrusts. But for the same reason, it was heavenly against her swollen nipples. She could feel her sphincter stretched wide, but the bizarre pressure of thrusts where nature never intended, wasn't that far separated from her dripping pussy which would have welcomed the invader. Still fantasizing of Andrew, she imagined it was his penis plunging into her ass, his hands in her hair holding her in place, head back and neck arched. Muscle gripping the fat shaft relaxed slightly as Jenny surrendered herself to fantasy and desire. Lust stirred in her exhausted body, heat spreading easily to her groin under the relentless pounding; anal sex strange and strangely stimulating.

Lady Isobell quickly rode her conquest to orgasm, on her side of the large strap-on-dildo was just a small projection that rubbed pleasantly against the user's clitoris; Jenny's lust fanned into an urgent heat in her groin, breasts swollen tender, and nipples achingly hard by the time she was finished with. Her Mistress unbuckled the dildo's harness from her hips and pulled away, leaving the fat, ribbed shaft still embedded between Jenny's buttocks.

"Thank you, My Lady," she said softly, even though her first, instantly quashed, reaction had been a moan of protest.

Knowing that if she wasn't respectful, there might not be a second opportunity to be disappointed, she kept her voice low, polite and subservient. She lay exactly where she'd been left, making no attempt to remove the dildo penetrating her. If Mistress wished to enjoy her a second time, then she would just be able to lie on top of Jenny, and buckle the harness back on. Jenny grunted, the air suddenly forced from her lungs, when a knee went down hard on her back and her wrists were quickly and efficiently handcuffed to her ankles.

"You know I'm going to miss you when we break contact," Lady Isobell said, holding up her head by her hair. "I've really enjoyed the novelty of having a lover."

The aristocrat kissed her lightly on the nose, and then let her head drop, settling herself on the sofa to watch a film. Jenny was left to lie where she'd been used, naked and bound, but strangely content.

FOUR
A PRESENT

JENNY EXPERIENCED THE USUAL moment of dizzying nausea when she stepped through the Gate. Resigned, she shrugged into one of the waiting robes with its built-in veil, and waited for the computer to recognise her voice and unlock the door.

A naked slave-boy with his arms secured tightly behind his back was kneeling outside the door, and stood when he saw Jenny. He was being tormented with clamped nipples. A bursting erection was swelling around a tight Arab-strap buckled and padlocked into place around cock and balls, and he had a feather duster held in his mouth by a head-harness. In thick black marker-pen, written across his torso, was: JENNY. SOUTH PADDOCK. LADY I. X.

In bemused wonder Jenny nodded to the slave, allowing him to return to whatever cleaning duties being a note-pad had interrupted. Pausing to admire the athletic slave-boy's nicely firm behind as he walked away, Jenny reflected on that the fact that being trusted to wander unsupervised was a definite step up. She was getting quite blasé about whip-marked flesh too, she realised. That was the true danger of the Slaveworld she was coming to realise. It was so seductive.

In the more public and frequently used parts of the house, glass display-cases held slave-boys and girls, some dildo mounted and chained in place with body-piercings, others so tightly bound with leather straps that their bonds dug into them with every breath. Toys with whip-stripes, clamp pinch-marks, rope-burns and bruises on their naked bodies, were displayed with pride by those who had abused them, until the marks faded and they were ready to be enjoyed again; a blank canvas to work on!

She stood aside, head lowered slightly in the proper attitude of a serf woman, when a uniformed man led a bound girl by with collar and lead. The voluptuous toy swayed past on tall stiletto heels, her wrists cuffed behind her, a belt digging deep into her waist dragging a cruelly tight, teasing, chain up between her sex-lips, a ball-gag filling her mouth. A key-ring, undoubtedly for the cuffs, and the padlocks on her collar and stiletto shoes' ankle-straps as well as the crotch-chain, was clamped to one fat nipple.

She was being taken to some aristocrat's bed or playroom to be sexually abused, Jenny realised with fascinated horror. The naked slave followed her lead placidly, without fuss; but what else could she do? This world was a terrible trap for someone born poor. No hope of escape, and she knew it; resistance pointless.

***

Jenny only got lost once in the huge rambling maze of the manor house. The basic shape was a capital E, the lab on the second floor of the centre projection.

Academic Franklin occupied the second and third floors of the top projection, his two sons and daughter the entire lower-wing between them. The rest was a confusing jumble; the main features a ballroom, dining-room and a small 50-seat theatre where slaves could be made to perform when cold weather or rain curtailed outdoor fun. Between and around, scattered seemingly at random, were guest suites, lounges, smoking-rooms, punishment rooms, playrooms, studies and three kitchens, house staff mostly occupying the attic. In the cellar, in row after row of cells, slaves not in use, or being given a chance for marks to fade from their bodies, slept, ate and were groomed. A detached stable-block was where most training was done.

In the south paddock a full-breasted blonde pony-girl was being pranced along at a smart breast-bouncing trot with the encouragement of Lady Isobell's whip, the petite aristocrat swinging her lash from the comfortable seat of the pony-trap the naked slave was hitched to. Jenny watched the tit-strapped, dildo-stuffed pony-slave with a mixture of sympathetic horror and green-eyed envy. Four more slave-girls in harness and bridle, three fresh, one sweat-sheened with fresh whip-stripes on her haunches, waited in a row hitched to a railing beside the gate.

In a sweeping turn, expertly weaving her mount in and out of a row of straw-bales, the aristocrat guided the blonde back to the gate and pulled her to a panting stop. The attraction of a panting, sweat-gleaming pony-slave was suddenly obvious, proof that the helpless slave was being made to exert herself to the utmost to please. The girl had reins clipped to her nipple-rings and also a strange bar linking the pierced nubs, wide blue blinkered eyes swimming with tears. Lady Isobell hopped lightly from the seat of her little two-wheeled carriage and ran a gloved hand lightly over the raised welts her whip had left on the taut curve of a buttock.

"What do you think Jenny?" she asked gaily, hefting and thoughtfully squeezing a bound breast.

"She's lovely My Lady. Is she yours?"

"They're all my brother's. He said I could try them out and borrow one. I need a hunter."

Lady Isobell removed a glove and ran a finger down the sweat-sheened slave's flank, tasting thoughtfully. Then she ran the same finger down the blonde's crotch-strap, starting at the girth, following the polished leather strap pulled into the girl's pussy between the folds of her sex-lips, she slowly savoured her flavour, and finally tasted her pony-girl's tears.

"Don't you just love the taste of subservience?" she said merrily, replacing her glove. "So anyway, here I am without a ride, and I get invited to a friend's hunt. Mortified? Well, who wouldn't be? And wouldn't you know it, I just sold the most perfect filly, not realising I wasn't going to have time to do the rounds of the auctions."

She winked at Jenny, their shared secret; the Gate, the reason she suddenly had no free time, and turned her attention back to her bound plaything. She nipped the panting girl's nipples between her teeth, first one and then the other, tonguing the trapped flesh, apparently seeing if they could be made harder.

She seemed disappointed.

"So, of course I own other girls, but three are just bed-warmers, pillow-trained, I've got several racing ponies but they're away competing and my pair of show-ponies are trained for a ten minute performance. Great tits and sexy as hell, but they haven't got the stamina for a day's hunt."

She tossed her head in petulant irritation and then licked the blonde's strap-bound breasts with long, slow strokes. The freshly whipped pony-girl moaned in delight.

"And my new toy's barely broken in. Daddy's hopeless; he likes the power of a pony-boy, so none of his girls has even tasted a bit, and I refuse to hunt a pony-boy! They're so clumpy. I like a dainty mount. My twin brother still won't let me near any of his anymore. Ever since I improved the tits on this girl he was planning to give to his girlfriend, without asking him. How was I supposed to know she liked willowy blondes?" she grinned, "Fortunately it's big brother to the rescue!"

Jenny felt her mouth hanging open. Everyone should have such problems! Lady Isobell stood aside to let a red-uniformed man unhitch the blond and replace her between the shafts with a slender brunette. She looked over the absolutely beautiful girl a moment with pursed lips, and then shook her head.

"No tits," she decided, waving the soldier back. "Let's have the redhead."

The uniformed man unhitched the girl he'd just secured between the pony-trap's shafts without complaint, and set about replacing her with Lady Isobell's next choice. They called themselves soldiers, but although no expert, Jenny didn't consider the alternate England's troops a real army. They drilled in regiments only twice a year; the Royal troops mainly policemen, the Household troops; security, enforcers and slave-trainers for the noble Houses.

"That's better," the aristocrat decided as she surveyed her next ride. "You're actually not supposed to hunt really top-heavy girls, but what the hell."

She stroked and then hefted the ginger-maned pony-girl's freckle-dusted breasts, the pink-nippled globes, squeezed and supported by harness straps, were large and heavy.

"Oh that's much better."

"Why does she have that bar between her nipples?" Jenny asked hesitantly.

"Makes her boobs swing together," the aristocrat said carelessly as she checked the attachment of reins to the redhead's nipple-rings. "Even with straps, top-heavy toys bounce about, and they look untidy with boobs swinging this way and that."

The top-heavy toy in question moaned in pained arousal when her huge breasts were lifted by her reins, Lady Isobell pulling up with both reins in one hand, the full weight of both bound melons hanging from pierced nipples. Tears of shame rolled down the obviously inexperienced slave's cheeks, her blinkered eyes, wide, green and frightened, darting back and forth between Jenny and the soldier in a silent plea for help. There was of course none. But interestingly, she made no move to pull away as she was handled, and when Lady Isobell's gloved hand cupped her clean-shaven pussy her hips twitched forward against the pressure and she whimpered with delight.

When Jenny had first encountered slaves, she'd assumed their apparent sexual arousal was faked; just keeping on the good side of the people who had absolute power over them. Each encounter had left her increasingly puzzled. Andrew, who she darkly suspected, but hadn't dared accuse, of having sex with slaves, had explained. As well as a contraceptive placed under the skin to slowly dissolve into the bloodstream when first sentenced, slaves also had an aphrodisiac implanted in them. In their minds slaves were still free to feel shame, humiliation, despair and fear, but the lust they felt, and the arousal and orgasms forced from their chained, bound bodies were quite, quite real.

Lady Isobell unbuckled the girl's crotch-strap, letting a fat heavy dildo glistening with the pony-girl's juices slide out for half its length to inspect, and then pulled up and buckled the strap tight again, driving the shaft deep back inside the harnessed girl. The slave groaned in pleasure, eyes half-closed. The aristocrat gave the red-head's crotch-strap a last tug to settle it into place, her harnessed and bridled plaything, mouth full of bit and arms buckled behind her, gasping helplessly. Lady Isobell stroked her naked prize with evident pleasure; the inexperienced slave whining plaintively when her bridle's collar was pulled a notch tighter, leather digging into her neck.

"She'll be drooling on those tits soon," the aristocrat confided happily.

The pony-girl waiting to be whipped around the paddock was about Jenny's height, perhaps a half-inch taller, the woman checking the fit of her bit appearing tiny, child-like by comparison, but Jenny wasn't fooled. She'd already experienced the woman's wiry strength and aggressive, fearless personality, and knew she would effortlessly dominate the bigger, stronger girl. Just as a child could ride a big powerful horse, it was partly a question of skill, training and equipment, but mostly, mind-set on the part of both. Lady Isobell believed she had the right and ability to control the pony-girl, and so did her big-breasted mount.

It was actually one of the fringe benefits of an SM relationship, unsuspected until she'd tripped over it, that Jenny found particularly attractive. Lady Isobell was the first lover she'd ever had who wasn't taller than she was. In her whole life she'd never been asked out by a man shorter than she was, and worse, she was too obviously bright, most men were intimidated by brains. But not just Lady Isobell, all the Lords and Ladies, simply didn't care if the toy on the end of their lead was bigger, stronger, more intelligent or even more attractive than they were. It was wonderful. She knew Andrew would find this girl attractive!

The freckled pony-girl's first squeak of pain as she was lashed into motion aroused instant sympathy in Jenny, reality overtaking fantasy. She stepped forward a pace, one arm going up, mouth open in wordless futile protest under her veil, but the pony-trap was already sweeping past. Another crack of leather on flesh drove Lady Isobell's young mount smoothly into a trot.

The endurance and speed a firmly whipped pony-girl was capable of surprised her. In black humour, the thought occurred that they should find some way to whip Olympic athletes as they ran. Guaranteed gold for Karen! She considered doing the decent thing and turning or walking away, but didn't want to offend her host. Besides, the girl's ordeal would continue whether she watched or not.

The way to watch was coolly, detached, like an anthropologist studying the rites of some strangely savage and barbaric tribe. Just like professor Phillips-Webber had advised. An uninvolved scientific observer wasn't accountable, need feel no guilt. And once you left moral judgements aside there was something quite primeval—compelling —about the spectacle. Young flesh straining against and constricted by a harness was strangely fascinating.

And somehow so right. The redhead just looked like she belonged in harness.

Of course no person, even a detached scientific adviser, could actually get used to, or fail to be moved by, the big-breasted slave's squeaks and yelps of distress. Of course her anguished cries of pain were horrifying. But—Jenny reluctantly conceded—the redhead, while making a lot of noise, could obviously take it. Tears were flowing and her flesh was marked, but she was being done no real harm and Lady Isobell was clearly enjoying her.

After watching a while, leaning up against the fence resting her chin on her forearms, Jenny suddenly realised with a guilty start she'd been watching the swing and bounce of the pony-girl's breasts with pleasure, dreamily thinking about the dildo she'd seen stirring the slave-slut's insides to jelly as she was forced to trot, prance and sprint against the weight of carriage and Mistress. The ginger-maned pony-slave soon gleamed as if oiled, a most attractive effect; and Jenny had to admit, her gasping squeaks and the crack of leather on flesh, were undeniably stimulating.

The pony, wide-eyed and bit foam-flecked, swept past, harness jingling merrily. She didn't need to feel guilty about enjoying the show Jenny decided. Her newly awakened submissive side was just responding to the dominant display. Imagining herself in the naked pony-girl's places, though not treated quite so harshly! Being aroused by sexual torment in no way meant she condoned the practice of slavery, she rationalised. The show would be the same if Lady Isobell's lush plaything was submitting voluntarily.

Jenny was actually disappointed when the gasping, sweat-lathered pony-slave, bound breasts heaving, was brought to a halt and Lady Isobell dismounted. The redhead obviously had a couple more laps in her.

Lady Isobell and Jenny took afternoon tea in one of her rooms; the study on the third floor, wood panelled and lined with books. A row of open French windows ran the length of the room, allowing in sunlight and a pleasant summer breeze. The aristocrat's chosen pony-girl from the morning's trials, the green-eyed redhead Jenny had been impressed with, stood naked in the sunlight with her arms chained above her for their admiration.

Jenny, allowed to remove her veil in the privacy of her lover's rooms, sipped tea from delicate bone-china, trying to carry on a normal conversation with a naked girl just an arm's reach away. She found herself very aware of the gentle rise and fall of the slave's large breasts, though she was no longer especially horrified by, or sympathetic towards top-heavy toys. She was getting acclimatised. It was a question of setting. Like a man wearing a tie looked normal in an office, but stupid on a tropical beach, so huge boobs didn't look out of place on a naked, collared and bound girl.

The young slave was actually quite lovely. Jenny had had a

school friend who was a redhead, with a mass of freckles over face, arms and legs. She'd always felt slightly sorry for the girl, only too aware even then how much importance the world she lived in attached to appearance. But the slave with her wrists secured to a winch above her, an orange ball-gag stretching her mouth wide and wearing stiletto heels, was a revelation. Without the distraction of clothing breaking the lines of her body when the eye naturally tried to follow a curve here and a swell there, the freckles that dusted her body were in no way a blemish. Quite the opposite, the effect was like a leopard's spots. She was simply gorgeous!

Jenny timidly said as much to Lady Isobell, knowing in her own mind she shouldn't be admiring a person who was property, should be nothing but emphatic in her disapproval. But what she really wanted to do was reach out and stroke that silky freckled skin.

"Oh you're right," the aristocrat agreed. "Freckled redheads are best kept totally naked. You saw even the harness and bridle detracted from her beauty, but here she's quite stunning. My fiancé's mother keeps a redhead as a pet actually. Never lets her wear anything or puts a harness on her; just wrist-cuffs, a lead clipped to her pussy and sometimes a black velvet hood. Takes her everywhere. Quite lovely!" She reached out and let her hand trail down the slave's hip. "I think that's what brother-dear's got planned for this. A present for one of his lady friends. She'll make a nice poodle don't you think?"

The aristocrat's hand lingered, slowly stroking down a firm thigh. The thick metal rings set through the gagged girl's pink nipples made the rise and fall of her breathing particularly noticeable, Jenny was actually close enough to reach out and touch the gentle swell and fall of her stomach.

She imagined doing so, feeling the slave's body-heat, and the way her fingers would indent soft flesh. The big-breasted slave had been hosed down and brushed up by one of the efficient grooms before delivery, and she smelled faintly of soap and shampoo, her hair, brushed into a shining wave, glinted copper in the sunlight.

"Would you like to fuck her?"

"You...I...I...what!"

"Jenny dear, you've been practically drooling all afternoon," Lady Isobell said with a fond smile. She reached out and ran the backs of her fingers down the gentle curve of the girl's belly, the young sex-toy quivering as fingers brushed her pussy. "If you'd prefer one of the others?"

"I... couldn't. It's not our way. You know... In our world..." Jenny stammered helplessly.

The aristocrat looked hurt. "Oh! I just thought you might like to try her out. A present, now that we're friends. She'll be tied down, and she's very docile," she encouraged.

Jenny's natural caution overcame her momentary stunned surprise at Lady Isobell's disappointed little-girl tone and her use of the word friend. Little girl nothing; she was 37! As for friend? Jenny wasn't stupid. The aristocrat did genuinely like her now, she was sure, but she'd never be seen as an equal in this world. Lady Isobell probably regarded her as an interesting diversion; a talking dog or a horse that could count, to be treated kindly as long as Jenny was clean, respectful and house-trained, but never a friend.

"Well, if you feel like that?"

Her host nibbled on a biscuit, looking at Jenny in puzzlement. Of course she might not necessarily have been teasing or manipulating, Jenny realised, but genuinely offering her what she'd thought was a treat, awkwardly, because she wasn't used to being generous to the lower-classes? Her next words confirmed it.

"It's just that some of your friends have been enjoying our hospitality, and you seemed to be missing out. I just thought you were too shy to ask."

"Really?" Jenny blurted.

Andrew, as she'd suspected, had been jumping anything that moved, but more surprising, the blond lovers Charles and Sarah had developed a taste for racing-ponies and had been tempted to try the playrooms.

"I'm sorry. You know me; I am a bit shy." Jenny apologised.

"Oh don't worry yourself. You have a closer look while I get you a strap-on."

Before Jenny even realised her refusal had been misunderstood, let alone had time to correct her, Lady Isobell had bounded out of the door. She stood, words unsaid, now alone with a ball-gagged, naked, girl with her arms pulled above her.

Wide green eyes watched her apprehensively. It was another popular bit of cosmetic surgery, Jenny had learnt. The actual size of the eyeball couldn't be changed, but by pulling the eyelids back a little, an owner could give his or her property that pleasing wide-eyed innocent look. The ball-gag increased the effect, giving the bound girl a look of doe-eyed submission Jenny recognised from a mirror. She understood the girl's apprehension. In her world women without veils were either slaves or Mistresses, and Jenny obviously wasn't a slave.

"Don't worry, I'm not one of them," Jenny promised, stroking her girl's copper hair. "I won't do anything to you."

Her hand slipped, so easily, from the girl's hair and down her back, fingers lightly tracing vertebrae. Long-lashed eyes half-closed in pleasure, the freckled girl arching her back as far as her bonds would allow. Almost hanging from her wrists she was forced to stand on her toes, body pulled taut, stiletto heels just brushing the thick carpet even though she was padlocked into 5" heels.

From behind, Jenny reached up to the thick padded bands buckled and locked around the girl's slender wrists, and slowly ran her hands down. Stroking slowly, sensuously, palms caressing velvet flesh, she slid her hands down the girl's arms, sides, hips, thighs, and down to the locked ankle-straps of her stiletto sandals.

Kneeling behind the helpless slave Jenny hesitantly stroked the welts that criss-crossed the young toy's haunches, most of the marks on her buttocks, but some on her thighs and curling around her hips. You could see by the gaps in the whip-stripes where, in addition to the thicker crotch-strap, the other straps of the pony-girl's harness had been; running up from under her up either side of her pussy, and behind, lifting and supporting each buttock, up to the sides of her girth. She only flinched a little.

Letting her cheek rest on the slave's back, Jenny let her hands stroke up the girl's stomach in dreamy contentment, scooping up large breasts without thought. Warm, heavy, flesh filled her hands, spilling and squeezed between splayed fingers. Surprisingly heavy. God, she was a big girl!

Jenny smiled lazily, realising she'd parroted a phrase from Professor Phillips-Webber that had horrified her at the time. But then she'd been automatically empathising with the slave; not the dominant! She had never touched any woman's breasts apart from her own before, not even her other-world lover now she thought about it, only a submissive's tongue required. She'd only scrubbed legs and back that first time in the shower, her hands subsequently secured or held neatly behind her. Now she was free to handle this girl as Lady Isobell had handled her. She had her first hint of power, and the emotional satisfaction that went with it, feeling now she might be beginning to understand Lady Isobell's attitudes to her human sex-toy's training, treatment, decoration and physique. Especially physique!

Ringed nipples rose obediently against her palms as she shifted her grip, squeezing, pulling and kneading, her hands simply too small to contain the heavy globes; only able to get a good grip when she sank her fingers deep into the flesh she held. The redhead moaned but with no hint of protest behind her gag. Jenny wondered idly how big her tits had been before they'd been enlarged. Leaning against the lovely body that was hers to play with was amazingly comfortable. Only a hint of guilt she couldn't quite push away spoiling the moment.

All too soon Lady Isobell returned, tossing a strap-on-dildo and its harness onto a heavy wooden desk. Jenny kneeling behind the almost suspended slave, her hands full of huge boobs, looked up, feeling herself flush scarlet. She scrambled to her feet.

"Strip off and get that on," her lover commanded cheerfully. "Unless you want to cuddle her some more?"

Wordlessly, without resistance, as in one of their games, Jenny obeyed, while the aristocrat arranged the entertainment into a more convenient position to be used. The winch was lowered to provide enough slack for the big-breasted plaything to be taken behind the heavy study desk and bent forward, Lady Isobell expertly looping rope around her ankles and tying them spread to the desk's legs. When the electric winch again pulled the red-head's body taut, the young slave lay on her stomach, bent forward over the desk, thighs up against its edge and with legs spread wide. The cable pulling her body forward and up, arched her body up off the desk, heavy breasts just brushing the polished wood surface. She was completely helpless, and ready to be taken from behind.

Lady Isobell reached under the bound girl and gave a breast a squeeze, her free hand stroking from the small of the bent-over slave's back, down between her buttocks, all four fingers sinking to the knuckle into the redhead's pouting pussy. The ball-gagged toy's head came up with a gasp.

"Head up proudly bitch!" the aristocrat ordered. "And don't be inhibited. When that dildo reams your snatch, I want to hear you. Understood?"

The freckled slave moaned something that might have been assent behind her gag. It turned into a rising wail of forced pleasure when Lady Isobell's fingers twisted deeper. Jenny, now naked, buckled the unfamiliar harness of the strap-on around her hips. At least it was unfamiliar being worn this way around. With the crotch-strap buckled into place, a fat ribbed shaft waggled obscenely between her legs.

Lady Isobell settled herself into a chair and raised a book. In a daze, wild excitement growing inside her, Jenny stepped up behind the bent-over girl, deliberately putting a swagger

83

in her step to make the black shaft swing more. This was fun! Her end of the dildo was just a small projection, barely more than a nub, which would rub pleasantly against her clitoris. Gentle stimulation for her, gasping, stretched impalement for the slave she was about to rape. The woman who had given her this wonderful present looked up from her book.

"Twist her tits or give her a quick spanking if she's not wet," the aristocrat advised.

Jenny nodded, disbelieving, an incredulous grin having plastered itself across her face. The tautly spread slave trembled lightly when Jenny laid a cautious hand on her hip. Bent forward across the desk, her pussy pouted between her thighs, humiliatingly exposed to Jenny's gaze. The tied down girl was very wet indeed thank you.

Jenny wiggled the tip of the dildo between plump sex-lips, and then simply leant forwards. The ginger-haired girl's body went rigid as she was penetrated, a long wailing moan of humiliated, pained lust forced from her. Looking down Jenny could clearly see how tightly her freckled pussy gripped the shaft. Bigger and heavier than the one Lady Isobell had used on her, she belatedly realised.

The slave's head jerked up with a whimper of delight as she was impaled to the hilt, Jenny's pelvis brushing marked buttocks with an electric touch. She was panting almost as hard as her now firmly stuffed and gagged victim, Jenny realised. Taking a deliberately calming deep breath, she relaxed her grip on the girl's hips. Her fingernails, sinking deep into firm flesh, had left marks. She leant forward with all her weight, pushing as hard as she could to force the dildo just that last fraction deeper. The impaled sex-toy cried out in delight.

Jenny found she had to squat a little awkwardly to shaft the bound girl, the desk height no doubt perfect for her shorter lover. Who knew how many lovely slave-girls had been raped over this very desk? Certainly not the aristocrat herself, for her it was just a pleasant afternoon's diversion, an act of no great significance. An ordinary day.

To the inexperienced slave Jenny was thrusting her dildo into, it was probably just another day too, though one of more significance to her. Jenny though, knew she would never forget riding the young slave to her first unwilling orgasm for as long as she lived, an impossible to imitate owner's-eye view. She thrust with long deep strokes, now teasingly trying to hold the lush-bodied sex-toy back from coming when she thought an orgasm approached, her hands free to roam the bound girl's body as she wished, delighting in her gag-stifled cries of pleasure. Occasionally Lady Isobell would look up from her book at a particularly shrill squeak or wail. Jenny's top-heavy plaything was unfortunately just too hot to be prevented from coming without permission.

Jenny deliberately pulled back from her own orgasm again and again, making her conquest moan in pleasure time after time. She rode her with slaps, pinches, handfuls of hair, her fingers hooked through the back of her ball-gag's strap buckled behind her neck, and with handfuls of breast. Just like her lover had ridden her, but harder. It didn't feel like rape, not here in this alternative dimension where lovely toys like this existed only to please, but she knew it was. And shamefully, that only added to her own arousal. She'd never dreamed how seductive power could be.

Eventually Jenny could hold back no more and had to give in to ecstasy. The first multiple orgasm of her life was quite shattering. But then, when she recovered herself, she still couldn't stop. The bound girl continued to docilely buck, gasp, and moan obediently under her. Thrusting the now dripping strap-on-dildo harder and deeper, Jenny discovered that if she threaded her middle fingers through the girls nipple rings, she could twist her nipples and squeeze her big tits at the same time.

***

Physical lust satisfied, she now learnt, that for the Mistress that was only half the picture. She felt empowered, thrillingly dominant, each time she thrust home the fat dildo and an unknown girl, bound and gagged, grunted or gasped. She was riding an emotional high that was almost as intense as her physical arousal had been.

Finally Lady Isobell called a halt. The top-heavy slave was spent, hanging limp, exhausted, in her bonds, head drooping barely responding to the most brutal dildo thrusts and hardly moaning at all when over-large breasts were squeezed.

"...I can give you some pin-lined gloves and a crop to perk her up, or a few volts to the nipples," she concluded, "but otherwise it's call up a replacement or call it a day."

Jenny remembered herself enough to decline, shame beginning to make itself felt as her physical lust and the emotional high faded. She dragged herself to one of her lover's en-suite showers, and stood under the cooling water for ages. God, what had she done? And worse, would she say no if the opportunity presented itself again? This place was a trap that would ensnare them, she was sure now, if they didn't quickly escape. When she returned to the study in a fluffy robe, nicely cooled off, the red-head was still lying limp as she'd left her, breathing slowly, head hanging and drooling on her ringed slave-breasts, sweat drying on her body.

"Tea Jenny?" Lady Isobell asked.

She rang a bell and a cock-strapped, tongue-clamped slave-boy materialised.

"I don't think I need to ask if you enjoyed her, do I? Such energy! You've nearly screwed her unconscious."

"No, she was wonderful," Jenny replied truthfully. "Thank you so much for letting me..." Jenny discovered she didn't know the right words but her lover waved her thanks aside. "What will happen to...?"

She gestured to the still-bound girl, realising she didn't even know her name. Lady Isobell pulled her belt-computer from a pocket, hooked a finger through the girl's right nipple-ring and lifted, breast and nipple cruelly stretched up. The machine beeped as it read the bar-code tattoo, hidden on the underside of the heavy globe.

"Sexual performance satisfactory; no punishment required. End," she dictated. "Hmm? Oh! It'll go in the cells or on display while the whip-marks fade. The grooms will trot her on a treadmill in full tack to keep her stamina up. She'll be toned and unmarked in time for the hunt, don't worry."

"Oh," Jenny managed.

***

A couple of days later, expressing casual interest, she persuaded Lady Isobell to take her on a tour of the cells. It was really the soldier's territory, apart from a once a month inspection by the master of the house, but the Lords and Ladies were of course a law unto themselves. She agreed, more for the amusement of seeing startled soldiers scrambling than for any other reason Jenny suspected.

The ordinary soldiers weren't allowed to have sex with their charges. A corporal could tit-fuck the girls, a sergeant was also allowed to come in the mouths of either sex. In theory only the Master-at-Arms was granted the privilege of full sex and was authorised to issue punishments; but there were probably one or two guilty consciences about. After all, if a hooded slave was taken from his or her cell one night, even if asked later, how would the hooded sex-toy know if the cocks that penetrated them, or the come coating their tongues in the morning, came from a soldier or a Lord?

Some of his men may have been nursing guilty consciences, but the Master-at-Arms seemed confident he ran a tight ship, and a surprise inspection would find nothing amiss. He was more than happy to indulge the whims of his Lord's daughter; in fact he seemed quite pleased at her interest.

The steel bars of the cage-like cells gleamed with polish—and saliva—as did the wooden floors. One or two slaves having been set to licking them clean. Naked flesh was on display between the bars, nervous eyes peering back at them.

Lady Isobell paused occasionally, checking a chart clipped beside each cell, but all the paperwork matched. This slave was having her nipples stretched on the orders of her owner, as was the girl with the stretching-plug chained into her ass, and the cock-strapped blond boy licking a pole-mounted dildo. If he didn't keep the entire surface wet, then sensors, via the electrodes attached to his scrotum, would deliver a painful shock, they were informed. Slaves were not allowed to be bad at oral sex!

Two new slave-girls swaying on 4" heels were being made to walk on treadmills, hobbled, hooded and hands cuffed behind backs. The luckier of the pair had a bar threaded through her nipple-rings, the other, nipples not pierced, had sharp-jawed clamps to hold her in place. They were undergoing normal, basic training, being taught to walk gracefully in stiletto heels. They came in three types Jenny had learnt; ankle-boots with 3" heels for show-ponies, 4" heels for everyday wear, and favoured pets were perched on 5" heels. A third slave, up to a more advanced level of training, had a dildo and plug strapped inside her as she walked, weights swinging from her nipples and her elbows fastened together behind her as well as handcuffs like the other girls.

In one of many punishment rooms a row of slave-boys who'd been found incapable of maintaining an erection for a satisfactory length of time were strapped in place, a wire pulled taut under twitching, flexing cocks. Any shaft that drooped would receive an agonising shock. It wasn't totally impossible to remain hard the required period. As a spur to greater efforts, they could see through the bars into the next punishment room, where a top-heavy blonde girl sitting on an icicle dildo was being tit-whipped; a punishment for being frigid.

Jenny gawked at the young slave, tightly strapped onto an almost ordinary looking chair, leather bands snug around her neck, waist, arms and legs, her clean-shaven sex stretched wide by the rubber-mounted pole of ice that rose up through an opening in the seat. A pair of automated lashes mounted on revolving poles flicked across her breasts at random intervals, the full globes quivering and dancing as she flinched, yelped and sobbed.

Jenny, now an experienced slave-watcher, figured out what she was watching almost immediately. There was a metal rod inside the ice-dildo, which combined with the electrode clamped to the blonde's tongue, would complete an electric circuit, and shut off the cat-o-nine-tails whips if the ice ever melted enough to allow contact with flesh. Certainly the punished girl was squirming, twisting and pushing down on the icicle shaft impaling her pussy as much as her bonds allowed, pale flesh already well marked with vivid red lines. And the ice-shaft's soft rubber mounting prevented her simply trying to break off the frozen invader. Cocks twitched and flexed as the whips suddenly, unexpectedly, swung again, smacking across trembling flesh; the blonde wailing helplessly as her large breasts were further reddened.

In the gym slaves toiled and sweated on exercise machines, the devices they were chained to automatically shocking them if they didn't keep up. Exercise and diet were closely monitored, no owner, many of whom were overweight themselves, was prepared to tolerate flab on property. Pony-slaves trotted on faster treadmills in full tack, other slaves had been set to lifting weights. To maintain muscle-tone, Lady Isobell carelessly explained.

***

Another punishment room, another sobbing girl, but this one's distress was being piped through the entire cellblock's Tannoy system. Jenny didn't know why she was shocked to find that the whimpers and pleas she'd been hearing was a live-broadcast rather than a recording, but she was. It was more real somehow. You could hope a tape was faked. The hog-tied girl with electrodes attached to tongue, nipples and sex-lips didn't even notice them, her ordeal authorised by the Master-at-Arms himself, for scratching one of his men.

Regular, measured shocks, every sixty seconds; and in a cruel twist, a ticking clock with a large sweeping second-hand had been placed directly in front of the bound girl. She could count down the seconds, see the pain coming!

As well as Academic Franklin, his two currently absent sons, and daughter Lady Isobell, there were his five resident lab-assistant/students; aristocrats one and all. Between them, even without the extra numbers Franklin maintained for the use of guests, that added up to a lot of sex-toys, Jenny discovered. Far more than she'd imagined!

Finally she found what she was secretly looking for in the shower block. Her redhead hung facedown in chains from ankles and wrists, having her teeth brushed and an enema tube pushed up her ass. The two girls hanging beside her were being soaped and shampooed by three pairs of hands each, the one on the end of the row hosed off with a high-pressure jet. The soldiers working the shower room all wore sleeveless waterproofs.

The top-heavy pony-girl seemed none the worse for her treatment at Jenny's hands she was relieved to see. She was bright eyed; breasts barely bruised at all. Guilt had been gnawing at Jenny. But more than ever the experience had convinced her that she and her fellow students were in a trap. This place was just too seductive!

And the trap door was closing.

FIVE
LONDON

THE COUNCIL OF WAR was held in professor Phillips-Webber's study. The topic was the likelihood that the alternative England would cut off contact. Most of the easily grabbable technologies had been secured by both sides, and what was left were guarded secrets; and the more intangible study of a new culture. Fascinating if you were an anthropologist, but worth the possible contamination for the Slaveworld?

"Incidentally, the Academic has now rigged his computer to shut down the Gate if it doesn't get a recognisable voice-print within 10 seconds of being used," Phillips-Webber told them. "He's been reading a book about the SAS, that someone happened to mention to him."

Andrew winced.

"Time to go public?" Jenny pressed.

"No. For two reasons. First, part of the reason they didn't shut us out after the first hello, is we're fellow scientists, just like them. Not official in any way; and I think we should keep it like that. They're leery enough of us as it is. I'm sure you've all noticed how I've been juggling the rotas around to try and keep one of them on our side at all times?"

Jenny and Karen nodded, Charles, Sarah and Andrew looking blank.

"And incidentally, well done those of you who've managed to persuade your guides to sleep over."

"They're so stuck up," Charles complained.

"And expect you to wait on them hand and foot," Sarah added. "Literally!" she chorused with her boyfriend.

Jenny caught Karen's eye and the dark-eyed girl looked away. She thought she could take a good guess at how her friend had been persuading Lady Sybill to tolerate the comparative squalor of Karen's flat instead of returning to the luxury of her own dimension each night. Pretty much the same way she'd been making Isobell at home at a guess. When

91

Karen had reached forward to put her glass on the table, her sleeve had pulled back revealing rope-burns around her wrist.

"It's confusing too sometimes," Andrew complained, shaking his head. "My chinless wonder asked me if I wanted to make love. So I politely tell him I like girls, and it's, '...no, no, no, my good fellow. You've got it all wrong.' Turns out he wanted to share a girl with me. Three in a bed!"

"Yes marriages, relationships and love amongst the nobles are primarily a meeting of minds," the professor agreed mildly. "Since artificial insemination was developed it's almost unheard of for a married couple to have sex even the once or twice that used to be necessary to ensure succession."

They all looked at her open-mouthed.

"But Lady Jane and Lord Albert are devoted to each other," Karen protested. "They're always kissing, touching and sneaking off together!"

"Yes, but what they call making love, we would describe as sharing the same slave together," their tutor explained. "And, while it's only polite to lend a slave to a friend, it is more unusual to share one. Your host obviously likes you and was paying you a compliment, Andrew."

He made a, "You-what!" face.

"She's right," Jenny confirmed, her lover quite uninhibited about discussing her own sex-life. "They're all too used to getting their own way. One would have to submit to the other, and by definition, aristocrats simply don't do that. So couples, husbands and wives, and sometimes close friends, share the same slave. Usually a girl in the sandwich, but sometimes a slave-boy."

"The two sometimes kiss over the slave's body, and of course there is pillow talk, but the chained slave endures any pain, humiliation and depravity. And of course licks up the semen afterwards. A very logical and satisfactory arrangement," their tutor said in a strange voice, eyes focused on something only she could see. "If you see nothing wrong with owning slaves," she added, suddenly aware of the silence.

92

All five students were staring at their professor in stunned surprise. She just kept amazing them. Before she'd opened the Gate, none of them would have bet on the cheerful old spinster not being a virgin, let alone having any idea what a sexual relationship entailed. That she could talk about the excesses of the Slaveworld so matter-of-factly, when none of them had thought she was even capable of mentioning sex without blushing, was baffling.

"You said two reasons?" Jenny changed the subject.

"Yes, the rejuvenation treatment! I really think we should get it for ourselves before we risk bringing in the government."

She looked around their faces, suddenly once again the razor-sharp scientist who could think in equations.

"Think about it. This world is over-crowded and under-fed already. People suddenly living longer will just make things a lot worse. The treatment's a secret, but its costs aren't. It's not that expensive, and we'd be doing it cheaper, in bulk. You know people would find the money. A new car, or a second-hand one and an extra twenty years? A colour TV, or a black and white one, and an extra five years to watch it? No contest!

"I could see a frightened government suppressing the treatment or pricing it out of almost everybody's reach, if only to stop the pension companies going bust. And I don't know about you, but I like the idea of those extra twenty years."

Phillips-Webber looked around the faces of her students, receiving solemn nods. She was right.

"And for all of you the treatment is even more dramatic. It's not just extending your lifespan like me, but extending your youth. The Academic has already agreed to pay for all our treatments if we can avoid official notice. I don't really think now is the time to go public. Do you?"

The nods this time were much more emphatic. The chance to keep the years back making them all greedy Jenny realised, even as she went along. And she'd come here to argue for closing their side.

"But what if they decide to cut off the Gate before we get

the treatment?"

"Maybe while we're on the wrong side?"

"And you can't pass for a slave. How will you get the treatment Professor?"

Their tutor shyly held out her hand, looking bemused but happy, as she displayed an engagement ring.

"Well as of this afternoon, I don't think my treatment, and the Gate being cut off on us, will be a problem for a little while. Lord Franklin has asked me to marry him!"

Jenny offered equally bemused congratulations. Poor cow, she thought. The plump tweed-wearing innocent was going to take it hard when this didn't work out. Christ, what would she do when he offered to share a slave with her; reality, not an abstract subject of study? All that brilliant intelligence, blinded by a foreign romance!

***

The next day Lady Isobell took Jenny on a trip to her dimension's capital city of Londinium which straddled the river Tamesis. It was not as large as their London, but occupied about the same position. In preparation for passing as a slave to get the youth treatment, Jenny wore 5" heels with a built-in hobble, a tight waspie corset and a posture collar under the mauve robes with the yellow trimmed cuffs of a secretary.

The corset was quite dreadful, squeezing her in two and she couldn't breathe properly, but it did look quite dramatic. It had inspired Isobell to give her a quick spanking and then push her to her knees, wrists tied behind her, and push her crotch into Jenny's face. For someone who had always been slightly revolted by the idea of oral-sex, though admittedly she'd been thinking of men, Jenny was becoming quite expert at pleasing her lover. Though she wished, just once, she could experience being the one tongued.

Forced by the corset to sit upright, her lover so taken with it that she suspected she was going to be wearing it a lot, Jenny perched on the edge of her seat, watching a strange England go by. The maglev train was really too fast to see much, but the neat, small fields and winding roads looked much like home. Only a half-seen pony-girl between the shafts of an owner's pony-trap, flashing past at a level-crossing, and occasional blurred glimpses of teams of powerful young men, harnessed naked to agricultural equipment, spoilt the illusion.

Jenny flinched with a gasp of pain, at an unexpected shock delivered to her left buttock. Also as part of her cover-training, she'd been made to wear a mesh body-stocking with small metal contact discs all over its inside, which gave her little electric shocks at random intervals. Supposedly in random places, but in practice, it seemed to be more on her bottom, pussy and breasts. Slaves didn't say no or make any more than the minimum of fuss when groped or unexpectedly hurt. Jenny had to learn.

"Anything wrong, Jenny dear?"

"No, My Lady. Just a hiccup."

"Try not to have too many more."

"Yes My Lady."

The aristocrat could also use her belt-computer to over-ride the random setting, guiding Jenny with remote control. She'd experimented around the house. A double shock between the shoulder-blades gave her notice she was now under control. A single shock to the pussy was, walk on, a double shock, stop, each breast left and right. The battery pack was a large ass-stretching plug filling her back-passage.

At the station a black-uniformed Royal trooper checking the passes and ID cards of the non-aristocrats riding the maglev totally ignored Jenny, obviously in the company of a noble. Isobell walked directly towards the exit, expecting underlings to get out of her way; which they did, Jenny scurrying along in her wake.

For Jenny the almost complete absence of traffic noise was initially the strangest thing about the Lords' and Ladies' capital city. Big steam-driven cargo carriers, powered by small fusion reactors, hissed past in a waft of humid air almost silently.

Smaller electric utility and delivery vehicles whined along softly, and only very occasionally, some young Lord in his private sportster, did you hear the rasp of an internal combustion engine. Most roads were two-lane, commercial traffic and trams kept to one lane, the other reserved for nobles. Where there was only one lane, it was for aristocrats.

Audible above the tyre noise were the squeaks of the whipped and shocked slaves, in the nobles' lanes. Pony-slaves pulling carriages pranced along between the occasional limousine as Jenny had expected, but in the city young Lords and Ladies in a hurry used tandem bicycles, weaving in and out of the slower trotting pony-traps and stately carriages.

The tandem bicycles looked normal at first glance, but of course weren't. In the front seat the young aristocrat just steered, braked and controlled the throttle, his or her feet propped comfortably on pegs. All the pedalling was done by the slave on the back seat, wrists, feet and waist chained to handlebars, pedals and seat. Many of the slaves were hooded, slavering down breathing tubes. Speed control was by means of graded electric shocks, increasingly powerful, through the slave's saddle or by electrode attached to their bodies. When the road-speed matched the throttle setting the shocks stopped, the bigger the difference between the speedometer and the throttle position, the more intense the pain.

Jenny watched a young couple, obviously racing, pull up at a red traffic-light with disappointed cries. They giggled helplessly at a sputtered, "Well, really! When I was a gel, we showed our elders some respect!" from a stern-looking matron driving the matched pair of full-breasted blonde pony-girls they'd just cut up.

The girl's slave was smallish, but with a huge cock pulled out in front of him, chained to the back of his tormentor's saddle with a ring set through his flesh. Surely such size wasn't natural? It wasn't only girls that were improved, Jenny knew. Whether big by nature's design or a veterinary plastic-surgeon, the thick meat shaft had shiny metal bands screwed down at intervals all along its length. Red wires trailed from the bottom of each band, disappearing into the bicycle's frame.

Her boyfriend's slave was another of the heavy-breasted blondes that Jenny was becoming so familiar with. She suspected that how to dye a girl's hair blonde, with matching eyebrows and, if any, pubic hair, was one of the first things a new soldier-groom was taught—right after being given a chart listing the recommended doses for boob enlargement. There were a lot of them about. Interchangeable toys.

The slave-girl's saddle formed a dildo that curved up into her, a red wire disappearing under it; a further two bundles of red wires running up to each breast. Both nipples and the areola around them were almost invisible under sharp-jawed metal clamps, many more biting into the soft flesh all over the large globes.

The light went green, no yellow on the Slaveworld, and both slaves cried out in anguish, instantly pedalling madly. The young Lord who had obviously picked his motor for her breast-size rather than her stamina, was soon falling behind.

With a haughty lift of her chin the stern-looking matron sniffed disapprovingly, and swung her whip hard across the naked buttocks of her pony-slaves, a triple lash, across, back and back again. The two golden-skinned sex-toys yelped, but were obviously superbly trained, and moved off smoothly without the slightest jerk, despite their Mistress taking out her frustration on their flesh. Both beautiful playthings had love-bites scattered over their heavy tits, rows of chastity rings set through their sex-lips and their crotch-chains were threaded through their dildos instead of mounted on the base. So that the dildo ends projected between their thighs, and passers-by could see and admire the size and weight of the shafts that impaled them. Standards were very strange things Jenny mused, as leather licking across taut buttocks took the pair out of sight.

It was harder to tell with the veiled women Jenny noticed, but without a doubt the working men going about their business, never looked directly at the naked slaves. They slid out of the way of aristocrats without thought, but were painfully careful not to notice the many slaves in the nobles' traffic lanes and on leads on the pavement. Scared to see a face they might recognise? Possibly. And also when the chained flesh was no longer young enough to enjoy, those toys they were so careful not to see would be returned to their families; and have to be accepted. Far more girls were taken than boys, but undoubtedly some of those drivers, shopkeepers, road-sweepers and merchants had once worn collars themselves. Or their wives had!

As in her own reality's feudal history, this world existed totally for the benefit of the ruling class, anyone not of noble lineage allowed only the scraps of happiness that fell from their betters' tables. Jenny saw a bound, tongue-clamped girl with a FOR SALE sign swinging jauntily from her nipples, being led along with a split lead clipped to her pierced sex-lips. And the worst thing about the feudal system was the way everyone from serf to Lord, not just the aristocrats, accepted it as normal. The way things were. No wonder the Lords and Ladies feared contamination.

After visiting a bookshop to pick up a copy on the care and maintenance of vehicle mounted fusion reactors, and several history books, Jenny followed obediently behind like a properly cowed servant/secretary, electronic note-book strapped to wrist and carrying the bags. She wished Isobell would walk slower, the hobble making her do a little short-stepped trot to keep up, occasional unexpected shocks and the plug filling her ass, more than a little distracting. She'd been very surprised to find she was able to come from anal sex; but surely it wasn't possible from just walking around in a butt-plug?

Jenny's shopping list now filled, her lover was free to do a little of her own.

Jenny liked shopping as much as the next girl, but really! She yawned safely behind her veil while her guide tried, and discussed with the proprietor, the merits of a dozen almost indistinguishable evening gowns. Apparently any old gown, and especially an old one, wouldn't do for a formal ball.

Convention required that Lady Isobell look the part of Lady of the House on a social occasion, but it wasn't all bad. At least she got to slop around in jodhpurs, old riding-boots and a scruffy pulley when she felt like it. Head held up by her posture collar, the damn heels killing her feet and squeezed in two by the iron band that her corset had become, Jenny was in a position to appreciate what Isobell's sex-toys had to go through every day to be pleasing to their legal owner. Only with more in the way of body-piercings, dildos, ball-gags and wrist cuffs!

She still remembered with dreamy pleasure, a toy she'd seen at the House once with a chain from her cuffs behind her pulled up between her legs and attached to a ring set through her navel. Now there was one ball-gagged plaything in no doubt about her station in life, and the appearance expected of her! Jenny quivered in delight, another little shock unexpectedly biting into her thigh. She was getting very good at not twitching and had trained herself to give silent gasps. Also the cream Lady Isobell had swiped from the vet's cabinet at the House had really helped her heels where the backs of the shoes had been rubbing, despite being a perfect fit.

She'd have to take some of that home with her too, Jenny decided. As long as women dressed to be attractive rather than for comfort, she suspected impractical shoes would always be involved. A cream that smoothed away blisters and made skin resistant to abrasion while still leaving it soft, was going to sell like hot cakes. It would be a nice little business to own, or have the rights to; her future would be assured. And she didn't feel at all guilty about her secret stash, assuming her friends were also tucking away little millionaire-making ideas for themselves. If they weren't, they weren't as smart as she'd thought. The cream was also quite good at soothing away whip-marks, but she wasn't sure there was such a market for that.

It was a measure of how acclimatised to the Slaveworld she'd become that Jenny found the slave-jeweller's and then the saddlery they visited much more interesting than the dressmaker's. The jeweller's wares were displayed on mannequins, Isobell selecting a set of matching diamond ear, nipple and clitoral pendants, some gold clamp-weights and a pet-tag with BUNNY engraved on it. Even more fun the retired soldier running the slave-outfitter's was also a licensed slave-dealer, so his mannequins breathed, his models naked and in chains.

Lady Isobell, with Jenny watching, spent a happy hour seeing a variety of restraints and instruments of sexual torture used on a pair of older slaves enduring their last few weeks of servitude before the ends of their sentences. The brunette had been lucky, already 27 when she'd fallen foul of the law, she'd only been given a five year sentence. The 28-year-old blonde, who moaned so enthusiastically when being demonstrated, had three more weeks of a ten-year sentence to complete. Isobell made several purchases, which of course Jenny carried. The steel dildo and matching butt-plug were particularly heavy, training aids for pony-girls, and she pitied the poor slave that was going to have to warm them up and carry them around inside her body.

They dropped off the bags and took a light lunch at the townhouse of one of Isobell's old school friends, who like many young Lords feeling a bit cramped under his parents' wing on the country estate, was experimenting with running his own small household in the city. Jenny knew from Karen that her guide, Lady Sybill, had the same arrangement when not living in at the Franklin estate.

The Master of the house was currently nursing a hangover and sexual exhaustion in the bath, but a beautiful young slave with her bracelet-like wrist-cuffs attached to her nipple-rings with short lengths of chain offered Jenny's lover refreshments, apologies and herself. The petite slave had the longest eyelashes Jenny had ever seen, creamy flawless skin, and of course her harem-pants left little to the imagination.

Jenny wasn't surprised when Isobell, after a moment's consideration, declined to enjoy the svelte slave's charms, now quite familiar with the aristocrat's tastes. In a world where no noble ever had to settle for second-best, the types they were attracted to quickly became very obvious. Lady Isobell, with a little variety, mostly liked the illusion of subduing and controlling a girl much bigger and more powerful than she was.

More important, the girl's breasts, delicately pointed with up-turned nipples, beautiful to Jenny's eyes, could be covered by a single hand. Not the thing at all. Isobell really, really liked big girls, in both senses of the word.

Jenny munched surreptitiously under her veil, passed tit-bits from her lover's plate while the slave was forced to face the other way, on hands and knees, functioning as Lady Isobell's footstool. The aristocrat's usually proud face was split by a naughty little girl look of mischief. The old thrill of risking being caught out doing something bad. How on Earth would she ever explain sharing food with an underling, to someone who wasn't in on the Gate project?

Jenny's eyes roamed over the curve of the kneeling slave's hips, the swell of her buttocks, pussy pouting between thighs under almost transparent gauze material. It was the sort of figure she'd always wanted to have herself; had dreamed of. She'd never been fat, just big, topping out at over 5'9", which was undoubtedly why Isobell liked her; but had endured enough 'clumsy heifer' jokes at school to wish for a fashion-model figure. Now she wouldn't want to trade places with the poor cow on her knees for all the gold in the world. Both worlds! It was funny how things went around.

***

That afternoon they toured one of the largest veterinary clinics in the south, Jenny tagging along behind her lover with notebook prominently displayed, totally ignored. It had started as Jenny's idea, Lady Isobell originally indifferent to how the process of turning people into sex-toys worked; just interested in the end results, but Jenny's questions had gradually intrigued her. The administrator, a retired Captain of Guards, had been only too happy to oblige.

An officer was the final rung on the ladder for a social climber. His children were now legally allowed to own slaves, and as such could marry into minor aristocracy. Their children would be able to marry into a Noble House. As commissions could be bought, it also neatly co-opted into the aristocracy's ranks any too successful merchant or bright inventor.

When they got there, the duty doctor, part of the small, free but precarious middle-class, seemed less keen than his superior on the tour, but had more sense than to object to a noble's whim.

All the other times she'd watched slaves being used and abused, her dutiful guilt and horror and been tempered with subversive fascination and occasional sexual arousal. She couldn't deny it any more, not even to herself. But in the clinic, she found a true nightmare. Jenny found herself feeling very definitely uncomfortable.

All the slaves undergoing modification at the clinic were heavily sedated, Captain McReaith explained, so that a smaller staff could more efficiently handle them. The restraints and chains they would see would be for the most part so that limp slaves could be winched from trolley to operating table and the like. Normal household restraints like hog-ties, and of course straps were important to insure the correct alignment of medical scanners and instruments, he added.

Did the Lady have a preference for studs or fillies? Fillies? Of course, My Lady.

In long rows, like specimens in jars, naked girls trailing wires and tubes hung from their wrists, immersed in a pinkish liquid in tall cylindrical glass tanks. Lab-technicians in white coats with electronic note-pads wandered this way and that.

All the slaves had respirators buckled into their mouths; a bundle of tubes pushed down throats as well as the air-hoses. Jenny could see how very slowly the drugged girls breathed by the bubbles.

The Captain cheerfully explained how once the correct doses of chemicals, drugs and hormones had been injected, force-fed to or allowed to soak into the helpless slave, she was then ready to be stretched. Twelve hours in the tanks gave them 30 minutes on the racks, a limber girl with some gymnast training probably needing two or three treatments. For a more heavily built girl, he tapped the tank of a strawberry blonde version of the redhead Jenny had raped, eight to ten treatments would be necessary.

At the end of which, muscles, ligaments and joints all loosened, the improved toy would be able to wear a ball-gag 22 hours a day without jaw-ache, sleep in total comfort hog-tied, be able to touch her toes, touch her elbows together behind her back and do the splits with ease. For the owner who wanted a truly double-jointed slave, wished to tie his toy's ankles behind her neck for example; a more intensive treatment was available. Stretching out the slave did make her slightly physically weaker than the norm, but the difference was only significant in an athlete; racing ponies, mud wrestlers and the like.

As they watched, a girl was winched up out of a tank; a steel cable hooked through both rings on broad, soft plastic wrist-cuffs, and lowered dripping to floor-level. Two lab technicians quickly and efficiently removed her respirator and intravenous needles, and then swung up first one leg and then the other, attaching similar ankle-cuffs to an overhead pulley. With her wrists unhooked the drugged girl hung upside-down, arms trailing, for all the world like a side of beef in a slaughterhouse. A touch of a button and the overhead conveyor swung her away, swaying and still dripping.

"Do mind your step My Lady. The surface can become a little slippery."

The floor was a grille to allow the tank's fluid to drain away. Getting to work on the girls as quickly as possible was the most important thing he explained. They followed the overhead rails, Lady Isobell occasionally pausing to admire the contents of this or that tank, usually full breasted.

In the next section they looked down on a series of smaller labs from an overhead catwalk. The girl they'd seen pulled from the tank was strapped to and being stretched on what looked like a perfectly ordinary rack, others, rag-doll limp, being pulled this way and that across bars and apparatus. The positions of the four winches attached to wrist and ankle-cuffs whined this way and that on railings, as did two medical scanners shifting position around each girl. The slaves looked soft and vulnerable surrounded by all the machinery.

Proudly the Captain explained that the process was now almost entirely computer controlled. In the old days there had apparently been the occasional pulled muscle, torn ligament and even rare cartilage damage, but all that was in the past. No slave had been even slightly injured for years. Almost the only thing the staff now needed to do was monitor malfunctions and manually fit jaw-stretching clamps.

All the girls had their mouths stretched wide open by metal frameworks, Jenny saw. "Got to be able to wear those ball-gags comfortably all day girls!" Jenny softly told herself. She watched in horror as a naked, wet girl was pulled back over a bar in the small of her back by her arms and legs. God, her back was going to break! But amazingly it didn't, and next the remorseless machines pulled the lolling, half-conscious sex-toy up against a stomach bar and proceeded to pull her legs into a wide splits. The winches paused a moment, a medical scanner whirring into a new position, and then the girl's legs were pulled wider.

In all the rooms below the catwalk winches hummed and whined, scanners whirring along rails, naked slaves hanging upside-down delivered to and from the tanks. They would ache for a couple of days, no more, their guide told Lady

104

Isobell, the tanks also soothing and healing, and they would remain supple for two to four years, depending on how hard they were exercised, before needing a second treatment. Jenny remembered that her lover had been surprised to find she couldn't get Jenny's elbows to touch together behind her back when roping her. This sort of explained it.

In a lecture hall she saw soldiers newly promoted to corporal attending a course on body piercing, and breast and penis enlargement. Under the eyes of two dozen uniformed colleagues a young soldier in his best dress-reds, had a chained girl carefully step onto scales, and then measured her breasts, the naked slave alone in a room full of dressed men. He checked a chart.

"22 ccs?" he hazarded.

"Idiot!" the drill sergeant barked. "You've got her weight wrong. You didn't take off the chains!"

In the next complex, unconscious and strapped in place to prevent mistakes, slaves were being tattoo branded. This process was also automated, a robot arm tattooing the bar-codes and serial numbers, to ensure the exact detail necessary. The back of the neck and the soles of the feet were the most common places for a brand, though some playthings were made to flaunt their owner's mark on highly visible places like stomachs, hips and buttocks. It was quite common for large-breasted girls to have the tattoo hidden on the underside of the breast.

The Captain also ruefully mentioned the younger Lords' and Ladies' current fad for branding the male slave's erect penis. He'd been given orders to try and tactfully discourage them because the bar-code could only be read if the cock was properly hard. It wasn't possible to transfer ownership of an exhausted or unconscious slave so marked.

For Jenny the surgeries were the worst part, all operating rooms were equipped with glassed off observation lounges so that those owners who wished, could see the changes they'd ordered being made on their property. There were contraceptives, aphrodisiacs, ID and satellite-locator beads, and sensors being implanted in slaves' bodies. The alternative England was also well ahead in cosmetic-surgery, a stark reminder of the realities of slavery for Jenny, just when she was starting to forget. Owners were able to choose the faces they wanted for their playthings.

Jenny shivered. Not just someone with the power over her to deny her clothing and say, "We'll have her hair longer and blonde, her pubes shaved and her make-up like this", as she'd fantasised. Not even just choosing breast size, which she still found worrisome. But the power to choose a complete new face out of a catalogue. "Oh yes, we'll have the green eyes, those cheek-bones, fuller lips and take a little off the nose!"

From behind glass they watched a newly sentenced girl won in a lottery being given a new face and having her skin cleaned up, a laborious and expensive process, freckles, moles and other blemishes surgically removed, and then every single hair follicle permanently stunned. No wonder Lady Isobell's toys had such flawless satin skin. Every last tiny body-hair had been removed, Jenny realised. The surgeons had already shaved a little off her hips, trimmed her waist down and lengthened her legs, lower-leg bones stretched, femurs actually cut in two and a coral insert placed in the gap, they were told.

The truly amazing thing was the Captain's bland assertion that she'd be on her feet in a week! They had all this truly marvellous technology, the power to heal, and they used it to create sex-slaves. The day-clinic was full of large-breasted toys having back problems remedied.

In the cosmetic labs semi-permanent make-up was applied, lip-colours and eyeliners, indelible inks that would last six months, and permanent enamelled nail-polishes, were applied. Genetic surgery could also make hair grow through the desired colour. No wonder there were so many blondes about! Jenny considered the technique for her millionaire-making collection, and then regretfully decided against it. Too complicated; mucking around with DNA for cosmetic reasons was way ahead of anything her Earth had, and the potential for some really grotesque mistakes all too obvious.

She liked the look of the drug that made hair grow through thicker and longer though. Waist length hair in a month? And all those male baldies were surely a ready market.

In the recovery-rooms behind two-way mirrors, newly modified slaves sprawled naked on a padded floor, huddled together in little piles for comfort. In the second-day recovery-rooms, more alert, they examined rings set through their flesh, the brands marking them, cradled unfamiliar large breasts, and studied new faces and bodies in the mirror. Some looked horrified, some sobbed quietly, but most just looked puzzled. Already some of the girls were surreptitiously touching themselves, or were flushed with shame, finding themselves rubbing up against each other.

In the third-day recovery-rooms the now bright-eyed sex-toys all wore ball-gags, chastity-belts and had their hands locked behind their backs. Lady Isobell paused in the tour, enjoying the show put on by three of the more assertive slave-girls who between them had trapped a smaller girl; destined to be a show-pony by the look of her, one sitting astride her face and one each astride a leg. All rubbing themselves up against her and each other.

A very subdued Jenny sat in the comfort of the borrowed limousine when they returned to the townhouse that evening. She just couldn't get the clinic out of her mind. These people could never, would never, give up slavery. Their whole culture was built around it. Full contact between this dimension and hers could only lead to civil war or invasion. And immensely satisfying as it would have been to see seventy-odd tons of Main Battle Tank crashing through the clinic walls; what about Isobell? What would happen to her if Slaveworld was liberated?

Jenny ate in the kitchen behind a screen so that the off-duty soldiers wouldn't see her face. Laughter, a cheerful bellow, and Lady Isobell's high-pitched peal, drifted through air-vents as old friends re-acquainted themselves. Their merriment was accompanied by occasional squeaks of female distress, and rarer, male cries of pain. After supper Jenny again donned her veil and waited in her lover's guest suite as she'd been told.

Also waiting, kneeling on a rug at the foot of the bed, her lead tied around one of the four-poster's poles, and with elbows touching, her arms strapped behind her, was a top-heavy slave awaiting Lady Isobell's pleasure. Their host was obviously familiar with, or had researched, his guest's tastes. Jenny couldn't tell if the girl was a blonde, her sex was clean-shaven and her head was encased in a tight form-fitting latex hood, the shiny black restraint broken only by nostril holes; but she probably was. Blonde toys were undeniably popular. Written in marker pen across one of the girl's big heavy breasts was: SHE'S NEVER BEEN TIT-WHIPPED. ENJOY.

Jenny lifted and weighed the full globes, as with her redhead, taking a guilty sensuous pleasure in the warm, soft weight she handled. A single decorative chain linked the girl's pierced nipples, and the weighty melons swung and bounced together wonderfully when she pulled up on it, nipples stretching prettily. Lady Isobell's bed-warmer moaned softly, helpless to prevent her arousal, as she was groped and teased.

Jenny pulled the hooded girl to her feet with her nipples and then pushed her back onto the bed, pushing her thighs apart so that she could examine her chastity-rod. A row of six interlocking rings had been set through each sex-lip, through which was threaded a curved bar with a T crosspiece at the top. The bar through the rings held her pussy-lips closed, and a simple small padlock set through a small ring at the base of the T-bar prevented removal. Simple, comfortable and attractive. The key to the padlock hung from a ring set through the top-heavy toy's navel, well out of reach of a girl with her arms secured behind her.

Jenny stroked and gently tugged at the elegant device and ring-pierced flesh, the naked slave quivering with pleasure, her hood muffling little moans of lust. In a dark sort of way it was strangely beautiful, not like hanging half a ton of steel around a girl's hips, and she didn't find the idea of wearing one for a lover, Andrew for example, totally repugnant. Again she was getting used to things; the first one she'd seen three weeks ago had been quite disturbing. Pretty really, and far more a symbol of devotion than a wedding ring, she decided.

The slave-slut moaned in pleasure again. Jenny was just reaching for the padlock's key lying on her stomach, with the intention of filling the girl's pussy with the fat candle on the dresser; a bit of hot wax dripping onto ringed flesh would make her more attentive and less inclined to just lie around enjoying herself, when she saw the brand. The bar-code and the serial number under it was tattooed on the underside of one of her large breasts, visible now she was on her back, the full globes flattened across her chest slightly from their weight.

Exactly like one the girls she'd seen, and pitied, being branded at the clinic today! Much as the poor cow would enjoy having her pussy filled, and the painful spice of hot wax would make her hotter, she didn't deserve it, which was what Jenny had been thinking. Her attitudes towards slaves were definitely getting a little schizophrenic, Jenny decided. Hating the clinic, but liking the toys it turned out? Knowing slavery could not be justified, but wanting her lover to give her another one to abuse? Taking pleasure in seeing slaves forced to display themselves, bound, in chains and humiliated, and then pitying them afterwards? And what had ever happened to getting the hell out of this trap?

But the hooded toy was so delicious! Jenny sat her up on her heels, and after a guilty look around, listening carefully, delivered half a dozen palm-stinging slaps to each big boob. The crack of the slaps was shockingly loud, heavy flesh bouncing under the blows and bright red splotches left behind on creamy, velvet skin. The helpless toy cried out at each slap, body jerking, breathing heavier, but made no real move to pull away. Flushed and breathing heavily herself, holding the slave-girl in place with her nipple-chain, Jenny stroked her cheeks and face up against the scarlet marks her hand had left; savouring the burning heat.

The top-heavy toy, arms strapped tightly behind her, elbows touching, probably a graduate of the limbering process Jenny had seen at the clinic, turned her hooded head blindly this way and that. Thighs widely spread, she was not only obediently thrusting her tits forward, but offering the key to her locked pussy, Jenny realised. She reached out again, but this time caution, not pity stopped her.

This might be a sexy, available and truly lovely toy, but she wasn't Jenny's toy. What she was was somebody else's legal property! In theory, without Isobell to bail her out, a working-class servant could get ten years wearing a collar just for touching. Unauthorised sex would bring the full weight of the law down on her. Probably, possibly, Isobell would cover for her, but it was still more trouble than it was worth to be caught having sex with the suite's assigned bed-warmer.

Jenny put the girl back on the floor where she'd found her and settled down to read one of her new books, only occasionally casting regretful glances at the gentle rise and fall of big, heavy, delightfully squeezable boobs; nipple-chain swaying enticingly. With a chuckle Jenny remembered the fuss she'd made about the name of that girl Academic Franklin had had serving on her second, or was it third, visit? How naive! She'd matured now, not caring in the slightest what the pussy-locked plaything she'd just handled was called, or even looked like. No point in getting bogged down in details. You either approved of legal slavery or you didn't!

"The brunette with the big tits," or "The blonde with the pussy-rings," were for the most part quite adequate labels. Suddenly it became clear to her; only a fool worried about how slaves were treated, Jenny realised, because there shouldn't be any slaves!

When Jenny felt her eyelids starting to droop, she gave up. To hell with slave-training! With a luxuriant sigh she removed her collar, corset, heels and plug. The body-stocking had stopped shocking her long ago, but she hadn't quite noticed when. Listening, the door open a crack, laughter and murmured conversation drifted up the stairwell.

"Looks like you don't get screwed tonight Boobie," she told the kneeling slave with a kiss on the top of her latex hood, giving one breast a friendly squeeze.

The bound sex-toy kneeling with head up and thighs spread, of course didn't reply, and Jenny settled down on the sofa and pulled a blanket over herself. The young plaything, nipples linked with chain and her pussy locked tight, probably no older than Jenny herself, didn't have the option of saying that's enough, and removing her bonds. She still looked delectable. God, slavery was so insidiously seductive! Head drooping a little when Jenny put aside her book, she was still obediently, helplessly, kneeling at the end of her lead, waiting to be put to whatever sexual use her owner's guest might wish, when Jenny fell asleep.

She was woken about four in the morning, when a very merry Isobell, much the worse for drink, tripped over the bound slave now lying across the carpet on her stomach.

"Oops!" she giggled, giving the naked slave an amiable pat on the behind.

The slave-girl, who had finally dozed off, scrambled back up onto her knees, hooded head up, thighs spread and sitting on her heels. The approved position for an owned girl to display herself.

"Nice boobies!" the aristocrat announced, still on one knee where she'd stumbled.

She reached out and scooped up the offered mounds, planting a wet, slobbering kiss on each ring-tipped melon. With a sigh Jenny threw aside her blanket and stood. She'd thought this only happened with boyfriends!

***

Jenny helped her plastered lover undress and poured her between the sheets, just like a boyfriend she could name. She turned her attention to the succulent slave with another sigh. She was tempted to have some fun with her anyway; the hooded girl wouldn't know who used her and Isobell certainly wouldn't remember, but regretfully decided it wasn't worth it. A servant or the Master of the House might unexpectedly enter. Having little that they were ashamed of and nothing to hide, the Lords and Ladies had next to no sense of privacy.

She unbuckled the straps around the girl's elbows and unlocked her lead and cuffs, the key hanging from her navel-ring being a 'one size fits all'. The girl placidly allowed Jenny to push her onto the bed and padlock her wrist-cuffs together through a ring on the bed's headboard. Isobell snuggled up to her naked form with a happy sigh, as Jenny had known she would. Her lover had never had to sleep alone in her adult life. In her world there was always a spare toy that could be chained to the headboard as a bed-warmer. Warm, gently breathing, velvet skinned cuddly toys.

She valiantly resisted the urge to unlock the girl's pussy, and pulled a sheet up over both, returning yawning, and alone, to her sofa. No fair!

Lady Isobell ate a late lunch off the slave-girl's body, played with her breasts in the bath, and eventually left her lying hog-tied on the floor. Neither hood or pussy-lock ever removed. It was another sobering close-up of the reality of slavery for Jenny, just when once again lust had been getting the better of morality.

When she dreamed of herself as a slave, she was the centre of attention, adored; a very pampered pet indeed. Obviously her loving and devoted owner would want to keep her naked and on a lead, and she would need training and occasional punishment, but never once in her submissive fantasies had she imagined a jaded or bored owner who couldn't be bothered to have sex with her. The world didn't work like that! Jenny didn't consider herself beautiful, more realistically pretty and middling attractive. 'Striking' was about the best she could do, but it was a fact of life that men would pay for sex or to

112

see women dance naked. Even pay for pictures, books and videos. It was common knowledge at the university that occasionally some students had made ends meet by table-dancing or soft-porn, and the entry requirements weren't exactly stringent.

It was impossible that an available, naked, girl in chains not be desirable unless she was dog-ugly! But then real owners, not her fantasy owners, also bought and sold slaves as an everyday act. Jenny had happily masturbated many a lonely evening away imagining being sold to the highest bidder on the auction-block, but the Masters and Mistresses of her fantasies always prized her too highly to sell her once they possessed her. No one with another person to play with should ever be bored! She didn't even understand how Isobell could leave her bed-warmer unused.

Disturbed, Jenny refused to put back on her posture collar and corset, and decided she'd rather be bare-foot than hobbled, only to discover she'd been on the end of aristocratic humour. To get the youth treatment, it didn't matter in the slightest if she could pass for a slave or not, whilst conscious. For security and ease of handling, all slaves being given rejuvenation treatments were delivered drugged in boxes. Safe in the arms of Morpheus, and quite dead to the world. Just a couple of nipple-rings and a fake tattoo brand would do it, her lover explained with a giggle.

SIX
MAKING UP

"OH, DO STOP sulking Jenny. It was only a collar and corset set, and you looked adorable."

"And the shocks?"

"Please! Static shocks. You've had worse off a car door!"

Jenny grinned wryly. It was true, and she knew real slaves got far worse.

She just hated being the butt of anyone else's humour. 'Good ol' Jenny,' who could take a joke, had been on the receiving end of one too many at school. Usually by the sort of person who thought it was hilarious when somebody else sat on a pin, but would slap you in the face if they were on the receiving end. Somehow she couldn't see Lady Isobell being amused at being tricked into wearing electric underwear.

They were returning to the Franklin estates from the city via the scenic route, puffing gently up the river Thames, what they called the Tamesis, in a beautiful steam-powered launch; all polished wood and brass. A muscular slave, his ankles chained spread to ringbolts set in the deck and his cock-strap to the centre of the wheel he held, mouth full of ball-gag, steered expertly.

Isobell had of course run her hands over his naked flesh on boarding, idly squeezing his strapped shaft and testicles while he'd negotiated two other taxis moored to the same pier she'd hired this boat from. He groaned helplessly as she toyed with his genitals, sweat dotting his brow. The other half of the crew was a slave-girl, surprisingly a willowy blonde, not Isobell's usual big-busted choice, trailing a rattling chain behind her when she cast off. One end of the chain was secured to a ringbolt set in the deck between the two facing passenger seats, the other padlocked to her ring-set clitoris. The aristocrat must be feeling like a little variety, Jenny reasoned.

She knew it wasn't illegal, aristocrats being free to do as they wished with their toys short of murder, mutilation or separating a married couple, but it was unusual for slaves to function as chauffeurs. One too many limousines had ended up in ditches or wrapped around the back of a bulk-hauler for all but the true thrill-seeker to consider letting a slave drive. The poor bimbo driving could be too easily distracted by the dildo she was mounted on, or by having her nipples pulled about by reins from the back seat. A slave crew in a boat, travelling at a more relaxed pace, was obviously acceptable.

There was no commercial traffic on the river, just sporting and pleasure craft. Taxis like their own puffed along sedately or here and there were moored to overhanging trees or jetties, their crews being teased, tormented and sexually abused. Isobell had picked a nice looking couple, but she'd had the pick of all-girl or all-boy crews, and additional crewmembers had been available for hire for a surcharge. Jenny watched a taxi pass in the opposite direction, four smartly dressed older men, each easily a pensioner in her reality, so God knew how old here, chatting animatedly under their boat's awning. The nearest tipped his top-hat to Lady Isobell. All four had a naked slave on her knees in front of them, hands cuffed behind backs, mouths full of, or tonguing, wrinkled, flabby, century old cocks. Jenny guessed none of the slaves would be older than twenty-five.

Oars flashing in perfect unison, students from the local university trained for the upcoming boat races; their long slender craft spearing through the water. The coxes calling time were the students, casual in T-shirts and shorts, male and female, the rowers all slave-boys. Naked, muscular forms sheened with sweat as they strained to keep time, electrodes attached to genitals.

Far larger than the taxis, luxurious cabin-cruisers with human figureheads strapped to the bows, left gentle wakes. Occasionally a naked slave, purchased at auction and being taken home, hung like a fishing trophy from the mast's crossbar. Sunning themselves on the foredecks or relaxing in the shaded comfort of well-decks, Lords and Ladies in swimming wear, loose shirts or sometimes simply and comfortably naked, were waited on hand and foot by variously, collared and restrained, dildo and plug stuffed playthings.

On the foredeck of a nearby cruiser another old man was enjoying a young slave, taking her doggie-style, the girl wearing a bridle, head pulled back, nipple-rings padlocked to a ringbolt to hold her in place. Jenny's lover returned a cheerful wave from the ancient pumping his cock into succulent, lush, flesh. Nipple-tethered, the girl's heavy breasts just wobbled under her, unable to sway normally, a ripple running across the creamy-skinned slave's hips each time his bony pelvis slammed up against her. Jenny shivered in revulsion, imagining wrinkled, trembling, liver-spotted hands on her body.

"They get to a certain age and they have to start proving how virile they are!" Isobell whispered, sotto voce, with a sly smile. The publicly screwed slave-girl's gasps of pleasure around her bit echoed over still water. "I'll bet he's had that top-heavy bimbo licking him half the morning to get it up; and kept the slut in a chastity-belt a week to boot, to make sure she was properly appreciative of his performance."

Jenny grinned helplessly behind her veil. "So what happens to all this healthy outdoor fun when the weather gets colder?" she asked.

"It speaks!" Isobell squeaked in mock surprise. "I thought you were going to sulk all the way home." Jenny started to look away and the aristocrat continued hastily, "Pack your three or four favourite playthings in pet-crates, and take a Caribbean cruise is the favourite. That's what I did last year. But if you're busy or have responsibilities, there's always indoor fun like the theatre, circus, and of course, the bed and playroom."

Isobell paused, arching her neck back to lick a bead of white wine from an offered nipple. The slender blonde slave-girl who'd come with the boat, kneeling beside and to one side of the aristocrat, arms neatly folded behind her, had been set the task of dipping her breasts into bowls of wine, one white and one red, and leaning forward to offer them to lick. One drip at a time. The lovely girl's nipples looked very hard indeed. Once again Jenny was impressed at the sheer amazing variety of humiliations in the Lords' and Ladies' repertoire. It came from centuries of practice, she was sure.

"And not everything goes under cover. You can still work pony-slaves in the cold, just not rain. Body heat keeps them warm with plenty of whip. You've just got to put them straight into a stall when you've finished with them; no hitching rails. In fact I love leaving tracks in fresh snow on a winter morning with my pony-girls."

"Sounds fun," Jenny said dubiously.

"It is. Of course you have to be taught responsibility. When I was nineteen and my first show-pony caught a chill, Daddy wouldn't let me near her, or any other toy in the house, until she stopped snuffling and sneezing. No sex for nearly a week!"

"That must have been a blow," Jenny said.

Isobell grinned, not missing the faint sarcasm. "It was actually. We all have urges, but I suppose your people have lower sex-drives, because your society makes you suppress your natural instincts. I'm used to a very active sex-life, when, where and how I like. I never, and never have to, suppress any desire, urge or fancy. It was a bit of a shock to the system to suddenly not be getting any."

Isobell had the slave-skipper moor them under the shade of a willow, and then the two hired slaves were set to screwing each other for her entertainment. The slave-boy was sat on the seat facing them, arms pulled wide and secured to the awnings poles on either side. The slave-girl was then sat astride him, also facing them, bending forward to hold his ankles, her own legs spread wide.

When the girl held her head up as ordered, they could look into both ball-gagged faces at once. Both had wedding-rings set through their noses, meaning they were a married couple, and had been when sentenced, and so as a pair, could not be

117

broken up or sold separately. Somehow Jenny didn't think that would be a problem. An inventive mind could think up humiliations available to a couple that would have no impact on two slaves who'd never met before.

***

The slaves were gasping and moaning more enthusiastically now. The slave-boy had his tattooed brand, presently hidden, prominently displayed on one buttock, his slave-wife on the outer-thigh. The chain that still padlocked her clitoris to the boat was an untidy coil at her slave-husband's feet.

"Slaves stop!" Isobell ordered.

The pair instantly obeyed, breathing hard around the identical red balls buckled into their mouths. Two pairs of eyes desperately pleaded.

"You may continue," she waved them on. "I've thought of a little treat for you," she said to Jenny.

"Really?" Jenny said guardedly. "You don't have to."

"No, I was cruel to trick you. I'm used to teasing property." The slave-girl's head drooped, and she flicked a lash across her breasts to bring her head back up. "And I know just how to make it up to you."

The thin whip had left a raised welt across both the girl's firmly pointed breasts. Isobell flicked it across her thighs, hips, and then breasts again. More for her own pleasure than any lack of effort on the girl's part. Jenny mumbled something ineffectual, cut off when the girl threw back her head and cried out in ecstasy, despite the lash biting into her flesh.

"Don't stop humping her!" she warned the slave-boy. "I haven't finished with her yet" She turned to Jenny. "See, I'm not totally heartless. I'm letting him screw his own wife before I do. And I'll bet this is the first time he's been allowed to have her in months."

"You said a treat?" Jenny asked.

"Yes. I can get you into bed with that cute Celt you've been drooling over," she replied triumphantly.

"Who?"

"You know. Pale, good build, black hair. Andrew something or other? The one you've got the hopeless crush on."

"Andrew! How did you know.... crush?"

"Jenny! The way you follow him around with puppy eyes whenever he's in the room? It's obvious! He knows it too. He just prefers our slaves."

"Andrew," Jenny breathed. "You really think so?" she asked, sulk totally forgotten.

"As easy done as said," her lover assured her.

Two naked slaves continued to perform sex right in front of her, but Jenny was seeing another scene. Herself, writhing in Andrew's arms, his lips on hers!

***

There was of course a small catch! Jenny stood naked in front of a floor-length mirror studying herself, her head encased in a shiny black hood. Isobell watched, but she didn't mind her proud lover's eyes on her; was used to it; in fact enjoyed the aristocrat's admiring gaze. What she'd subliminally been aware of each time she saw a sex-toy in a hood, now hit with full force! No personality, not even a person almost, just a lovely plaything waiting to be used without guilt or responsibility, deserving of the name sex-toy. The girl in the mirror was a very sexy toy indeed.

The hood had dozens of tiny pinholes over the eyes, invisible except close up from the outside; to Jenny, like looking through gauze. Slightly fuzzy, soft focus, but clear enough vision, while leaving her own face hidden. Stark black against her flesh, there was a brand on her belly, above and to one side of her pussy. A transfer that would wear off over a few days, used by Lords and Ladies when deciding where they wanted to put a bar-code and serial number on a new plaything. Her wrists were handcuffed behind her back.

Jenny's pubic hair was now a neatly trimmed and shaved vertical tuft above her pussy, the work of Isobell's own hand.

Most slave-girls were clean-shaven, but enough owners liked a little decoration or a remaining little tuft to yank, for her to now pass without comment. Her lover had been quite adamant. If she was to pass for Andrew's evening slave, the bush had to go! The fact she'd been wanting to 'tidy Jenny up' for ages, just a nice bonus. In fact several weeks of being able to look at clean-shaven and trimmed pussies on an almost daily basis had acclimatised her. Jenny actually thought she looked quite smart.

The latex-like hood was held in place with a shiny stainless-steel collar snug around her neck, threaded through loops around the neck of the hood, a padlock hanging at her throat. It also looked good. Smart. Businesslike. Not so pretty, a ring-gag held her mouth wide open. An integral part of the hood, straps ran across her cheeks, a snap-lock on one side, holding a plain metal ring behind her teeth, and making her mouth gape obscenely wide.

Jenny was quite used to ball-gags now, seen on other girls and wearing them herself, and was only too well aware of how pretty a girl with a large pink, orange or red ball filling her mouth looked. That helpless, pleading look of doe-eyed submission was so appealing, and sexually, just yummy! But the ring-gag? She'd used the word 'obscene' deliberately. It was after all a device originally invented so that a reluctant slave's mouth could be used for oral-sex without fear of sharp teeth. And wasn't even pretty.

Isobell hadn't insisted. Like her trimmed bush, she'd let Jenny see the necessity for herself. She had. If Andrew was to accept her as a slave, he would expect to have access to her mouth. Or, if she was delivered in a gag, the ability to remove it, even if he didn't get keys to the cuffs or hood. If Jenny spoke, or even just cried out in passion, she would be recognised. The solution had to be a locked device that would allow in a penis but let only unintelligible sounds out.

She wiggled her tongue back and forth, watching it dart from side to side inside her wide-open mouth, able to push it out beyond her lips only if she stretched really hard. Obscene? Probably, but less so if she imagined she was looking at a slave-girl instead of herself in the mirror. It was strangely erotic, and Andrew would never connect her with this hooded, naked, branded sex-toy with her wrists handcuffed behind her.

It was exciting! She barely recognised herself!

Jenny turned away from the mirror and walked back to stand in front of her seated lover, swaying across the carpet in padlocked-on 4" stiletto heels. She whined plaintively, and then eagerly rubbed herself up against the hands that stroked her naked form, her breasts squeezed and her newly trimmed pubic hair yanked before her lover consented to unlock her ring-gag.

"Oh," Jenny said, experimentally working her jaw. "That thing's going to make my jaw ache."

"Don't worry. It won't be an all-nighter. I'll have you collected after a couple of hours." her lover assured her. "Time to complete your disguise?"

Jenny closed her hidden eyes in resignation, and obediently held open her mouth. The ring-gag locked back into place, she was led over to a heavy study table, where all too recently she had fucked a bound girl to exhaustion. Where hood, cuffs, heels and handcuffs had lain, beside discarded clothing, now only remained a cane. Jenny shivered just slightly as she let herself be bent over the desk, polished wood chill on her naked body. Waiting for the final detail that would ensure that Andrew would never even consider the girl he was going to sexually use was a fellow student from his own reality.

She flinched, catching her breath, when her aristocratic lover lightly let the cane rest across her backside. Taking aim for the first stroke!

The cane hissed through the air; and landed with a crack. Jenny gasped, the air driven from her lungs, unable to even cry out at the pain. A sharp biting sting, followed with a slow spreading burn. She wailed helplessly, half rising up off the table when the cane touched her bottom again, but Isobell lifting her arms up behind her by her handcuffs forced her body back down onto the table.

The cane cracked down again, and again, Jenny twitching and jerking, voice found now, squeaking helplessly. Each stroke was a sharp, vicious pain, followed by a slow deep heat burning into her abused buttocks that earthed itself in her groin. Jenny was surprised to find herself becoming aroused, the cane much more intense than being spanked. She moaned in pleasure, pain and lust strangely combined, when Isobell stroked her handiwork.

A squeaking gasp was forced from Jenny as another cut followed, and then another, and in delighted disbelief, she felt burning pain pushing her slowly but firmly towards climax, she was forced to admit to herself how hot this was making her. It was strangely delicious, the way throbbing pain went on long after the cane had landed, allowing her to savour all the strokes at once! Jenny squirmed and twisted, but only to force Isobell holding her handcuffed hands up behind her to push her arms forward and her body down harder. Squeezing lust-swollen breasts, flattened under her on the desk.

Her lover stroked the cane between Jenny's sex-lips, twisting the rod this way and that to Jenny's delight, then briefly holding the glistening-wet cane before her tear-filled eyes.

"It hurts more when it's wet!" the aristocrat whispered.

The cane hissed through the air, and landed with a crack. Jenny squealed, rearing up off the desk until forced back down, the pain atrocious. She was amazed that she could be turned on by her punishment, the pain quite real, but in some strange way pain and pleasure merged and became one. Isobell put aside the cane and opened a desk drawer. Jenny wailed in delight as a fat dildo was plunged into her dripping pussy. Her arms were pushed forward above her by the links of the handcuffs again, metal biting into her wrists, sweat slick on the desk under her now. Jenny tried to grip the dildo inside her sex, muscles spasming helplessly as the cane landed again, and again, feeling the shaft slipping out of her dripping pussy even though she was desperately trying to hang on. So desperately that she lost count of how many strokes she took, arousal growing with each biting lash.

At last she was pulled to her knees by the ponytail projecting through a hole in the back of her hood, sitting on burning hot buttocks, which only made her hotter. The dildo was pushed into her mouth.

Jenny squeaked in protest, tasting herself, trying to twist away, but was held easily in place by her hair, and she couldn't close her mouth because of the ring-gag. Her wrists jerked against her cuffs as she instinctively tried to bring her hands up to protect her mouth. Isobell pushed the dildo to the back of her throat, twisting it this way and that to coat her tongue completely in her own juices. Jenny whined softly, realising she was further turned on by the taste of herself. Not only had the punishment stopped before she could come, leaving her desperately frustrated, but also Isobell knew she hated licking dildos clean!

"I think you look authentic enough now," Isobell smiled, pulling Jenny back to her feet with her hair. She brought a small syringe out of the drawer. "Just a little aphrodisiac to keep you on heat like the real thing."

Jenny, her mind a whirl of shame, arousal, humiliation, lust and eager anticipation, barely even noticed the pinprick on her upper arm. She stood quite docilely as her lover had a male slave tightly lace and padlock into place the waspie corset she'd refused to ever wear again.

***

Jenny, hooded and with her arms locked behind her, knelt on a sheepskin rug at the foot of a huge bed in one of the guest suites, just like countless real slaves she'd seen. Even better, waiting for Andrew! She was sitting on her heels, the corset holding her breathlessly upright; the small padlocks of her stiletto pumps' ankle-straps digging into the still throbbing flesh of her freshly caned buttocks. The discomfort was delicious. She'd just had time to see the stripes criss-crossing her own backside in the mirror before being led here.

She was breathlessly excited, and not just sexually. She'd dreamed of being in Andrew's arms a thousand times. Not always quite like this, holding hands across a candle-lit restaurant table more often than not, but more recently Isobell's training/love had prepared her to accept more restraint in her fantasies. More restraints! It didn't matter that he would see just one of many sex-slaves, bound, hooded and mouth stretched wide open for his use. She would know!

Her heart leapt, excitement and fear sending adrenaline coursing through her veins when she heard Andrew's voice. Oh Christ, what if he recognised her, like this? Her nipples so hard they ached, she looked up, straining for the first glimpse of his dark God-like good looks through her pinhole-restricted vision. Three figures entered the room.

Isobell, you complete and utter bitch, Jenny said to herself.

"I thought we were getting that blonde with the huge tits tonight?" Sarah complained, tossing aside her robe and veil.

"She's got flu," Andrew said dismissively. "I don't really see what that's got to do with it, but these people have this thing about only playing with healthy toys." He shrugged. "This is it."

"Oh I think she'll fill in nicely," Charles said positively, reaching down to handle Jenny's breasts. "Looks like she's got a bit of stamina. Carriage-pony do you think?"

Jenny's last chance to explain, to tell them it was her and get out, ended in a rising wail of pain as she was pulled to her feet with a painful grip on both her breasts. Her fellow student bent her forward from the waist, still with a cruel double handful of breast, his girlfriend's sharp nailed fingers roughly probing her pussy from behind.

"Nice and wet," Sarah said approvingly. "I like the way they keep the sluts on heat. Always ready to be used."

"I've got the formula," Andrew confided as he undressed.

"Going to be worth a fortune."

"Damn! Why didn't we think of that one?" Charles muttered.

With easy confidence, they'd done this before Jenny realised, the two slight blond lovers and Andrew stripped off in front of each other. All three examined her body with an easy familiarity, not at all inhibited by having to deal with a hooded stranger instead of the girl they'd been expecting. Two cocks were pushed through the ring holding her mouth open, one after the other, her nipples twisted to encourage her to better transform the meat shafts from merely hard, to rigid, with her tongue.

Andrew's cock was thick and heavy, bumping against the back of her throat before even half its length had penetrated her mouth, his taste sour, a faint unwashed smell filling her nostrils. Charles was much smaller in length but almost as thick, circumcised, and he smelt and tasted of soap. While the two took turns to be tongued, Jenny was mercilessly spanked by Sarah, her own brand of foreplay.

They tied weights to her nipples and Andrew and Charles held her legs spread wide while a laughing Sarah brought a broad strap down again and again across her pussy. Jenny shrieked and thrashed to no avail, her pleas distorted by her ring-gag and interrupted by her squeaks and yelps, amazed that the angelic looking Sarah could be so sadistic. Through it all she was aware of the way the weights tied to her nipples dragged her breasts out of shape, the strings' constriction a sharp, painful bite on the swollen nubs.

Jenny cried out wordlessly as the strap cracked down once more, licking across her belly and curling down over her pussy, plump lips and clitoris stung with a vicious kiss. She squeaked, jerking and twisting against the hands tight around her calves. Having mostly been spanked, caned or whipped on the backside, Jenny knew from that experience that a whip-stoke would continue to burn deliciously into her buttocks long after the lash had fallen. A second or third stroke wasn't just a repeat of the original pain, but added to it! Bucking and trying to twist away from the hands that held her legs spread wide, crying out as the broad strap again smacked down on her wetness, Jenny discovered with horror and delight that the same held true for a pussy-whipping. Each stroke hurt and aroused with a new and added intensity!

Sarah swung the strap down between her twitching thighs again. Her sex-lips throbbed with an unquenchable heat that was only half pain, Jenny's pretty fellow student giggling as she paused to lick the broad leather band before swinging it down again. The blows landing squarely on her unprotected clitoris brought pleasure that the most sensitive fingers or tongue could never match, a starburst fusion of agony and ecstasy. Despite tears, shrieks and very real pain, Jenny realised she could come from this; she really could!

The three didn't seem to realise that although Jenny continued to twist and cry out when the strap smacked down, their hooded and corseted toy, with arms bound behind her, had stopped trying to beg for mercy around the obstruction of her ring-gag. Still surprised herself at how hot being lashed between her legs had made her, Jenny didn't know whether to be relieved or disappointed when Sarah tossed aside the strap, again before she'd been made to come. She didn't even know if she wanted to be made to come like this; sure at least that she liked not having the choice, but God, she was horny!

When Jenny's tears flowed freely and her body shook to sobs, breasts quivering, she was ready to be mounted. On the huge bed she was sat astride Andrew, sliding forever down the thick length of his cock, until thoroughly impaled, she at last sat panting astride him. Sarah kneeling behind her, thrust into Jenny's ass with a strap-on-dildo, laughing at another squeak of pain, driving cruelly to the hilt with three quick thrusts. Uncomfortably stuffed, stretched to the hilt, her corset's constriction making it worse, Jenny's forced-open mouth was still available for Charles standing astride Andrew to thrust his penis into.

126

"Lick me bitch!" he ordered, twisting tightly held nipples for emphasis. "Don't just sit there!"

"Hey slut. Are you tit-trained?" Andrew demanded from below her, squeezing her breasts to get her attention.

Jenny gurgled helplessly around the hot meat in her mouth, Sarah stroking her sex-lips tight around his cock. He took that as a yes.

"Good! Work your hips in time with my squeezes," the man of her dreams ordered.

With Sarah now scattering slaps across her thighs to encourage her, deep painful dildo strokes stretching her back-passage wide, Jenny mindlessly began thrusting herself down on Andrew's cock in time with his fingers sinking into her breasts, still desperately tonguing the cock in her mouth. Charles would give her tied nipples a little twist if she forgot. Three pairs of hands were free to roam her body once Jenny, like a wind-up toy, had been obediently set in motion. All occasionally stopped on her handcuffs, her corset-nipped waist and the steel collar padlocking her hood in place, but she liked it best when three pairs of hand fought for possession of her breasts.

Jenny came and came again, the tight corset seeming to intensify and amplify her orgasms, while her formerly oh-so-innocent seeming friends discussed her merits as a screw. Of course she wasn't giving the conversation her full attention—she loved her corset; was never going to take it off! —but she caught bits. All were agreed she was more responsive than the top-heavy blonde they'd been expecting, and had sampled before, but not as good as the brunette with the pierced clitoris.

Andrew and Sarah though she was better than the girl with the pearls hanging from her nipples, but Charles thought that slave had a better tongue. The merits of two other blondes with nipple rings, one with a brand on the soles of her feet, the other behind her neck, and a brunette with an ass-brand, were also discussed. All were agreed Jenny didn't compare to a spectacular heavy-titted redhead they'd had once, and were hoping to sample again.

***

Jenny lay sprawled limp on her bound arms, thick, slimy, semen coating her tongue and dribbling out of her ring-gagged mouth, her unknowing friends sitting around her body sipping iced drinks while they recovered their stamina and discussed how to use her next. She found she preferred the taste of Isobell to semen, and had been surprised at how hotly Charles's come had splashed into her defenceless mouth. But drenched in satisfied pleasure she was trying to recall the disgust and revulsion she'd always felt at the idea. Before, she'd only ever reluctantly taken a man in her mouth, and then on the strict understanding that he didn't, and often jerking away in fear that he might, come in her mouth!

Sarah's fingers penetrated her again, scooping mingled semen and her juices out of Jenny's pussy, which she was using to trace abstract patterns on her belly and polish Jenny's fake brand and serial number to a shine. Andrew had hold of one of the strings tied around her nipples, idly pulling her breast this way and that, Charles stroking a length of thigh. Her unsuspecting fellow students' conversation returned to an obviously favourite topic: first, how to get the youth treatment, and second, how to remain in the alternative England.

"This pretending to be slaves stuff is for the birds," Sarah said dismissively. "They're just trying to put us off. Overseas aristocrats arrive for treatments all the time, and there's masses of different accents, languages and customs. We could pass for some of them, no problem."

"They're not even as totally exclusive as they make out. You can marry in. Professor Phillips-Webber's officially one of them from the moment they tie the knot."

"Think that'll go through?"

"She's got no idea what she's getting into, but it might. Meeting of minds and all that. It might even work out. I mean it's not like the physical stuff matters all that much in an aristo' marriage. And he's already got kids, he's a widower, so her pedigree is irrelevant and won't raise any eyebrows. It's going to be my way in, anyway!" Andrew stated.

"And how is the lovely Lady Sybill?"

"Eating out of my hand. Nobody in this reality knows dick about romance. They're polite to each other, but they've never even imagined having to charm an uptight looker out of her panties. I'll get her down the aisle, no problem, and before the Prof'. Still going with your adoption plan?"

"Sure," Charles agreed. "We've already talked around it, and she doesn't seem to mind."

Charles and Sarah intended to become members of the aristocracy by having Phillips-Webber legally adopt them, Jenny learned. So when she married, they were in too. Her friends' lack of caution and almost open disdain for the Lords and Ladies appalled her. All bedrooms were wired for vision and sound so that those special moments enjoying this or that slave could be treasured forever. She could only hope the aliens from the alternative dimension didn't consider them worth the bother.

Her desire to warn was of course tempered by how mortified she'd be if they ever suspected she'd been pretending to be the slave they'd just enjoyed, and the fact that she had a ring-gag locked behind her teeth, but mostly by their secret opinion of her. Karen was judged not bright enough to want to stay and live like a King, or even figure a way in, and Jenny herself, too much of a mouse to really understand the joys of owning people or to leave behind the moral baggage of their own reality.

And then the games recommenced. Jenny's breasts, still dragging weights from her nipples, were whipped, and again she succumbed to the dazzling blend of pain and pleasure as they rippled under the lash. Sharp-jawed clamps were attached to her sex-lips. Charles sampled her anally, Andrew coming in her mouth, and then she had to awkwardly lick Sarah's pussy, her own filled with a vibrator, for what seemed like hours.

Two was enough for Charles, but Andrew managed one more, Jenny again sat astride him, her breasts now roped, while the sweet-looking couple, Charles and Sarah, swung crops across her buttocks from either side of the bed to encourage her to thrust herself down onto Andrew's cock with greater efforts. The fluttering of her cuffed hands, trying to shield herself from their strokes, was a source of some merriment. The former White Knight of her fantasies, the perfect gentleman of her dreams, put a shock dildo up Jenny's ass to punish her because the clamps decorating her pussy had scratched him.

Jenny did everything that was required of her. Moaning, gasping, crying out in both pain and pleasure and tonguing anything that was put into, or pushed up against, her mouth. Nothing further was required of her but that she should be there, hot, wet and firmly bound. Afterwards, the two sated men sipped iced beer and watched while Sarah was first licked by, and then proceeded to screw the toy they'd been provided with, into exhaustion with a strap-on, a plug filling Jenny's ass and many encouraging slaps, squeezes, pinches and twists.

Jenny was only mildly surprised when her lover Lady Isobell forgot to come and rescue her from her ordeal at midnight. But by dawn even her aching jaw wasn't the worst of her problems. Her whole body felt black and blue. No wonder real slaves were given a chance to recuperate in the cells, or on display, after being used. She lay on the floor where her fellow students had discarded her, aching, but totally content. And now she'd finally got it out of her system as well; knew exactly what it was like to be a real slave. Now she could find a nice Master and Mistress to voluntarily submit to.

SEVEN
ESCAPE

SLOWLY, RELUCTANTLY, Jenny pulled herself from the bath. Her bottom, caned, spanked and whipped was bringing new meaning to the word tender; her strapped and pummelled pussy, quite swollen. Inside she felt a little raw, anus throbbing uncomfortably after being so hard used. Her jaw still ached, her nipples were very sore and her breasts felt strangely swollen, heavy almost, as a result of all the squeezing, roping, slapping and whipping. Emotionally she was blissfully relaxed and content, the cares of the world just stripped away.

To hell with it. Jenny hooked her foot around the plug chain and let some water drain away, fumbled it back into place, toed on the hot tap, and luxuriated another half hour, until she was totally wrinkled. Finally, in danger of becoming a prune, she forced herself from the bath, reluctantly dressed, and made her way to the university lab. Her fingers were still slightly wrinkled when she stepped through the Gate and identified herself to the computer.

Isobell wasn't in her chambers, just a pair of slave-boys slumbering entwined in a corner cage, and a naked slave-girl, hooded and with her arms bound behind her kneeling at the foot of the bed. Remembering, she couldn't help smiling again. Jenny couldn't tell if the girl was finished with or waiting to be used; her skin unmarked, but Isobell could be gentle when the mood took her. A single rope, looped tight around each heavy breast, and criss-crossed over both, secured the girl to one of the bed's posts.

Jenny wished Isobell wouldn't do that. She loved breast bondage, securing pony-girls to a hitching rail by pierced nipples was obviously just fun, and she'd got used to most of the things that could be done to slaves. But tying girls to things by their breasts disturbed her in a way she couldn't quite define. It crossed a line somehow! Her aristocratic lover knew it disturbed her in some way, and although she had no intention

131

of stopping, had asked Jenny what the difference was from securing a slave-boy to something with a rope tight around his cock and balls, which didn't bother her at all!

Perhaps, because men being led around by their penises wasn't so far away from normal life anyway, she'd replied. She tracked down Isobell in one of her three playrooms, torturing a new slave-girl who hadn't been satisfactory in bed.

"You sound chirpy," the aristocrat told her. "And how was the lovely Andrew?"

"Fun!"

"Just fun?"

"Well I'd imagined more in the way of romance, and a little more privacy, but the sex was better than my wildest dreams," she admitted. "Big fun!"

Isobell grinned.

"What are you doing to her?" Jenny asked.

"Just teaching her to be a little more appreciative of dildos," the aristocrat said casually.

The ball-gagged girl was kneeling upright in a small cage on a waist-high stand, mounted on a fat, heavily ribbed, dildo, and with electrodes clipped to erect nipples. Her lovely baby-blue eyes, that had probably been dyed a colour chosen from a catalogue, were wide with fear.

"Daddy doesn't really approve of my using this; it's a very powerful shock," Jenny's lover explained off-hand, "but he can't really complain. It was my mother's."

Isobell's face clouded momentarily. Some illnesses even the alternative England's advanced medicine couldn't cure unless caught early enough. She shrugged and continued.

"It's quite a clever toy actually. The dildo is a mechanical pump, see? Like a car jack?" Jenny nodded. "Each time she thrusts down the ratchet turns once and she cranks up this little weight hanging from the pulley? But the weight is slowly clicking down all the time, and has to be constantly jacked up just to keep it still! With me?"

Jenny nodded again, beginning to get the drift. The gently

spinning weight was suspended above a metal pad, slowly clicking lower and lower as she watched. The naked slave, obeying an order, thrust herself down hard on the shaft, the ribbed invader disappearing inside her sex, and the weight was ratcheted up a notch.

"All set," the aristocrat declared with satisfaction. "If the weight touches the metal contact pad, it completes an electrical circuit, and she'll think her nipples are being burned off." She patted the girl's creamy, satin thigh. "Come on Bunny. Start fucking yourself, or you're going to find out what pain really is."

The weight which had continued to slowly click down, swung perilously close to the contact pad for a moment, the pretty young slave with her wrists locked through the bars behind her, thrusting down frantically on the dildo that filled her. Slowly, with much effort, and despairing lust-forced moans, she jacked the weight up away from danger, and then settled into a steady rhythm. The red wires running to her cruelly clamped nipples swayed as her breasts swung, the little metal jaws biting deep into the fat nubs, as her hips slowly but firmly thrust up and down. As ordered, she was fucking herself. Jenny watched the dildo sliding in and out of her, entranced.

The girl's nametag 'BUNNY' hung from her left earlobe like an earring, and Jenny suddenly remembered her lover buying it. Isobell handled the girl's large breasts a moment, and then swung the cage door shut.

"You get lovely skin, stamina and really perky nipples on an eighteen year-old, but they're so repressed; inhibited, when we first get them," she complained dismissively. "Now a twenty-two year-old, who's been wearing a collar at least two years, preferably three, then you know the sex is going to be good."

"Do you ever use the same pet names on different property?" Jenny wondered.

"Oh no. No one does. Obviously plenty of other owners

will have pets called Bunny, but this is the first and only Bunny I'll ever own. It would be disrespectful to the memory of a pet; if a girl's worth being called more than 'hey you',"

Jenny was still trying to figure that one out as she was lead from the room, a gentle gag-muffled panting fading out of earshot behind her. Both science teams were getting together for a pow-wow on the future of the Gate today. Crunch time. But as they still had an hour or two to spare, they took a stroll around the grounds. Jenny gently steered her lover towards the stable-block.

A Lady she didn't recognise was on the front lawn throwing a stick for a naked slave-boy to chase and lay at her feet. Her collared pet was a huge powerful man, easily 6'6", heavy straps around his wrists chained to the back of a tight belt. Bells hung from his pierced nipples, a dainty chiming accompanying his eager dashes, cock and balls padlocked into a small pouch. A very small pouch, Jenny realised. An erection inside that leather bag would be painfully impossible. He whimpered helplessly when the aristocrat exercising him stroked a whip-marked buttock approvingly.

Behind the stables they paused a while admiring a pair of dressage pony-girls in training. The large-breasted, wasp-waisted, dildo-stuffed playthings with white and purple plumes on their bridles, the Franklin colours, prancing in perfect step, only a week away from an important national competition.

Less overtly sexy than the top-heavy show-ponies, but still quite lovely and graceful to Jenny's eyes, a racing-pony was being tacked up. The slave-girl, slender, smoothly muscled and with high firm pointed breasts, pranced out proudly onto the track where other racing slaves were being limbered up. The harness digging into her skin, unlike the ornate dressage-slaves', was utilitarian, plain and slightly worn, the uniformed soldier driving her from the lightweight trap she was hitched to grinning from ear to ear, his lash licking across her firm rump.

In a nearby field an unfamiliar Lord was driving two male

hunting-hacks. The paired pony-boys were weaved in and out of a course of straw-bales and poles and yanked to a cruel stop. One of Isobell's brothers?

"Pull!" the middle-aged and slightly chubby Lord called.

From a little half buried hutch-like shed down the course a naked girl with her arms secured behind her bolted, breasts swinging. The Lord raised his hunting rifle, squeezing off careful shots, his well-trained ponies not even flinching as tranquillising darts whipped past between them. The running girl suddenly staggered, stumbled to her knees, and then flopped to the ground.

"Henry. Second cousin," Isobell whispered. "Poor soul actually managed to shoot one of his own ponies on a Royal hunt once." She giggled. "We all lend him spare slaves to practice on."

"Pull!"

Another naked slave with bound arms and an eye-protecting visor dashed across the grass and was brought down.

They encountered Academic Franklin and professor Phillips-Webber taking a stroll by the gallops, where racing-ponies were timed or run against each other. The professor looked very at home in a Lady's semi-formal garb, Jenny had to admit, arm in arm with Lord Franklin, a slave-girl's lead looped around her wrist. Isobell smiled at her father and exchanged cautious but polite greetings with her soon-to-be stepmother. The two seemed to have reached an understanding.

Jenny let her eyes roam over the almost naked slave-girl her tutor had on a lead, and found herself a little surprised. For one thing the blonde was a woman, not a girl, the oldest slave Jenny had yet encountered by far. Late thirties, Jenny guessed, though wearing her years well. There was a definite curve to her belly, breasts probably not as firm as they'd once been, and up close there were lines around her eyes and her skin wasn't quite the silky, flawless, velvet Jenny was used to seeing on displayed property. But she was still undeniably attractive, and she must have been totally stunning when she was younger, Jenny thought.

The slave was perched almost on her toes in 5" heels, ankles linked with a short hobble, a heavy black leather collar holding her head up and with her wrists and elbows cuffed together behind her. A pair of chains looped under her between her legs, swinging against firm thighs when she moved, linking wrist cuffs to a pair of shiny thick rings set through each sex-lip, ensured that her arms would stay neatly down her back.

A third ring pierced the slave's clitoris, which Phillips-Webber's lead was clipped to, and a nametag hung on a short length of chain from a navel ring. It was difficult for Jenny to judge exactly how firm the woman's breasts were, the full globes appearing the equal of many of the younger slaves' she'd seen though slightly marked with pale blue veins, because of her restraint/torment.

The bound woman held a bar between her teeth, like a bit but not buckled into place, with a too short chain running down from each end to her nipple-rings. Her large breasts were not being allowed to droop, they were held up and swinging suspended from the chains by cruelly stretched nipples, she was being made to hold up the weight of both heavy globes with her bit and pierced nipples. And, being able to drop the bit at any time, she was being tempted into disobedience!

Academic Franklin cocked his head, listening to something only he could hear from a directional collar-mike, and pulled out a perfectly ordinary looking stopwatch. Again Jenny marvelled at the differences and similarities between two worlds whose histories had diverged in Roman times. His fiancée, Jenny's tutor, looked on indulgently as he nodded to himself and started the watch. The slave she led, lead looped around her wrist almost forgotten, had calm, placid eyes. Jenny, used to seeing exciting fear, shame and uncontrolled lust on the faces of toys, found her calm serenity almost frightening. Could being owned ever become merely normal?

A half minute later a racing-pony, squeaking in high-pitched yelps as she was lashed, flashed past, pulling carriage and driver. Franklin stopped his watch. It took skill and practice to whip a racing-pony he explained to Phillips-Webber, having to time the lash to land just as she was exhaling. You got a breathless pony-girl if she was trying to breath in just as the whip forced her to yelp. Of course a well-trained girl would let the whip control her breathing as well as encourage her, he added.

"Good time!" he called to the soldier circling his human mount back to the gate.

"My Lady. My I borrow Pretty?" Isobell asked.

The professor looked to her fiancé, who shrugged carelessly.

"Of course dear," she agreed, handing over the woman-slave's lead.

They moved about ten metres up the course, Isobell now leading the naked slave, Jenny not even sure if her tutor had recognised her under her veil. Jenny and her lover leant against the fence, waiting for the next pony-girl to be whipped past. Down the track at the finish-line she could see her professor, under the direction of the Academic, handling the harnessed body of the last slave, being shown what to look for when buying a racing-pony?

Isobell looped Pretty's lead around a fence post and scooped up her nipple-suspended breasts, carelessly squeezing them together and kneading creamy flesh. The placid slave sighed softly in pleasure, partly relief that her nipple-torture was brought to a momentary pause, but mostly because she genuinely enjoyed being handled by the aristocrat, Jenny suspected.

"This is the first slave I ever had sex with," Isobell told Jenny. "My brothers too. She was a present from my mother to my Daddy. The first time I ever had sex, actually," she admitted.

The blonde gasped in pain as her breasts were dropped, jerked to a cruel halt by her nipple-chains. Isobell gave the suspended globes a few slaps, heavy flesh bouncing and swinging. The bound woman held herself obediently still.

"Early conditioning I think," Isobell continued. "I like to ride a slave-boy's shaft on occasion, and I have a slender girl every now and then for variety, but I always come back to a docile, sweet-faced, top-heavy pet who loves sex."

"Taller than you?" Jenny asked.

"For preference. I just love big dumb animals."

She laughed, remembering.

"Oh Gods, you should have seen me. It was so embarrassing! It's my eighteenth birthday, I've had a couple of celebratory drinks too many, and there's a naked Pretty kneeling at the foot of my bed waiting to be used." She shook her head, stroking the blonde slave's flank now. "So there I am with half a mile of rope in one hand, and enough restraints lying around to secure her fifty times over. Birthday presents. And in my other hand, a slave-training manual that some well-meaning great-aunt has given me!"

Isobell laughed, an uninhibited peal of delight.

"Gods, I was actually standing there with a slave-training manual in my hand. Can you imagine?"

Jenny couldn't help laughing with her. It was a lovely image. STEP 1. OPEN SLAVE'S MOUTH. STEP 2. INSERT AND BUCKLE INTO PLACE BALL-GAG. STEP 3. SECURE SLAVE FIRMLY TO THE BED FACE UP, AT WRIST AND ANKLE WITH ROPE PROVIDED. NOTE—FACE DOWN—SEE ANAL SEX, CHAPTER FOUR.

"Fortunately I had the sense to read it later, and Pretty knew what was expected of her. I had a wonderful birthday."

The aristocrat turned the naked woman's name-tag over in her fingers, patted the pussy her lead was clipped to, and lifted a large breast to inspect the bar-code and serial-number tattooed on the creamy globe's underside.

"Do you know I doubt if I'd even recognise a quarter of the slaves I've enjoyed over the years, let alone remember what I did with them, but that night's still clear. You never forget the first time you make another person squeal in pain, or the way rope digs into flesh and what a girl trying to plead past a gag sounds like. Especially, you never forget the first mark you leave on another person's flesh, and the first time you force a bound, utterly helpless sexual plaything to have an orgasm. Gods know how often I've used her over the years since then, it's not important; but that first time? You never forget your first slave." Isobell let her fingernails trail across one of the docile toy's buttocks, and then stepped back. "How old do you think she is?"

Jenny let her eyes roam over the helpless woman, forced almost onto her toes, hobbled, her arms secured behind her back and with her wrist-cuffs chained to her pussy. A collar to force her head up, nipples-tormented, branded and pet-tagged, a lead clipped to a ring set through her clitoris. Quite, quite naked, and humiliatingly treated, discussed and handled. A pet.

"37, 38?" she guessed, so used to slaves now she could study one without the least trace of embarrassment.

"She's sixty two, and still got a few good years in her yet," Isobell corrected. "Daddy wanted to keep her, so he appealed against her sentence and had it increased. Listen to me carefully Jennifer, and listen good! The only reason to give the rejuvenation treatment to a peasant is if you've got a favourite pet you want to keep. Every new slave on this estate would rather have a leg amputated than be given the youth treatment. Toys come and go, but this is Daddy's pet. He can keep her as long as her likes!"

"It's hardly fair," Jenny said softly.

"Of course it's not, though Pretty here, did get down on her knees and beg, without permission, to have her sentence extended when Daddy was considering keeping her. But then, the system's not really fair. You think we don't know that? I'm starting to suspect you people don't. Our lifestyle is more important to us than abstract moral arguments, is all. Now, how do you think I see you?"

Jenny didn't need to think too hard. The question had already occurred to her.

"Like a family dog," she replied. "Loved, but it's still your right to smack and train; expect obedience. I expect you'd prefer to feel free to punish me, have me wear a collar, and for me to be house-trained. Not uncover my face or answer back my betters, sort of thing? Outside sex, I don't suppose you'd punish me for the fun of it like a slave, but the training would be real?"

"I knew you were intelligent," her strange, proud lover nodded. "Ah, here's the filly I wanted you to see."

The next racing-pony swept down the track, harness jingling merrily, leather cracks on flesh accompanied by gasps and squeaks. The pony-girl was very unusual, being dark skinned, the row of silver chastity-rings set through her sex-lips and the nipple-rings her reins were attached to, standing out vividly. Coloured slaves were rare and very expensive, usually the gifts of African or Arabian rulers to European Royalty. There had never been any large-scale immigration on this world except to Australia and the Americas.

"Oh god! Karen?" Jenny whispered.

Isobell scooped up Pretty's lead and led the way to the finish line, where professor Phillips-Webber was examining the sweat-sheened, harnessed and bridled girl with interest.

Karen's brand was prominently displayed high on her right hip above the buttock, showing clearly against coffee skin. She was blinkered, so couldn't see Jenny and Isobell standing off to one side at first. The bound student was panting helplessly, slavering on the breasts her tutor was handling so enthusiastically. Racing ponies didn't run in dildos, it interfered with speed, but the crotch-strap's friction against the slave's clitoris would still keep an aphrodisiac-treated girl's mind where the owner wanted it. Karen moaned in despairing protest when her teacher gave the strap a tug, settling it even deeper between the folds of her pussy.

The black girl's hands on the shafts of her pony-trap, broad bands tight around her wrists, secured to the poles with

140

padlocks, were clenched, white knuckled, as professor Phillips-Webber stroked the rings set through her sex-lips. She tried to take a step back, but a lick of the driver's whip, across her already marked behind, reminded her to keep her ankles together. Karen wasn't just panting, she was sobbing, Jenny realised.

"Professor," Jenny greeted her neutrally as they stepped forward, Isobell handing back Pretty's lead without comment.

"Jenny? Is that you?"

Karen's eyes went wide, a plaintive, bit-muffled cry cut off when her driver gave her reins a sharp pull, jerking her bit back into her mouth, breasts bobbing as her newly ringed nipples were cruelly yanked. Pony-girls were never allowed to talk!

"Karen's going in for the youth treatment tomorrow," their tutor announced cheerfully. "I think she'll pass as a slave, don't you?"

The professor's hand, totally unconsciously, slid down Karen's flank, tracing the straps of her harness when her fingers found them. Isobell's grip on Jenny's elbow tightened warningly.

"She looks every inch a real slave, "Jenny agreed, glad her veil hid her face. "I thought the rejuvenation treatment was done unconscious?"

She carefully didn't mention the brand and rings. They had discussed such things amongst themselves to appear authentic, but somehow she didn't think slaves came any more authentic than this.

"Just so that she can pass if some nosy type wakes her up," the professor said airily. "But mostly, would you believe she actually likes this, and might even want to stay on when we leave? Did you know Karen was a masochist?"

Another wail of protest from the naked, harnessed student they were discussing was cut off by a flick of her driver's whip up between her legs and into her crotch. Karen squealed, Phillips-Webber, unconcerned, twirling her nipples between thumb and fingers.

"I thought she might be sexually submissive," Jenny allowed.

"How fascinating! I must admit it would have never have occurred to me she'd want to be publicly treated like this, would find slavery so fascinating; or would want to be one," Phillips-Webber said, painfully squeezing her student's breasts to make her meet her eyes. "A dark horse, you might say."

They all chuckled dutifully, Jenny was then forced to stand and watch her friend run the course twice more. Karen's light coffee skin gleamed as if oiled by the third run, and she was totally unresisting when Franklin waved away her driver, positioned himself behind her, bent her forward and unbuckled her crotch-strap; Karen still harnessed to the pony-trap.

The Academic's hands on her hips and his cock sliding easily into her sex, were by contrast with Karen's darker skin, startlingly white. Jenny watched mesmerised as his cock plunged in and out of the bound girl's pussy, the hard-worked pony-girl's gasps for breath slowly becoming gasps of pleasure; Jenny suddenly realising she was standing beside her middle-aged, frumpy, teacher watching someone having sex. She looked up, Isobell having long ago drifted away back in the direction of the house, watching a family member having sex being one of the few perversions the Lords and Ladies didn't indulge in.

The estate's newest pony-girl was too exhausted to respond to her rape with proper enthusiasm, though as Jenny watched she spread her thighs wider, thrusting back to meet the strokes of her Master's cock, her moans becoming more urgent as her nipples were yanked with her reins. You didn't make a slave in a day, Jenny knew only too well from having visited the clinic; the brand, the rings and surgically implanted aphrodisiac, and probably an ID tag as well, not an overnight job. She suddenly realised she hadn't seen her friend for several days.

Her teacher watching with a strange smile, Jenny turned

142

away and hurried after Isobell. Behind her Karen was squeaking in pleasured lust, the cracks of the Academic's hands on her freshly whipped buttocks, encouraging her. Isobell had paused to let her catch up.

"They didn't think they fooled you, but they don't think it matters either way," the aristocrat told her. "I'm giving you fair warning. From a lover. We're going to go straight to the Gate now, and you are going to leave, and then take a long trip away from your Gate. And before you say anything, it's too late to save your friends. Walk, don't run!"

"But...?"

"Oh, the goons won't look twice at you with me. I'm the one supposed to be delivering you."

Jenny swallowed a sudden lump in her throat. Two unfamiliar limousines were parked in the drive, the chatting drivers wearing the black of Royal Security Police. In the main hall slave-boys were licking the marble floor clean, a slave-girl strapped to and mounted on the stone penis of a statue as decoration. All six glass display-cases in the hall contained naked flesh, and heart pounding, she was suddenly afraid to look inside them. Only Isobell walking two paces ahead of her with a measured tread prevented her breaking into a run when she remembered the acceptance in the placid Pretty's eyes. Forty years a sexual plaything!

The lab computer wouldn't respond to Jenny's voice and unlock the door, but Isobell over-rode it. She swatted Jenny on the behind. "Goodbye Jenny. Remember, keep walking. I have to go and distract Daddy."

Jenny sobbed with relief when she stumbled through the Gate, tripping over her robe. She grabbed Andrew's cassette player, and wrapping it in a towel to cushion the blow, turned it on and tossed it through the Gate. She knew what would happen, and counted down to herself as the computer in Franklin's lab got a voice it couldn't recognise, and knowing something had entered through the Gate, shut it down! Unsupported now, the Gate in the professor's lab winked out of existence in the blink of an eye.

All that was left was a copper framework supported between poles. Quite unthreatening. Jenny slumped into a chair, letting the panic she'd been holding back overwhelm her. Now all she had to do was explain to the authorities the disappearance of four friends and one teacher. Yeah, right!

With trembling hands she put the kettle on. Fantasies were wonderful, the chance to act them out even better, as were sexual games, but you had to think carefully about your place in reality. It was like those people who wished they'd been born in different times, as a cowboy, a pirate, a warrior storming the walls of Troy, or people who wished they'd been born in the days of chivalry, knights in armour. But of course the unspoken assumption was that they would be the hero on the white charger, or the beautiful maiden he rescued, not, as was more likely, one of the countless illiterate peasants up to his or her knees in mud ducking their head and tugging at forelocks as the armoured man rode by.

As she calmed down, regrets started to replace relief. She'd never had a chance to sleep with a human cuddly toy as Lady Isobell had promised. She'd wanted to see one of the dairy-slaves she'd heard about but hadn't seen, being milked. And she'd almost worked up her courage to ask if she could have a go at driving those cute little paired show-ponies Isobell owned. With the eyes of a free woman, she still found pony-slaves quite delectable. Even Karen had looked good.

But she'd come much too close to tasting a bit herself there. Too real. Much too real! One day she would find a nice Master or Mistress, preferably a couple, with a pony-trap and a nice quiet meadow; who would pet, groom, spoil, pamper and very gently..."

"Jenny! What the hell happened to the Gate?" It was Andrew's voice.

She turned to see him, Charles, Lady Sybill, and Charles and Sarah's appointed guide, a Lady called Constance.

"Oh shit," Jenny muttered.

EIGHT
SAFE

JENNY WOKE SLOWLY, relaxed in the comfortable safety of her own little flat. The couple below were screaming at each other again, rap music was drifting in the open window and from above came the rhythmic squeaks of a bed seeing action. Home sweet home.

The marks and aches of her night of passion with Andrew, Charles and Sarah were fading, except for her breasts which still felt uncomfortably swollen and heavy. She pushed a stray worry to the back of her mind. Maybe her breasts were bruised on the inside, more delicate than she'd thought; the way owners in the Slaveworld treated their toys making her forget that. She grinned. Or as Andrew had called it, Tit-world. Getting out of bed she spared a moment's sympathy for all the slave-girls she'd seen Isobell tit-training, teasing and tormenting.

The worry gnawed at her through breakfast, all through a long cup of tea and while she dressed. Her breasts; a little tender maybe, hadn't swollen like this before, and her other-world lover had frequently wrapped them in rope, squeezing and slapping them hard. She dealt with her worry in the time-honoured way of ignoring it, and hoping it would go away. No way was she going to try and explain this one to her doctor!

She could feel herself flushing scarlet just thinking about it. No way! Back at the lab Charles, Andrew and the two stranded aristocratic Ladies from the alternative England were trying to re-establish contact. Jenny was soon feeling distinctly outnumbered.

Charles had no intention of leaving Sarah behind, or being left behind by her; it depended which side of the Gate was your final destination, and that was the limit of his thinking. The two Ladies of course wanted to return home to their own dimension. And Andrew, sure he had Lady Sybill eating out of the palm of his hand; though Jenny suspected it was the other way around, saw no personal danger, which was the limit of his thinking. Idiot, she muttered. The 25-looking Lady Sybill was in her late forties. Don't let the age-gap fool you! Though it was possible her own judgement was being clouded by jealousy there.

None of them really seemed to believe Isobell had told her to run for the hills. Jenny had obviously misunderstood. A joke had backfired.

Karen with a brand on her being publicly fucked by Lord Franklin, Jenny demanded? Lady Sybill shrugged, making no attempt to deny it had happened, just Jenny's interpretation of events.

"I don't want to live in your world, so she had to come to mine. She loves me; and as my property, it's the only way to be with me," the aristocrat explained.

Jenny even felt a little doubt herself. She knew Karen had a sexually submissive streak in her, like she did herself, and knew again the black girl had had the same sort of relationship with Lady Sybill that she'd had with Isobell. The only relationship possible with a Slaveworld aristocrat who didn't consider you a social equal. She'd been fascinated by slaves herself. And the Lords and Ladies, practised people owners and mostly all older than they looked, were expert manipulators. Could Karen have been persuaded that wearing nothing but a collar and having the chance to stay young, was worth it to stay with her lover? Might Isobell have been able to talk Jenny into becoming her pet if she'd put her mind to it?

No! She remembered the very real fear that had gripped her as she'd finally seen the trapdoors springing shut, the pleading in Karen's eyes, and Isobell's actions were the clincher. Deciding to be kind, her lover had chosen to set her free. That didn't imply a choice. That last meeting would have seen them all shot with dart rifles, and waking up naked in chains. Making sure nobody in this world even knew the existence of their world was a safer bet than just shutting down

146

the Gate.

She considered sabotaging the equipment, but didn't think she needed to. It was keeping the four busy and off her back. And their chances of hitting the right Gate again at random were worse than winning the lottery. Billions to one, not millions. It had been all very hit or miss in the first place. Oh, they could get a Gate, with all the possible probabilities there would be untold labs experimenting so that the two could join.

But to hit the right one? Imagine throwing a dart at a wall 20 metres away with your eyes closed. And then trying to hit exactly the same hole in the wall doing it again. It wasn't going to happen. The last little bit of fear she'd felt when she'd found two aristocrats trapped on her side of the Gate, faded. Lady Sybill and her snooty friend would just have to get used to a world in which they had to work for a living, and ask for sex.

Karen had been beyond saving, but she did feel bad about Sarah, for which Charles would never forgive her, but all in all it hadn't worked out that badly. She'd saved herself and two of her fellow students, and they still had the advanced technology they'd brought back. No matter what they said, Jenny still believed she'd done the right thing shutting down the Gate.

***

The next day her breasts had swollen more, and Jenny pushed dawning suspicion away. By the next day she was spilling out of her bra, and could no longer pretend. Not swollen, growing! She remembered the injection, almost unnoticed at the time; Isobell's last gift. Her haughty lover had always said she needed more up top.

"Fucking bitch!" Jenny muttered under her breath for the hundredth time.

By the end of the week her old bras lay unused under new purchases, her eventual new size a 38D cup, and even that

147

was a little snug; though she flatly refused to even consider that she was a larger size.

All women knew and got used to the fact that men's eyes, lascivious, admiring, lustful, hungry or just plain appreciative, would occasionally be on them. The nature of the beast. It was even more noticeable when you watched men watching women. Sometimes it was fun, she liked having her legs admired, sometimes humorous, like when you saw the male of the species dreamily following the sway of hips down a pavement, totally absorbed by the flick and roll of a bottom in a tight skirt. Unless you were interested, eyes going to your breasts before your face was a little annoying; and the compulsive starers ranged from creepy to scary.

But this was ridiculous! Even wearing what seemed to be an industrial bra, they bounced, wobbled and swung. Men openly drooled down her cleavage and talking to her nipples. She turned heads just walking down the street and trotting up and down stairs was worse. The one time she'd run for a bus, to her lasting embarrassment, workmen swarming over a scaffolding overhead had openly clapped and cheered. And even that wasn't as bad as the snide way in which female acquaintances asked her if she'd had a boob job.

The tightly buckled, clinching, criss-crossed straps of a show-pony's harness were looking more practical all the time. Except that would only make them stick out more. Suddenly she was wearing a lot of loose tops.

Summer holidays arrived, the university mostly emptied, and she spent less and less time in the lab. The other four, knowing she wasn't committed, didn't seem to care about her drifting away. Jenny had been right. They'd opened dozens of new Gates so far, all quickly closed after a quick hello, not one the correct one.

She did initially consider talking to her doctor about breast reduction surgery, but every day, despite a certain amount of new awkwardness, it seemed less important. She was growing to like the increased male, and sometimes even female, attention, and certainly didn't mind being asked out more often. Even if it was for the wrong reason. Her adventures in the Slaveworld had even given her the confidence to allow herself to be picked up by a woman twice her age. The lawyer had called several times since, but Jenny had put her off. It had been wonderful to finally experience cunnilingus, but she missed the ropes.

As a substitute for a Mistress Jenny had discovered self-bondage. She'd bought a pair of handcuffs. With her feet tied wide to the bottom of her bed, a vibrator tied against her pussy and a blindfold over her eyes, she could happily lock her wrists to the headboard, deliciously helpless, until the handcuffs' key tied to the headboard with a length of string, and encased in a block of slowly melting ice, was freed.

And maybe she couldn't walk down a street without her breasts jiggling, but with a rope tight around each full globe and a clothespin on each nipple, her self-bondage was wonderfully, fantastically, complete.

* * *

The doorbell rang as Jenny was about to secure her ankles to her bed. The handcuffs' key was set frozen in the centre of a block of ice under the bed, not even yet started to melt, the string to the key tied securely to the headboard next to where her hands would be locked. The shiny metal bracelets that gave her so much pleasure waited open on her pillow. Jenny suppressed a yelp of panic. It was part of her ever-more complex ritual now to leave the front door unlocked, the thought that somebody might walk in on her, up to now, very exciting indeed.

Jenny ripped away the blindfold resting ready on her forehead as the bell was rung again, more insistently, panicked fingers scrabbling at the knot of her gag behind her neck, panties tied into her mouth. Clean underwear at the moment, but the seductive thought of dirty underwear, as Isobell had used, was growing on her. She had two regular boy-friends and a possible on the go at the moment, but none of them she wanted to see her like this yet.

She snatched clothespins off her nipples, gasping in pleasure as blood rushed painfully back into crushed capillaries, her breasts were too elaborately and complexly roped to quickly release. Her self-bondage had become more and more adventurous with each attempt, rope now looped around her torso and up around her neck, so that as she writhed in pleasure, by arching her neck back she could pull on her bound breasts.

Padlocked tight around her waist, polished leather digging deeply into soft skin, was her new toy. She'd taken a train 50 miles to make absolutely sure that there was no chance someone who might recognise her would see her going into a sex-shop. And still she had nearly died of embarrassment buying the thing for herself, so hot was her shame that it had nearly made her come on the spot. Fortunately the sweet old chap who ran the place had been nothing but helpful, not the dirty-raincoat brigade she'd been half expecting.

As well as the padlock on the belt, the chain that ran down between her buttocks and up under her to the front, holding a vibrator inside the wearer, was also locked. The plastic invader that impaled her could not be removed without a key, and they were both embedded in ice with the keys to her handcuffs! Once its base was twisted to turn the vibrator on, its wearer would just have to moan in delight until the battery ran down if she'd tied herself to her bed.

The doorbell rang again, the ringer more insistent still. Shit, shit, shit! Jenny pulled on her robe, splashed her hair wet in the sink and wrapped a towel tight around her neck to hide the bondage-bra's cord looped around her throat. She hadn't tied her breasts that tightly, especially compared with some of the slaves she'd seen, but they still bulged noticeably against her robe. No time! To her horror Andrew and Lady Sybill were at the door, and invited themselves in.

"I was just having a shower. Can't talk. I've got to go out and I really don't have time...."

Her protests were brushed aside. Apparently it was urgent; and her date would have to wait. Still in her hidden bonds, Jenny reluctantly found herself making coffee, offering biscuits and obediently admiring Lady Sybill's engagement ring. Andrew looked smug.

It was important. Karen's parents had reported her missing. Stories had to be matched before the bored, uninterested, but no doubt methodical, detective who had questioned Andrew got around to her. And as he tried to question known acquaintances, he was going to discover a missing professor and another missing girl, Andrew concluded grimly. Jenny, who'd once been all for bringing in the authorities, was now less than keen. She'd been the one who had trapped the three in a parallel universe. And it was such a fantastic story anyway! Who would believe her?

The agreed story, thin but difficult to disprove, would be that Karen and Sarah had said they were going to accompany professor Phillips-Webber hiking around Scotland for a week before going home for the holidays. Very thin, Jenny agreed, but as long as no one made any disprovable claims, like they'd seen them off at the station, just stuck to "That's what they said, officer,", then hopefully it would be enough to keep the long arm of the law at bay. Getting deeper! Was this what quicksand felt like?

Lady Sybill's eyes were on her like a cat, Jenny realised, and catching sight of herself in the mirror it wasn't hard to see why. With her increased bust augmented by her bondage bra, and her robe pulled snug around a very slender waist, the vibrator's harness belt acting like a corset, she was displaying an hour-glass figure of almost cartoon proportions.

Or an owner-modified slave-girl's!

Jenny pulled her towel tighter around her neck to better hide the rope around her throat, and let the loose ends hang down over her breasts.

"Jenny dear, I can't help noticing you seem to be a little more prominent than I remember you?" the aristocrat purred.

Andrew's eyes widened, as he noticed what his worries had so far distracted him from.

"Yes, your friend thought it would be amusing to slip me a little injection to improve my appearance," Jenny tried to say with quiet dignity, but afraid it came out a mouse's squeak.

She had no trouble getting an authentic amount of bitterness and anger into her tone; it was how she still felt despite the very real improvement in her sex-life. Andrew sniggered behind his hand, and then started to laugh helplessly.

"That explains it," the cat said, buffing fingernails on a silk blouse. "May I see?"

"Certainly not!" the mouse squeaked fearfully.

Lady Sybill shrugged as if it was unimportant, and then stood, looking closer at a picture behind Jenny's chair; an old print that had come with the flat. Jenny felt her heart pounding, treacherous sexual excitement which had already built to a peak as she'd bound herself, mingling with her fear; knowing that she should run, order them out, that there could only be one outcome when a cat played with a mouse.

"You have lovely hair," the aristocrat told her stroking Jenny's wet locks. She started to pull away, but rattlesnake fast, a fist was wrapped around a loop of her hair. "When it's dry of course. Dark, shiny, just a hint of a wave and those lovely copper highlights. I was discussing you with Isobell. We both agreed if we owned you, you'd be one of the ones we didn't have made blonde."

As she spoke she slowly pulled Jenny's head back over the back of the chair, neck arched, and Jenny knew the cord around her throat was visible. The haughty aristocrat gave her hair a little jerk to make Jenny meet her eyes.

"Fold your arms behind your back, Jenny," the woman standing behind her ordered. "Andrew. Open her robe."

"Oh Christ, yes!" the former man of her dreams breathed as her belt, the chain pulled between her sex-lips and the ropes criss-crossing her breasts, all digging deep into her flesh, were revealed.

Mentally, Jenny stamped a foot. She'd been as nice as she knew how, she'd always tried to be casually attractive, she'd listened attentively, always ready to talk, and had even learned the rules to rugby and stood freezing on the sideline watching several games. And all it really took to get his attention was big boobs and a phallus strapped inside her!

She was pulled off the chair and onto her knees, still controlled with a handful of hair, subserviently letting her robe and towel fall away to tangle on her folded arms behind her, making no move or protest as her clothing fell away. It was what she wanted anyway, she realised.

"Thighs wider, head up!" Lady Sybill snapped.

Nipples rising, heat stirring in her loins, Jenny obeyed, sighing happily when her breasts swelled against the cat's cradle constriction of the cords she'd wrapped around them. Andrew was sent to fetch something to tie her hands with, not even seeming to notice how naturally Lady Sybill was giving him orders. He returned grinning, with Jenny's handcuffs.

"Souvenirs from our travels Jenny?" he teased.

Still held in place by her hair, Jenny was bent forward and her robe pulled away, cold metal snapping shut around her wrists behind her. She couldn't help flinching slightly at the familiar sound, even though she craved it. Lady Sybill decided she wanted her toy properly dressed, and once again Andrew was sent off to hunt for the stiletto heels the aristocrat was sure Isobell's old plaything would have lying around somewhere. The 4" heeled sandals were found, and the ankle-straps padlocked around Jenny's ankles.

"Jenny. Stand!"

Naked, cuffed, her breasts in rope and a vibrator belted and padlocked inside her, Jenny obeyed. She groaned helplessly when the aristocrat reached out and switched on the plastic invader, the buzz clearly audible around the room. The tingling, throbbing, stimulating vibration was far more powerful than her old vibrator, the one she was used to. This device was designed to tease or torment a submissive, not something a woman used to gently pleasure herself. The pulsating, powerful, vibration reminded her of the times she'd surreptitiously let a petrol-pump hose rest against her crotch, but this was inside her!

Jenny gasped in mingled relief and disappointment when Lady Sybill reached out and turned off the tormenting device, this was very clearly the way it was meant to be used. She was obediently still when the aristocrat stroked and squeezed her breasts, pulled and twisted at her nipples.

"Very nice, though I'm surprised Isobell didn't make them bigger. She always did like her toys large and heavy."

Her fingers trailed down the chain digging into Jenny's belly, switching the vibrator on and off, and on and off again.

"Please!" Jenny begged, powerless.

The aristocrat touched a finger to Jenny's lips and shook her head disapprovingly.

"Bad girl. Sexual playthings do not speak without permission. You know that."

Jenny let herself be bent over the back of an armchair and spanked by the aristocrat without resistance. Lady Sybill was much bigger than the petite Lady Isobell, but Jenny still had a couple of inches on her, and the weight. It made no difference. Domination wasn't about strength, it was mindset that counted, and the Lords and Ladies practised effortless domination. Besides, she did know better than to speak without permission in restraints, this was the woman who could turn her vibrator on and off, and being spanked had always made her horny. When her hand became sore, Lady Sybill used a slipper.

She hadn't wanted to resist, Jenny admitted to herself when the punishment was finally over, her behind throbbing, burning hot and her pussy dripping. Her yelps, and twists and squirms, meant nothing; just flesh responding, not mind. Andrew was watching spellbound she noticed, almost drooling over her bound nudity, and not even realising he'd seen her naked and bound before. Strangely it never even seemed to occur to him to grab, even though it must have been obvious to him that

Jenny was totally incapable of resisting. She has got him well trained, was Jenny's stray thought.

"You may thank me by licking my shoes clean."

Jenny dropped to her knees and hesitantly reached out a tongue, gingerly licking hand-tooled leather. Licking feet made her hot, but you never knew where shoes had been. The heady smell and the taste of leather assaulted her, and like being made to lick a dildo clean, disgust and humiliation only added to her arousal. It wouldn't be humiliation if she didn't mind. Licking with broad, deep strokes, Jenny let her nipples trail through the rough carpet.

"Stand! Cunt!"

Jenny scrambled to her feet and pushed her vibrator filled pussy into the aristocrat's waiting cupped hand.

"Rub yourself."

With a sigh of pleasure Jenny obeyed eagerly, her hands locked in the cuffs behind her clenched into tight fists. This was even more shamefully exciting than Isobell's training. At least Isobell had liked her, not just wanted her, had allowed her the pretence of consenting. And Andrew was watching!

"Kneel! Tits!"

She dropped to her knees and pushed her breasts into the waiting cupped hands to be squeezed and pulled again.

"Good puppy! Reasonably obedient. You'll have to do," she decided, idly rolling Jenny's nipples. "The reason I'm bothering with you at all is my fiancé and I want to make love. I've decided when necessary you'll be the meat in our sandwich. Second. I'm sick of you skulking off when there's work to be done. I want your ass in the lab tomorrow at nine-sharp, helping me to get home; and wear just heels and panties under your lab-coat. Understood?"

"Yes Mistress," Jenny agreed happily. She did so love subservience, when it was in the safety of her own reality.

"Good. Now you're going to suck off Andrew to calm him down a little, and then we'll both give you a nice long shafting. You will be punished if your sexual performance is not satisfactory! Andrew, don't touch her yet, just sit there. Begin!"

Jenny unbuckled his belt and pulled down his fly with her teeth, once again amazed at the hold Lady Sybill had on him.

"She's really going to do it," he said in wonder.

He just didn't understand sexual submission at all, Jenny decided, pulling apart his trousers with her mouth; only ever seeing slaves as toys to be used, never considering someone might want to be dominated. His erection made a tent of his briefs, and being careful not to nip him, it took her four bites to get a good enough grip to pull them down. Jenny, under orders, opened her mouth wide and let the hot shaft rest on her tongue. Andrew's cock twitched. He was keeping better personal hygiene since he'd started trying to get Lady Sybill into bed, Jenny thought.

"You may begin now," the aristocrat told her.

Jenny closed her lips around the shaft in her mouth, and slowly slid them down its length until he bumped against the back of her throat. Andrew made a noise halfway between a groan and a sigh. Jenny let her lips slide up and down the heavy shaft in a slow rhythm, each time docilely taking him as deep into her mouth as she could, until, following the orders of her new self-elected Mistress, she was instructed to began alternately licking and kissing his balls and shaft.

It quickly became obvious to Jenny that cock-sucking was a lot more fun if another shaft was simultaneously buried in her own sex; as she'd already learned, two, and even three, into one, went quite easily. Whereas here, on her knees and with her hands locked behind her, she was just being made to service Andrew. Pleasing him, of no more emotional importance to him than the frustratingly turned off vibrator inside her was to Jenny.

But to her surprise, as she slowly brought him to orgasm, Jenny found she was thoroughly enjoying herself, not at all reluctant. A participant, not just a mouth, delighting in the simple joy of providing another with pleasure, Andrew clearly loving every second of it. Jenny was also basking in the far from simple pleasure of having Lady Sybill's critical eyes on her subservient, humiliating obedience, knowing she was under control, and then there was anticipation! Waiting for revolting, slimy, disgusting come to splash into her mouth, and knowing she wasn't allowed to pull away.

"How is she Andrew?"

"Incredible! What a mouth! I always thought she was frigid until Lady Isobell got hold of her. But she must have swallowed gallons of spunk to get this good!"

"Sod you," Jenny whispered quietly around the cock in her mouth, sound lost in her obedient slurps.

"No, not experienced," Lady Sybill judged. "Just enthusiastic and eager to please." She patted Jenny's behind. "Which is all I require in a toy besides a decent body and a pretty face."

Once again Jenny was taken by surprise at how hot the gelatinous, salty, sour fluid that splashed into her mouth was. Following the aristocrat's orders, she didn't swallow, but sucked and licked up the last drop, and then held out her tongue pooled with come and saliva for Lady Sybill's inspection. The woman let Jenny sit a moment, the mingled mess in her mouth running down her chin, and in long slimy strands, dripping onto her bound breasts, before reaching between her thighs and turning on the vibrator. When Jenny was moaning in delight, only then was she ordered to swallow.

Once the keys had been broken out of the ice, the betrothed couple enjoyed her doggie-style, tied down over the end of her low coffee table. Lady Sybill sat in front of her, thighs spread, crotch pushed into Jenny's face, allowing Jenny to hone her oral skills. The aristocrat, heads, that left Andrew kneeling behind her, tails. Mostly he pumped into her pussy, but occasionally, again prompted by Lady Sybill, would withdraw and plunge his shaft deep into Jenny's back passage.

Jenny's thighs were tightly tied to the table legs, spread wide, the thin cord they'd used digging deep into her flesh. But the rope just as tight around her waist, holding her arms bound behind her back, was, perhaps on purpose, only loosely looped under the table itself allowing her upper body to squirm and twist. Head between Lady Sybill's thighs, her nose mashed into the woman's pubic hair, her nostrils full of the scent of her, Jenny savoured the aristocrat's taste; sweeter than Andrew's come.

Her dream-lover's thrusts; powerful, deep, hard strokes, to the hilt, made her gasp in delight, and kept pushing her face into the aristocrat's crotch. Despite involuntary bucks, twists and squirms, as both delivered occasional slaps to her backside and reached under her to squeeze and pull her breasts, twist and pinch her nipples, Jenny's lips never left the aristocrat's sex. Throughout the delicious shafting, hard meat rammed again and again into her dripping pussy, Jenny never allowed her own pleasure to distract her from serving her new Mistress. Between squeaks and moans, she flicked her tongue back and forth across the seated woman's straining clitoris, tonguing and sucking labia, and licking deep inside her.

Jenny stifled a disappointed moan as Andrew withdrew, his hands hard on her hips, and then gave full vent to the sound in a flesh-muffled wail of delight as he plunged his cock into her ass again; pain and pleasure as inextricably bound as she was between the two lovers. She was so learning to love the novelty of having her still-inexperienced sphincter stretched wide.

Lady Sybill came with a genteel sigh, her fingers twisted in Jenny's hair. Used to the much more vocal Isobell, whose sex would pulse and spasm, fingernails usually painfully deep in Jenny's breasts, Jenny wasn't even totally sure Lady Sybill had come until she pulled away. Andrew, after several more energetic thrusts, his fiancé now stroking his balls, withdrew, and deliberately splashed hot semen all across Jenny's dripping pussy. He slammed the softening shaft into her in one last brutal, squeak-forcing thrust, remaining inside her as he went limp.

"Well Slut, that was...adequate," Lady Sybill decided,

kneeling down beside Jenny and stroking semen and Jenny's own juices up between her buttocks, fingers trailing up under Jenny's bound arms to her collar and then back down her spine. "Though I will expect an improvement the next time I use you!"

"Yes Mistress," Jenny agreed subserviently.

"You were making quite a bit of noise there actually, Slut. How many times did you come?"

"Three times, Mistress," Jenny admitted in her best husky, pleading, voice.

Out of the corner of her eye she saw the aristocrat nod thoughtfully, either missing or choosing to ignore Jenny's unspoken plea to make it four.

"You can lick Andrew clean now," she decided.

"Thank you Mistress," Jenny agreed placidly.

Her fellow student pulled his now shrunken penis out of her pussy and sat on the table in front of her. Jenny took the shrivelled, soft, fluid-glistening shaft into her mouth without hesitation. Tasting herself and semen, she licked and sucked; and knowing where his cock had been, she felt only continued arousal. With growing pride as she tongued Andrew's balls, Jenny realised that this was a landmark; she had graduated, evolved. No longer just playing at SM, she was now a fully-fledged, true submissive.

Andrew and his Lady didn't bother to thank her, barely even acknowledging her, just slowly kissing over Jenny's tied down body when they decided they'd finally satisfied themselves on her flesh. Almost as an afterthought as they left, Lady Sybill remembered to tell Andrew to untie one hand so that Jenny could struggle loose, leaving her lying panting on a layer of her own sweat. She only got six hours sleep that night, having to get up early to meticulously wash, shave, shampoo, blow-dry and apply make-up.

***

The next morning Jenny reported to the lab at 8:58 exactly,

after the most humiliating and exciting journey to work of her life. As ordered she was wearing just the stiletto heels with padlocked ankle-straps and the skimpiest pair of panties she owned under her white lab-coat. Lady Constance and Charles had the morning shift.

Charles gave Jenny a stiffly polite nod. Being pleasant, but obviously he still hadn't forgiven her for stranding Sarah in the alternative England. Perhaps not yet appraised of Jenny's new place in the scheme of things, he looked at first puzzled when she didn't respond, presenting herself to Lady Constance, and then faintly intrigued. Perhaps he did know; just hadn't really believed it. Already aroused by her bus journey, sure everybody had been able to tell she was naked under the lab-coat, his eyes on her only made Jenny hotter.

Nipples already hard, heart pounding and licking nervous lips, an unmistakable stirring in her groin, Jenny presented herself for inspection.

"Well?" the aristocrat demanded, looking up from a printout.

"I was told to report for work at nine by Lady Sybill," Jenny said hesitantly.

"Mistress Sybill," the aristocrat corrected.

"Yes Mistress, sorry Mistress," Jenny agreed, the word slipping so easily off her tongue as the woman's cold eyes inspected her critically.

"And didn't Isobell tell you how a sex-slut not in use waits to be noticed?" she asked, raising one perfect eyebrow.

"Yes Mistress. Sorry Mistress!" Jenny stammered again.

Desire growing, and very conscious of Charles's avid, disbelieving, but increasingly delighted gaze on their little drama, Jenny unbuttoned her lab-coat, folded it neatly and placed it over the back of a chair. Now standing naked except for the high-cut panties and stiletto heels, she was aware of their eyes on her body long before she looked up.

As her lover had taught her, Jenny set her feet apart, legs straight, stomach in and held her head up with her hands neatly folded behind her neck, properly, looking straight ahead and

160

taking slow, deep breaths to make the rise and fall of her chest more noticeable. Her nipples were so hard they ached now, her newly enlarged breasts lust swollen, and a raging heat between her legs was begging for attention. Firmly reminding her, as if she could ever forget, how much she really did love submission.

Charles's eyes roamed over her nearly naked form in open delight, no doubt thoroughly enjoying her display of humbling obedience just as much as her body. Lady Constance, after a far more appraising glance, left Jenny to stand in place for another fifteen-twenty minutes or so, while she finished what she was working on.

Then she stood, walking slowly over to Jenny and then around her. Jenny caught her breath as fingers stroked down her spine.

Hands reached around Jenny's body, examining, then lifting and squeezing together her breasts from behind.

"Lick your nipples now. Bite them!"

Jenny obeyed, flushing with exciting shame when she caught Charles's eye, ducking her head down to trap her nipples between her own teeth, tonguing rigid flesh and biting down a moan of pleasure as her breasts were squeezed harder. Teasing her own desperately sensitive flesh with her tongue was making her incredibly horny.

She let the full globes she was squeezing and holding up to Jenny's lips fall, nipples yanked painfully from between Jenny's teeth. Stroking down her stomach., the aristocrat's hands delved inside Jenny's panties, Jenny, expecting a caress, gasping in shock and pleasure as her sex-lips were roughly seized and yanked wide apart.

"It's for stranding me I'm going to punish you," Lady Constance concluded. "And I don't expect to hear one peep of protest out of you!"

Jenny groaned as rough fingers penetrated her, stirred her and then withdrew; her juices wiped off the aristocrat's fingers on one of her thighs, and then her panties were pulled down

161

to her knees. She was obediently still as her buttocks, thighs, stomach, breasts again, hips and neck were stroked, patted, squeezed and pinched. Finally, panting with lust by the time the aristocrat had finished her inspection; Jenny was held in place with a handful of tightly gripped pubic hair, hands still behind her head.

"I'm used to using prettier, hotter, toys for sex, but I suppose you might do," Lady Constance allowed. "Charles! Find me some rope."

Jenny's fellow student was too busy watching, mesmerised, to heed the aristocrat's orders. Almost drooling as Jenny's panties were removed, and pushed into her mouth!

"Don't drop!" Lady Constance ordered. "Charles!" she snapped again.

"Huh?"

"Rope! How am I supposed to punish her properly without rope?"

Charles scurried away to obey. Jenny could taste herself; her juices soaked into the white satin, and also a sour hint of urine she hoped was just her imagination! The dreadful, revolting, humiliation as always only made her hotter.

Like any good scientist, to document the original experiments, Professor Phillips-Webber had had a railing installed overhead to mount video-cameras on out of the way. Lady Constance tossed the length of rope Charles had produced over the railing, tugged down hard to test how much weight it would hold, and nodded in satisfaction. The end of the rope went down between Jenny's legs, up between her buttocks, and was tied tightly around her waist.

Jenny was then made to lie on her back and arch her body up into a bridge on hands and knees, groaning in pleasure as the rope was pulled up harder and harder between her pussy-lips, her hips pulled higher and higher. In the awkward position, her legs and arms were soon feeling the strain, almost all her weight on the rope dragged painfully through her crotch, tender flesh crushed as she settled into position. A second rope linking wrists to ankles ensured she would remain bent over backwards and not be able to just raise herself up.

"Good! A little harder. Okay. Tie that off," the aristocrat instructed Charles.

Jenny moaned as her hips were dragged a little higher still, and then there was only exquisite, torturous, pressure. From her upside-down viewpoint she watched Lady Constance's feet moving past her face as the woman who now had total power over her walked around her again. Admiring her prize? Jenny hoped so, shivering in delight as her stomach was stroked and her pubic-hair was ruffled. Then she sighed in pleasure as the aristocrat stroked the plump lips on either side of the cruel rope that was now supporting her body.

Jenny squealed in unexpected pain!

She didn't even realise she was being lashed until the second and third strap-strokes, so overwhelming was the pain; thinking her cruel bondage had injured her in some way. Something had been pulled or torn inside her! Another stroke followed, and then another, cracking down across her taut belly and on her pussy-lips, puffed plump and defenceless on either side of the rope that dragged up her hips.

"Please stop!" she desperately cried. "Please!"

Mercifully, the strap stopped falling.

"You dropped your gag," Lady Constance said mildly, trailing the belt she was using as a lash over Jenny's breasts and face before crouching down beside her to push Jenny's panties back in her mouth. "Don't do that again, or I'll really hurt you."

"I think you are hurting her," Charles protested.

"And I think I'm probably a better judge of what she can take than you. Besides, it's not polite to interfere when someone's disciplining a slave," the Lady said matter-of-factly.

"But Jenny's not..."

A slave? His half-hearted protest tailed off.

Jenny's tormentor gave her breasts a good half-dozen hard slaps each—the enlarged mounds already feeling noticeably strange hanging upside-down because she was bent over backwards—bouncing and swinging this way and that under the blows. Sting faded into throbbing burn with each loud crack as a palm struck her defenceless flesh. Again Jenny's bondage allowed no escape; she was capable of no more than twitches, whimpers and squeaks. The aristocrat delivered one last stinging slap to each reddened globe, Jenny's flesh quivering under the blows.

"And you, Slut. Don't ever protest when I'm enjoying you," Lady Constance warned, twisting Jenny's nipples for emphasis. "Understood?"

"Yes Mistreessssss!" Jenny squeaked helplessly in a rising wail as the rigid nubs were squeezed and twisted.

Eyes tear-bright, she obediently held her mouth open so that the gag she'd dropped again could be pushed back into her mouth. The crotch-whipping went on, the lash teasingly smacking down on her inner thighs and belly, Jenny swaying on the rope pulling up her hips lost in delighted lust; and then again the belt would bite into the sex-lips that rope parted.

She squealed. The strap teased her thighs and belly again, building back arousal, making Jenny squirm on the taut rope now dripping with her juices, before biting agonisingly back into her pussy-lips again. And again! The pain was unbelievable, blood rushing to her head with her whole body swaying, pulled up, into this unnatural position, leaving her incapable of rational thought. Eventually there was only pain and pleasure, strangely intertwined.

Panting helplessly, blinded by tears and desperately wishing she'd been allowed to come, Jenny slowly realised her punishment was over. Someone was stroking her pussy-lips, hands sliding along her body to her breasts, fingers kneading and pulling. She realised it was Charles's feet she was seeing upside-down.

"Are you alright?" he asked softly.

Jenny moaned.

***

"That was really amazing," he said enthusiastically. "I wouldn't have believed you could take it."

Her breasts were pulled up by the nipples, stretched into cones.

"Gosh, they're much bigger now aren't they?" he said happily. "So red; and you've got stripes all over your cunt!"

Her legs and arms trembling quite badly now, Jenny bit down harder on her panty-gag as her throbbing breasts were bounced together as her squeezed nipples were swung. Charles slid a hand up her body, fingers stroking her whip-tender pussy-lips on either side of the rope now almost totally supporting her weight.

"She said I could.... have you," he concluded, eagerly but almost apologetically.

Her fellow student's trousers and underpants fell down around his ankles in front of Jenny's face, her breasts squeezed together around a shaft that felt hot even on her slapped flesh. His cock?

Charles quickly settled into a rhythm, thrusting between the slap-reddened mounds he'd squeezed tightly together around his penis. He came quite quickly, hot semen splashing up her stomach and coating Jenny's breasts as he thrust a last few times, her flesh sliding easily together and against him now.

Jenny was still in her bent over backwards position, hips dragged up to the railing by her crotch-rope, and still hadn't been allowed to come, when Charles and Lady Constance opened the Gate on the next alternative world. Jenny couldn't see her from her bondage-position, but the next visitor through the Gate sounded quite shocked at what was on display in Professor Phillips-Webber's lab.

***

Jenny slipped into the role of laboratory sex-slave with ease and pleasure. It was just the sort of relationship she wanted, none of the guilt, unease, and later, fear, she'd had to push to

165

the back of her mind in the Slaveworld. Just total, wonderful, joyful, sexual submission!

Her lab-coat was taken off her within 5 minutes of walking through the door the next day, after which she worked, was admired and handled, performed service; maid, secretary, waitress and sex-toy, wearing only the stiletto heels and panties around four fully dressed colleagues. In the days that followed she learned to hang up her coat and present herself for inspection in just panties and heels to whichever Lady was on duty, the aristocrats splitting shifts to try and check more Gates.

She was made to wear a hobble, her hands usually handcuffed in front of her so that she could use her computer keyboard, but always behind her for sex, and from somewhere Lady Constance produced a broad double-padlocked collar. The high leather band, worn almost permanently, chafed under her chin to start with, until she learnt to hold her head up high and still; and it was a source of open irritation to both Ladies that jaw-ache prevented them keeping her in a ball-gag permanently.

"Girls are physically much better trained where I come from," Lady Constance said irritably, before the next of many punishment whippings.

Jenny became quite proud of her ability to hold position, legs straight and slightly spread, back dipped the better to present her hindquarters, bent over the back of a chair when being whipped. She performed oral sex for the two men on demand, Andrew and Charles apparently readily accepting the limitation on further sex, Jenny quickly and firmly established as the Ladies' plaything. She was a toy they were allowed to play with for the moment, but the use of which might be withdrawn, if they didn't behave themselves.

She was quickly tit-trained to serve men, by Lady Constance, just a variation on Lady Isobell's first lesson. Slide her lips up and down the cock; get it as deep into her mouth as she could, in time with her breasts being squeezed. Twisted nipples meant lick and nibble the shaft, squeezed nipples, kiss and lick his balls. And always swallow unless told otherwise. It was easy.

The two aristocrats occasionally shared her for sex, and more rarely she was the meat in a slave-sandwich between Andrew and Lady Sybill, but mostly she was enjoyed one on one by the two women. Lady Sybill liked elaborate bondage and humiliation, Lady Constance the more sadistic of the two, happy with just a simple piece of rope if it meant Jenny couldn't escape her whip or dildo.

She used and thought to herself the aristocrats' Slaveworld phrases, 'being enjoyed' and 'being used for sex' with delight not shame. Stupid not to be realistic. Certainly they weren't lovers, neither women even offering the pretence that Jenny was of any importance to them except sexually. It wasn't making love, it wasn't even animal-sex, passion without love, she was simply being used and enjoyed by the pair when, where and how they wished. And she loved it.

***

Also a source of smug satisfaction was that neither Andrew or Charles had recognised her as one of the slaves they'd sampled in the alternative dimension, even when she'd been fitted with a hood by one of her two Mistresses for whatever reason. Were larger breasts and a fake brand no longer on her belly all it took? Had they used so many girls they could no longer tell them apart? Or, delicious thought, they just couldn't imagine prim, proper Jenny putting herself in that position in the first place, despite her current display? Whatever, Jenny remembered her one four-in-a-bed experience with glowing pleasure, the more it receded, and hoped the Ladies would one day share her with one of her fellow students, but unfortunately it hadn't looked like happening yet.

It was clear that Andrew, focused on his aristocratic bride-to-be and the luxurious, rich and powerful, slave-owning lifestyle he thought he deserved, no longer saw Jenny as he had. She was closer to being one of the ubiquitous slaves in what he called Tit-world, than a fellow student and friend. A sex-object! Charles on the other hand, not so jaded, still considered her enough of an individual to feel guilty about cheating on Sarah when she knelt at his feet, cock in mouth. He'd threatened, more than once now as Jenny swallowed his semen, that when they got the Gate back if Jenny even breathed a word to Sarah, he would personally drag her into the Slaveworld, see her branded, and give her to his love as a birthday present to abuse for the rest of her life.

Days drifted into a week and then two in contented servitude. Jenny was sitting at her keyboard, as usual almost naked and in restraints, when the idea came to her. Her wrists were cuffed together in front of her, her ankles chained to her stool, the tube of an inflatable butt-plug, currently deflated, that Lady Sybill had forgotten or couldn't be bothered to remove, trailing from her anus like an obscene tail; when the light dawned. Out of the blue! Up until then she'd been more focused on trying not to drool on her computer's keyboard, the usual result of the ball-gag buckled into her mouth, and trying to see past twin bundles of clothespins biting into her nipples, areola and the soft surrounding flesh.

The nipple-torture was Lady Constance's punishment for pulling away from a pussy-whipping, not an unusual occurrence; yesterday she'd been breast-whipped for having the wrong colour eyes. The important thing was not to let ongoing punishments distract her from working, or the sadistic aristocrat got really inventive. The tips of her firm, full breasts were throbbing, pulsating, pain, but arousal and pain, as always, had become strangely entangled, and fingers poised and staring blankly at the screen, at least looking busy, she'd idly compared sensations.

She liked having her now-large breasts clamped, the wooden jaws bit so deeply into soft flesh that it looked far more painful than it was, and so she pleased her Mistresses with her obedient endurance. She didn't like having her sex-lips clamped too much, especially where weights were involved, but clothespins on her nipples were heavenly. A clothespin on the clitoris could be nice, but unlike nipples, only during sex.

And that was it, she realised. Different results from the same instruments. She'd always liked puzzles and problems, for a moment even her bonds and nipple-punishment forgotten. Yes, that worked!

Lady Sybill, no doubt attracted by the sudden urgent clicking of her computer's keys, came up behind her, cupping and rhythmically kneading her breasts. Jenny, used to being handled, moaned her approval behind her ball-gag.

"Oh that is clever. Good slut!"

The clothespins decorating the tips of Jenny's breasts rattled together as the aristocrat playfully hefted her breasts, bouncing the full globes in her palms and against each other.

"Has she got something?" Lady Constance asked, now looking over Jenny's other shoulder. "Oh! That might work. I told you a little pain wouldn't inhibit her intelligence, just rational thought."

She didn't even seem to be aware of her hand resting on Jenny's naked thigh, though Jenny was. It was the same hand that had fisted her the night before last! Lady Constance stroked idly between her legs, lightly probing between Jenny's sex-lips, and then stroking her wetness into her pubic hair.

"If this works we'll have to get her a gold collar and hang the biggest diamonds we can find from her nipples," Lady Constance joked, fingers roughly penetrating Jenny's pussy.

Even as she sighed in pleasure, Jenny suddenly realised, she wasn't joking at all. Terror killed her lust stone-dead, one second basking in the attention of her Mistresses and enjoying their touch, the next just a frightened victim of sexual abuse; and suddenly her bonds and tortured breasts weren't fun, and never had been.

Realising what she'd done, chasing scientific discovery without thought, caution lulled by sexual arousal, Jenny tried to crash her computer, but almost gently they pulled her stool out of reach. Her handcuffs were unlocked, and then refastened behind her back. The two jubilant aristocrats touched palms victoriously over her head once they'd secured her, grabbed a breast each and then each sucked a deep purple love-bite into Jenny's flesh, concluding with a victory slap, Jenny, an experienced enough sex-slave by now, to know a hand-print had been left on each buttock.

"Yes!" they cried together.

Jenny felt a pit opening up under her, tears welling in her eyes. Stupid!

Like all good ideas, it was basically simple. Contacting and opening each possible Gate in the hope of hitting the right one, was as she'd already realised, impractical. It would take a thousand lifetimes. But, if each Gate was just slightly and subtly different, different equipment used, the way it was set up, and the power, volts and amps used, different again, then you had a fingerprint. A way to look for just the Gate you wanted, she'd realised.

You didn't have to open each possibility in turn; just let the nexus skim across all the countless possibilities, seeking a lock. Knowing the pattern you were looking for, the two Gates would find each other, like magnets in a huge box full of shaken plastic look-alikes. The four worked through the night.

Two black uniformed soldiers stepped through the newly formed Gate, and instantly shot a very surprised Andrew followed by an equally surprised Charles. Another pair carrying tranquilliser dart rifles stepped through behind them. Jenny recognised the Royal Security Police uniforms. Academic Franklin followed, then a Lord she didn't recognise, and then a very familiar aristocrat indeed. Two more soldiers came through behind Lady Isobell.

Under Lady Sybill's and Lady Constance's direction, the soldiers tossed all computer disks, printed records and the technological gadgets and books professor Phillips-Webber's students had gathered, through the Gate. While the lab was being trashed, Lady Isobell wandered over to Jenny's bound nudity, walked slowly around her, and then stroked her spine from behind.

"Silly bitch. I told you to run. Guess you didn't want to be free." Jenny pleaded behind her gag, a stinging slap to the backside silencing her. "Tits came up nice though."

Jenny groaned in mingled pain and growing lust, as her breasts were brutally mauled.

"And did I say close the Gate? You wouldn't believe how much grief I got over that. I hope your owner's willing to lend you to me, because you really deserve punishing for that." She let her fingers trail down Jenny's stomach, pulling sex-lips wide apart. "In fact, on the subject of borrowing you, do you remember I once said you had the makings of a half decent pony-girl? I think I might enjoy training and driving you. Do you think you'll like prancing in dildo and bit? Lots of whip?"

Jenny nodded obediently. The soldiers left behind several drums of oil, a spreading puddle across the floor and three firebombs, bundling Jenny through the Gate stool and all. She watched the Gate in Franklin's lab wink out of existence, as professor Phillips-Webber's was destroyed by fire, and knew there would be no going back.

NINE
OWNED

JENNY WAS GIVEN A SEDATIVE by the estate vet, a needle plunged into her thigh, and immediately packed off to the clinic in a travel cage. She lay on her side in a dreamy haze, letting her eyes roam over the other bound, naked property in the maglev's baggage car. They were being posted not just to the clinic, but around the country; mail-order and shopping-channel purchased slaves as well as those whose owners didn't want the inconvenience of holding a lead during a journey.

Charles and Andrew, fear and anger perhaps allowing them to more effectively fight sedatives, and they had been shot quite a while ago now, were especially vocal in their claims that a mistake had been made. Finally the supervising soldier, trying to read his pony-slave racing form, got tired and gagged them, brutally squeezing testicles as a punishment.

Her time in the clinic was mostly a drugged haze, but occasional moments of lucidity stood out. She remembered hanging suspended from her wrists in a tank of liquid, one of a row, alongside other girls, and one incident, a lab-technician giving her a furtive grope as she swung past upside-down for another stretching session, stood out clearly. Dreams, fantasies and nightmares merged, so she really couldn't be sure if a uniformed soldier actually had had sex with her as she lay semi-conscious, strapped to the cold, bare metal of a wheeled trolley between treatments.

Consciousness returned slowly, fuzzy, but for the first time in she didn't know how long, Jenny could think. She tried to shake her head to clear the cobwebs, but just tugged on her hair. Puzzled, she tried again, remembering.

Oh! The bondage was actually quite familiar. Lady Isobell had been quite keen on hog-ties. She ached, every single muscle, but strangely there was no strain, even though a ball-gag stretched her mouth wide and her wrists were not just tied to her ankles, but strapped to them, ankles also strapped together, body arched.

It was the ache of a long and strenuous workout, nothing to do with her restraints. 'What do you know? It works' she thought to herself. She didn't doubt she'd now be able to touch her elbows together behind her back, do splits, wear the ball-gag almost permanently and touch her toes with straight legs even in 5" heels. The Lords and Ladies liked their playthings supple.

Her hair was somehow also tied to her strapped together ankles and wrists, forcing her head up high and arching her back up even more, and a strap tight around her waist glued her tummy to the bare metal surface of the wheeled trolley she lay on. Jenny lay on the trolley for several hours, staring at a bare room in perfect comfort, but increasing boredom. She flinched once when an unseen hand lightly stroked her vulnerable pussy, but eventually dozed off. When she woke, the only thing that had changed was that another naked girl, strapped to a trolley as she was, had been left in the room with her, and her head was clearer.

The hog-tied blonde, broad strap digging deep into her waist had big baby-blue eyes, a ball-gag as large as Jenny's filling her mouth and over-large breasts. She'd thought the redhead she'd enjoyed had been impressive, but if anything this slave's bust was fractionally larger. Even with her spine arched back hard enough to break an unmodified girl's back, the heavy melons lay on the table, partly flattened under their own weight. The creamy mounds quivered slightly when she tossed her head against the rope woven into her hair, trying to see something behind Jenny, fat pink nipples adorned with shiny rings too large and heavy to be just decorative.

In sudden terror Jenny looked away, unwilling to meet the blonde's eyes, grateful when a lab-technician came to wheel her trolley down a corridor. Her body heat had long ago warmed the trolley's metal surface to body temperature so couldn't feel how much skin touched the surface or where, but with a sudden sick foreboding, she thought she felt heavy flesh wobble as the trolley rattled over tiles. They couldn't have! There was no reason to! Her breasts had already been enlarged!

In a comfortable suite Academic Franklin, professor Phillips-Webber and Lady Isobell sipped drinks, waited on by a body-harnessed slave-boy, his cock straining to escape an open-ring chastity device. A doctor stood respectfully to one side of the seated aristocrats, pad poised.

"Thank you, Saul. My Lady, your property, modified as per your instructions," the kindly looking vet said. "And the rejuvenation facility reports she responded exceptionally well to treatment. I've enclosed their report with her medical file. You may get quite a few more years out of her than the norm."

Jenny, parked in the middle of the room side-on for their inspection, couldn't see which woman he was talking to. Who did she belong to? She desperately needed to know! Lady Isobell clearly hadn't expected to be owning her in the lab, but perhaps she'd found a way? God, she hoped so. Surely kindly professor PW hadn't gone native to that extent, but if Jenny was legally her property, in practice that had to mean she was Lord Franklin's! Jenny realised she was sobbing quietly in terror, and her breasts were definitely quivering as her silent cries wracked her body.

"Excellent work as always. Have it delivered to my estate after the usual recovery period," Franklin ordered. He turned to Jenny's former tutor. "And now my dear, we still have to pick out wedding rings."

The two stood over her a moment, kissing, and then left, Lady Isobell lingering a moment, running an appreciative hand over Jenny's now silky smooth buttocks. And then, as she'd known she would, the aristocrat slid her hands under Jenny's breasts and hefted, weighing the flesh she held. Jenny's breasts were squeezed, fingers sinking deep, then hooked through her nipple-rings, both globes were lifted off the table and idly bounced together.

"Please, please, don't make then bigger," she tried to beg

around the gag, enunciating as slowly and as clearly as she could with a large ball strapped into her mouth.

But sobbing without restraint now, she already knew it was far, far too late for her pleas, and she'd been given a second dose. Probably a show-pony's dose. The nipple-rings were new, but she knew what it felt like to have her breasts lifted with clamped nipples, and there was much, much more weight hanging from the ring-set nubs. She could feel her flesh spilling out of the aristocrat's cool hands, acres of flesh seeming to touch when they were squeezed together, and the humiliating thump, a definite quiver, when her breasts were dropped back onto the trolley could mean nothing else.

"Lovely. These are going to be great fun to play with," the almost flat-chested aristocrat decided.

Jenny's slave-breasts, lubricated by her tears, slid and slipped easily against each other as they were handled.

***

Jenny woke with her usual gasp of pain in the now familiar environs of the Franklin estate's cellblock, a double jolt of agony delivered to her humiliating, huge slave-breasts. Her alarm clock was electrodes clipped to her nipple-rings; all slaves woke to face the trials of another day with a jolt of electricity to some body piercing or other. Her waking mind recalled the whimpers and yelps of other sexual toys shocked into alertness.

She didn't bother to raise her head, knowing what she would see through the bars of the cells beyond hers. Naked girls, sleeping hog-tied and ball-gagged, lying with breasts flattened under them, red wires trailing away from various rings set through their flesh; like the pair that trailed away from her own adorned nipples. Some slaves, being stretched to make them more convenient to bugger would have slept in butt-plugs, but otherwise the picture was the same in each cage-like cell.

Now in her sixth day on the Franklin estate, Jenny still didn't know if she could touch her toes in heels or do a full split, but she slept hog-tied without discomfort, and her ball-gag had only been removed for food, semen, having her teeth brushed and exercise since she arrived. She wouldn't have believed it was possible to drool so much. Nobody told slaves anything, it had taken her three days to discover her tattooed brand was on the underside of her left breast rather than on the back of her neck as she'd hoped, but she'd overheard a corporal explaining to a new recruit why slave-girls slept hog-tied. A hog-tied girl could only sleep face-down, and so was in no danger of choking, it being family policy on the Franklin estate that all slaves wear ball-gags whenever possible.

Jenny had arrived back on the estate in a state of almost total panic, raging sexual desire, and a sneaking curiosity as to who was actually her legal owner. Now, though still horny, she just felt humiliated. Her owner, whoever they were, was free to do absolutely anything they liked with her, put her to any sexual use no matter how degrading, and she'd been ignored! Or forgotten. A toy not even interesting enough to take out of its box.

Metal crashed, soldiers appeared and opened cell-doors, girls were unstrapped and their electrodes removed, allowed to use their cell toilets in full view of their fellows and the uniformed men. Girls on order, wanted for use by a particular aristocrat, were taken to the shower-block first. On past form, terrified of being chosen but chafing at the indignity of being left out, Jenny expected to be taken to the gym first and then cleaned up, not one of the chosen playthings. She flushed the toilet and then stood and reached up on her toes to the pair of cuffs hanging from the ceiling, snapping the metal bands locked around her wrists. Naked, a large orange ball buckled into her mouth, and now almost hanging from her wrists, forced to stand on her toes, she looked up with fear and longing when the duty sergeant paused outside her cell, clip-board in the crook of his arm.

"214," he said, the blonde in the cell opposite, "Carriage-pony. Standard tack, shock-dildo and full-sized butt-plug. To be paired with 454, on the number 7 carriage, main entrance, at 10:15"

His eyes lingered on Jenny's displayed nudity a moment, and then he moved on. She slumped in relief and disappointment. Another ordinary day. They usually took her to the gym first and then the shower-block, to prevent having to groom her twice after Jenny had been worked to sweat-lathered exhaustion, strapped and chained to various torturous exercise machines. The PT instructor had decided her thighs and buttocks needed to be firmer and wanted to flatten out her tummy a little. An anal shock-dildo was making Jenny a very willing student.

She'd made another discovery in the gym. Once when waiting to be put on an exercise machine, just for a moment she'd been stood alongside another naked girl with a bridle like hers holding a bit between her teeth. It was the redhead she'd so enjoyed shafting across Lady Isobell's desk, though fortunately the freckled slave didn't seem to recognise her. Finally Jenny had a frame of reference for what they'd done to her. Jenny was now taller, her waist about the same, breasts definitely slightly bigger, so she knew the clinic must have lengthened her legs by at least an inch, maybe an inch and a half. So in the 4" heels they habitually made her wear, she must now be topping well over six foot! No wonder that sergeant had said she'd make an impressive carriage-pony, but one that would be hard to find a match for.

She looked up in surprise when another sergeant followed by an enlisted man squeezed into her cell. Oh, contraband search, she realised. She'd seen two searches so far, a regular feature of cellblock life, slaves' cells and body cavities searched at random. A comb, a sweet or a note from another slave, and it would be Jenny sobbing over the Tannoy from one of the punishment rooms. Slaves were permitted absolutely no possessions. They were possessions!

Two more men made a leisurely inspection of her naked

body, the sergeant's eyes lighting on the rise and fall of her heavy slave-breasts. He was a heavyset, hairy, ugly man with heavy jowls who never seemed to shave properly, his belly resting on his belt, the buttons above straining. Jenny could almost feel the trails of slime she imagined his eyes left on her flesh, knowing from past encounters his palms were sweaty. She moaned in lust, nipples rising, her desire making her bite down hard on the ball strapped into her mouth when the gorilla-like sergeant squeezed her breasts.

Her arousal was almost instant, total and completely involuntary, the result of the aphrodisiacs they'd implanted in her body slowly dissolving into her bloodstream. Jenny, feeling like a bitch on heat, was sure she'd been given a double dose by mistake. Surely it wasn't possible for slaves to endure being this hot, wet and desperately frustrated for year after year, never mind the couple of days she'd suffered, without going totally insane.

She had a dreadful suspicion it was possible though, because although she felt like screaming, kicking and tearing the walls down, what she'd actually been doing was meekly submitting to every indignity in the desperate hope someone would make her, allow her, to come. Just like all the docile, placid, obedient slaves she'd admired as a free woman. She sighed in delight, hips twitching and swaying, when the Neanderthal with stripes on his uniform searched her, blunt fingers roughly probing deep inside first her pussy and then her ass.

"Can you believe I actually had to give some mouthy serf the back of my hand in the tavern last night," the sergeant asked, his subordinate left to search the cell while he groped Jenny. "Drunk, but that's no excuse, actually said to my face that what we did to his little girl was cruel."

"Yeah?" the enlisted man said without much interest, but knowing better than to ignore a superior.

"I mean look at this slut." Jenny wailed in ecstasy as her clitoris was squeezed. "She loves it. Is that cruel? My wife would spit in your eye, but this top-heavy fucking-machine?"

178

He lifted Jenny's breasts by her nipple-rings, "She just lives to have her tits squeezed, her ass spanked and her cunt filled. I ask you, is this cruel?"'

Panting gently as her breasts were handled, Jenny briefly wondered how the redoubtable Mrs Gorilla would manage this feat with a ball-gag buckled into her mouth, before having her ringed nipples rubbed together caused her to lose track of her thoughts. When she recovered herself, so very near to an orgasm, but not quite there, the search was over and she was alone. The really grotesque bit was not how horny having her boobs groped made her, but that while every man in the cellblock had had a feel, she had yet to touch the large globes herself. If you didn't count being made to tongue her own nipples and lick semen off the heavy mounds.

Finally, about mid-day—some slaves being fed—she found herself hanging face-down from four chains, broad, soft plastic cuffs around wrists and ankles, in the shower-block. No gym? She hung about chest height to the three men tending her.

Considering how much time they spent in gags, and how little contact except physical the guards allowed, Jenny had been surprised at the extent of the slave grapevine; a snatched word here, a whisper there, and at every opportunity experienced slaves had gone out of their way to comfort, reassure and just explain what was going on, to the new pillow-slave.

Too big to be a show-pony, breasts too large to be any other sort of pony-girl but a carriage-pony; and they were all matched pairs and blonde, on the Franklin estate, her fellow toys had convinced themselves that Jenny would be a purely sexual toy. Perhaps they were right. It would at least be nice to know. Most of her fellow toys also enjoyed the shower-room, she'd learnt.

Jenny was starting to agree. The guy with the toothbrush tended to be a little rough, taking literally orders to brush gums as well as teeth, and you had to keep your eyes closed being shampooed as they made no special effort to keep the stuff out of your eyes. But the enema was relaxing, the soap-on-a-rope dildo for internal cleanliness delicious fun, and three pairs of hands simultaneously kneading soap into every crevice of her suspended body, just heavenly. If only they didn't hose you down with cold water afterwards, the process could have sold as a health treatment to rich old ladies back home.

Jenny, hair blow-dried and brushed into a wave by a surprisingly gentle soldier who rubbed his crotch against her breasts as he worked, Jenny on her knees, wrists locked behind her, joined a half-dozen other slave-girls and two slave-boys for lunch. Like her, they all had their hands handcuffed behind their backs. Their heads were in a single trough that ran the length of the room, all were gobbling down a salty white gruel with the consistency of babyfood, but no doubt very nourishing. The whispered topic of conversation, around slurps and slimy mouthfuls, was the Master's upcoming wedding.

Four blonde pony-girls had been selected to pull the bride's carriage, sent off in chains to the clinic's cosmetic surgeon to have faces and bodies matched. The only genuine team of quadruplets in the country was owned by Her Majesty the Queen, and was not for sale or hire. Pony-boys for the Master's carriage had still to be selected, and possibly were going to be hired in, she learned. And it was rumoured, but not confirmed, bride and groom were going to have their wedding-rings set through the nipples of the Master's favourite plaything, Pretty, at the ceremony; to symbolise his desire to share not just his life, but everything he owned, with the new Mistress of the house.

On the girl's side of the trough, at intervals, poles ran up from the floor, bending towards the trough and dildo-tipped. Jenny positioned herself on her knees in front of one, spread her thighs, and slowly edged back until the tip of the shaft rested against her pussy.

"Permission to be shafted, Sir?" Jenny called out.

"Carry on," a bored corporal with his nose in the racing form agreed.

With a groan of delight, Jenny leant back and let the dildo slide into her. The pole was another mechanical pump. Each time she thrust back onto the shaft filling her pussy, a tap pumped food into the trough in front of her. Jenny leaned forward, balance precarious with her hands locked behind her, but gripping the dildo as tightly as she could with internal muscles she'd never suspected she had, and slurped and licked at the sticky, gelatinous gruel, occasionally thrusting back on the dildo to get more. She supposed the little crunchy bits were vitamin and mineral tablets.

Jenny thrust back again, and again, moaning in pleasure.

"Careful!"

A whispered warning from the heavy-breasted show-pony with the tiny waist and whip-marked buttocks beside her. You had to be careful not to get carried away. Every last slimy drop a slave pumped into the trough with her dildo had to be licked up, or severe punishment would follow. Hunger strikes were never likely to be a problem. Slave-girls kept on heat by their implanted aphrodisiacs would often slurp and slobber in the trough until their stomachs bulged, if they didn't keep a tight grip on themselves. The unappetising stuff may have given energy, but it certainly wasn't fattening.

Jenny threaded her nipple-rings through two waiting hooks, and pulled back, raising her head to the water-tap. When her breasts were pulled into cones, nipples painfully stretched, cool clear water splashed into her mouth. Naked, on her knees with her hands cuffed behind her, impaled on a fat dildo, eating a thick white slime, that no doubt deliberately tasted like and resembled semen, and now forced to torture her own nipples, Jenny who had once dreamed of winning a Nobel prize, wanted nothing more than to be brutally ravished.

She settled for another slow, deep thrust back on her dildo, and yanked back on her nipples for another drink. That was another world. And she would do well to remember she wasn't now owned, by whoever it was, for her mind. Just her body.

The slave-boys didn't have as much fun being fed as the

girls, for them getting enough to eat was more of an ordeal. They had to thread their cocks through upright rings set into the floor, and lift, to turn their taps on. Slightly hard wouldn't do it; an erection had to be rock-solid to pull up hard enough and not slip out of the ring. And of course an erection on demand was an integral part of being a slave-boy, so it couldn't be called cruel, any slave-boy starting to look a bit gaunt was clearly in need of further training.

A perfectly judged system that balanced humiliation against sex, encouraged sexual subservience, and kept the slave-girls sleek and the slave-boys lean, Jenny had realised. She felt the duty soldier's eyes on her, racing form put aside, as she licked the trough clean of white salty, gloop.

"You! Tits. Heel!"

With resignation and a shameful spark of eagerness, Jenny obeyed, already used to her new nickname, which thankfully she shared with several other girls, or she might have died of embarrassment. She'd also learnt to respond to "Boobs, Jugs" and "You, the top-heavy one."

Jenny placidly crawled to his feet, ashamed and aroused by her own docile acceptance. The corporal unbuttoned his fly, and squeezed her breasts together around his cock, the heavy, creamy mounds completely enveloping his not insubstantial shaft. His flesh against hers was hot and hard. The unknown man thrust away happily between her boobs, Jenny enjoying having them squeezed but knowing she wasn't going to come, thinking longingly of the trough-pump dildo now glistening with her juices. It was Pretty's job to lick them clean first whenever she was fed.

He was the eighth man she'd been tit-fucked by in her short stay, by some of them two or three times, and all six sergeants hand come in her mouth at least once, the eligible soldiers all eager to exercise their right to sample the new spectacularly top-heavy plaything, in case she was unexpectedly sold. In her own world she'd quietly disapproved of the glass ceiling, pay and opportunity inequalities, and the boy's-club mentality of so many firms, but all that paled into insignificance against a corporal's right—down in black and white in his pay and conditions—to use her breasts for sex, a sergeant's right to come in her mouth, and any uniformed man's perk, the legal right to handle her as he wished.

She felt heat, and then moisture, the shaft between her breasts suddenly sliding easily, lubricated, in the channel the soldier had squeezed her flesh into. Finished, his softening member still hanging out for all the world to see; knowing he was doing nothing wrong, he held up Jenny's heavy breasts so that she could lick off his come. The corporal watched with pleasure as Jenny's tongue left broad trails over the come-spattered mounds he held up for her. It wasn't that she didn't like licking her own breasts; she just wished it wasn't so easy to lick so much of them. Wished there wasn't so much of them, period.

Her only consolation was that there were a couple of girls if not bigger, then at least as big. Certainly the three dairy slaves when they were due a milking, and their udders when painfully swollen, were bigger.

***

Later that afternoon Jenny was taken to the Master-at-Arm's office, initially she thought so that he too could exercise his right to have sex with her, which would explain the break in her normal routine. A row of five tall cages lined one wall, each just large enough for a slave to stand upright in, a naked slave-boy in one. Jenny, knowing what was expected of her now, stepped into the indicated cage and obediently reached up and snapped the pair of ceiling cuffs closed around her wrists, securing herself in place with arms above her. Like the ones in her cell, they locked like handcuffs, but snapped open when a soldier chose to press the lock-release button beside the cage's keyhole. She was wearing nothing but the regulation ball-gag and 4" heels.

After slowly, and with evident pleasure, working his fingers into her sex and planting a light kiss on each breast, the uniformed man who'd delivered her shut and locked the cage door, then pushing, pulling and squeezing her breasts between the bars, he padlocked her nipple rings together. The heavy mounds bulged between the steel bars, obviously an attractive effect, because her keeper was inspired to give them a second round of kisses. Jenny's nipples sat up and begged, and she herself would have if that was what it took to be allowed to come. She had to settle for a plaintive, pleading moan.

The soldier sauntered out without a backward glance, Jenny left frustratingly alone. She turned her head to look at the other sex-toy awaiting the Master-at-Arm's pleasure, like her, his arms pulled above his head, mouth filled with a large orange ball, tightly buckled into place. After a quick guilty look to the door, he leaned up against the bars, his erection poking through into Jenny's cage. She knew the pleading look in his eyes was a mirror for the one she'd just given the guard.

She tried to look directly ahead—there was no room to pull away in the narrow cage—but it was hard to ignore a rigid penis poking you in the hip. Relenting, she met his eyes again, he whined, and she shivered her eyelids in acquiescence. Knowing she wouldn't be able to squeeze her breasts between the bars again without hands, she didn't dare face him, but could twist around enough to push her backside up against the bars. The hot shaft pushed up between her buttocks, probing vainly at her anus, but without hands, lubrication, and in an awkward position, it wasn't possible. He soon settled for just pushing his cock up between her cheeks, and very quickly, heat splashed up Jenny's back.

He must really have been desperate, she thought, surprised at how far his come had jetted up her spine. As she stood, gently panting, her own lusts unsatisfied, she finally thought to wonder how she was going to hide the semen on her body. Oh God, this was going to get her punished! The naked, ball-gagged slave-boy's come dribbled slowly back down between her buttocks.

The Master-at-Arms with a recruit-soldier assistant eventually appeared and took her from the cage. She held herself still for inspection, trembling slightly, while another unknown man who had the legal right to rape her, slowly looked her over. He took the dried come on her tush quite calmly, though Jenny quaked inside when she learnt the slave-boy she'd helped to come was the soldier's special pet, a perk for the senior NCO, and he'd been deliberately keeping him from coming as part of a training regime. He lifted a breast by its nipple-ring, his belt computer beeping as it scanned Jenny's bar-code, and started to dictate.

"Unauthorised sex. This slave to be kept in blindfold-hood and earplugs when in the cellblock for the next month. Sixty minutes in the broadcast-punishment-room," he looked at the readout, "but as it's a first offence, reduced to fifty minutes. Punishment authorised by RSM Collins. End."

She'd been warned, by both her uniformed keepers and her fellow toys. She'd heard the live broadcasts of slaves in the punishment rooms. But what she hadn't fully realised was how very deliciously easy it was to earn a punishment when lust overwhelmed thought.

"Now this is a nice slave," he said to his... son, Jenny realised. She could see the resemblance. "What do you think she'd fetch at auction?"

Jenny stood naked in the room's centre, head up, arms folded neatly behind her back and ankles together, her ball-gag making her drool helplessly.

"Two thousand crowns?" the boy hazarded, his face serious, not looking with lust or even attraction, certainly not seeing beauty, just judging her worth on the block.

"Closer to three thousand, I'd say," his father corrected. His hand under her chin turned Jenny's head this way and that. "Pretty face, and nice heavy tits." He lifted one and bounced it in his palm. "Plump haunches with a trim waist," he stroked Jenny's flank and then squeezed a buttock. "You can see she'll take the whip well; and those legs go on forever.

185

But none of that makes her unique does it?"

"No Sir."

The Master-at-Arms nodded approvingly to his son. "It's in the eyes. This one was born to be owned. And see how proudly she holds herself for inspection? My next month's pay against yours says she'll soon be a tagged pet, not just a pillow-slave any guest or family member can use. Bet?"

"I trust your judgement," the recruit soldier said.

Jenny was prepared by the boy under his father's direction. Her ball-gag was left in place, she was fitted with a broad leather collar and her wrists and elbows were cuffed behind her, elbows touching. A waspie corset was laced tightly around her waist with a flap padlocked down over the laces. Jenny took an experimental deep breath. A bit breathless, but not really crushing. The cosmetic surgeon at the clinic had trimmed her waist down to about twenty one, maybe twenty two inches, she guessed, so being squeezed down to the standard slave-size, an owner-pleasing 18", was just a pleasant constriction.

She'd seen enough slaves in corsets and broad girths, and once herself in a mirror, to know what she looked like, though Lady Isobell had only been able to get her waist down to 20 inches then. She knew a corset made the flare of the hips much more dramatic, buttocks appeared plump and especially spankable, and by contrast her slave-breasts would appear even bigger. The suspenders hanging from the corset and the sheer stockings the Master-at-Arm's son rolled up her legs, were a bit of a puzzle though.

Lady Isobell had briefly experimented with lingerie, but delicate, coloured, satins, silks, velvets and lace didn't really figure in the Lords' and Ladies' desires. In history serfs had just tied rags around their bodies for underwear, in more prosperous times plain cotton briefs were available, but only aristocrats themselves had ever worn attractive garments made of expensive materials. Naturally the majority didn't find dressing up their toys in their own clothing particularly stimulating, preferring leather, latex, rope and polished steel.

186

Finally she was made to step into 5" stiletto heeled pumps and was fitted with a too-short hobble, shiny steel bands locked around her stockinged ankles. Her heart pounded faster. The cute little show-ponies pranced in 3" heels, 4" heels were for everyday wear, but only special orders were perched uncomfortably on their toes. She was finally about to meet her owner! Her hair was brushed again until it shone, dried semen brushed off her back and bottom, the Master-at-Arms humiliatingly trimmed tidy the small vertical tuft of pubic hair she was still allowed, and a lead was clipped to her collar.

The heels were higher and the hobble-chain shorter than she was used to, but she'd already spent several hours walking in standard heels and hobble on treadmills with her elbows strapped together behind her, being trained to put a fuck-me sway in her stride, and that all important tit-jiggle bounce in her step, so she managed easily enough. She was led up and down the corridor past the Master-at-Arms twice before he nodded in satisfaction and the young recruit soldier led her into a service elevator.

In the small confines of the lift the boy let his mask of cool detachment slip, lust raising an eager head. Timidly at first, and them bolder when Jenny just stood placidly in place in her bonds, his hands explored her body. She carefully didn't notice his erection, just staring placidly ahead while she was groped. What was it Isobell had said? "She just loved big, dumb animals."

"Huh. You don't look that special to me," he lied.

Offended, Jenny just managed to hold back from moaning in pleasure when he squeezed her breasts, the boy probably thinking he was hurting her. A gentle chime, the doors opened, and he was all business again. It had never occurred to her before, but of course hobbled toys needed an elevator.

Being led down familiar deep-carpeted, statue and picture lined corridors, chipped the first crack in her stoicism, reminding her of what she'd lost. Her eyes shied away from glass display-cases, mostly empty in the evenings, slaves not in use being bedded down, where once she'd have paused to admire the contents. It could be her. A floor length mirror at the end of a corridor drove the full horror home.

At first, just for a second, she thought she was seeing an aristocrat's plaything being led down the corridor towards her. It was the first mirror she'd seen since the drugged haze of the clinic's recovery rooms. The sort of gorgeous, breathtakingly sexy plaything on a lead she'd encountered on several occasions in Lady Isobell's company or when allowed to roam the house alone.

Just a sex-object, placid in her bonds, who Jenny's experienced eye judged would take a whip well and a cock or dildo plunging into her pussy, with delight. Jenny felt herself flush scarlet, realising her first reaction had been pleasure; approval of the obviously deserving sexual plaything's dress and treatment, and envy for the Lord or Lady who would use her. She recognised the soldier holding her lead before she recognised herself. It was just and ample payback for every bound, naked slave Jenny had ever admired.

Jenny stumbled, almost falling before her captor pulled her back to her feet with a hand on her upper arm.

"Concentrate, stupid!" he barked, delivering a slap to her backside.

Jenny obediently squared her shoulders, holding her head up proudly, showing she was ready to be led on. He gave her behind another slap for emphasis, Jenny giving an obliging yelp, but remaining in place. The sting was actually quite stimulating; pleasant, the inexperienced harem-keeper yet to learn how hard he had to strike to cause pain. She hadn't wanted to hurt his feelings too much though, hence her little squeak.

Jenny followed the mollified soldier's lead on towards the mirror. She didn't want to see herself like this, so she didn't, remembering instead; looking with a free woman's eyes at the type of sleek, top-heavy plaything Lady Isobell was drawn to when clicking through 3D images of slaves for sale on her

TV's home shopping channel. Memories came to her rescue. A darker haired version of the sort of breathing doll the aristocrat had once admired in a shop-window, dildo-mounted, a candle-holder buckled into her mouth and with hot wax dripping down her large breasts, in Jenny's company once. She'd expressed her intention to casually mention the expensive displayed sex-toy to Daddy as a present for her up-coming birthday. Jenny remembered how hot the blonde had looked. She didn't remember feeling sympathetic, though perhaps she had.

This new slave, led by a uniformed soldier, tall, with long, long legs, swayed enticingly towards her perched on ridiculously high stiletto heels. A polished stainless steel hobble, chain taut between her ankles, forced her to take small, neat, restricted steps. The ball-gagged brunette had huge breasts, rings set through nipples; surprisingly firm but obviously very heavy, jiggling, wobbling and swaying as she walked. Her arms were secured behind her, elbows touching, which thrust the creamy mounds into greater prominence, and allowed no distraction from a tiny waist. Her waspie corset and collar were both polished black leather.

It was no good! Jenny was only too aware she had looked at herself. And had just seen a sex-object. If you didn't want a person, a relationship with an individual with their own agenda, just an incredibly sexy body to enjoy; then she had to concede that the top-heavy, wasp-waisted chattel in the mirror, was quite perfect. With her wide, intelligent light-hazel eyes just waiting to fill with tears, flawless peaches and cream skin that would mark beautifully and her plump clean-shaven pussy, just a decorative tuft of pubic hair above, just waiting, needing and deserving to be deeply filled. Anybody not in chains would like what they saw.

Jenny knew she would look superb chained to a bed, would be a delight to fuck and torture, how much pleasure her owner would take in her cries of pain and ecstasy, in leaving marks on her flesh, and the pride that person would take displaying her naked and bound in public. She couldn't help thinking it. It was self-evident. She tried to tell herself it was fear of punishment that made her so docile, the drugs that made her so compliant and helplessly horny and the satellite tracking device implanted in her breast, that would track her anywhere on the planet, that was responsible for the fact she didn't even think about escape.

All true, but none of it changed her humiliating owner's-eye assessment: and her secret shame. Under fear, forced arousal and the knowledge that escape was impossible, there was also excited anticipation. Like a bored horse hanging its head over a paddock fence watching cars go by, the price of stimulating activity, a little kindness and any feeling of worth, was being harnessed, bridled and ridden by her owner, encouraged with crop and spurs. Or, whoever her owner chose to lend her to or sell her to, the mare never getting to choose her rider.

Jenny had no illusions that her upcoming sexual ordeal would be anything other than degrading, painful and humiliating, or that there would be any limits other than those her abuser chose to set him or herself. And in the abstract of course she didn't want to be chained, totally controlled, naked property for the next 30 or more years. But now, at this moment, like a newly broken horse, she'd tasted the bit, her girth had been tightened, and she was eagerly waiting for her unknown Master or Mistress to mount her.

Once broken in and trained, the horse could enjoy being ridden.

***

Jenny was a little disappointed when she was taken towards Master Franklin's wing of the house, and not to Mistress Isobell's chambers. She'd been secretly hoping she was owned by her former lover. The soldier knocked respectfully on a door unfamiliar to Jenny, opened it, and pushed her gently in with a hand in the small of her corseted back.

"There's my toy! All together at last," Professor Phillips-Webber called out jovially.

Oh! That explained the stockings she'd been made to wear. Mistress Phillips-Webber, Jenny mentally corrected herself.

"Jenny. Heel!"

Jenny obediently swayed across the carpet and knelt at her tutor's feet, sitting on her heels, head up, thighs spread wide and breasts in reach, as she'd been taught. Her teacher, hard as it was to believe, now her owner; lounged in a comfortable chair, glass in one hand, remote in the other, wearing an embroidered silk robe that hung open, revealing drooping breasts, rolls of fat on her stomach and chubby thighs, quite un-self-consciously. The aristocrats never judged each other's appearance, Jenny remembered, just their properties.

Jenny's last hope, the secret hope she hadn't even dared look at too closely in her own head, in case scrutiny made it evaporate, died. The tiny, forlorn, last hope that professor Phillips-Webber was biding her time, would somehow find a way to rescue her students, was gone. Mistress Phillips-Webber wouldn't be setting anyone free. Now there was nothing but the knowledge that she would be owned and used by the Lords and Ladies for as long as their medicine could keep her young.

The realisation was surprisingly liberating. Now there was no reason to try and cling to the old Jenny, slave number 673 could learn to placidly accept submission, and find contentment in docile surrender, like the older, experienced slaves did.

"Isn't this nice?" her tutor said happily. "All my toys together for the first time. A full set of subservience." Talking more to herself than anything, Jenny realised, she happily rambled on. "Of course Sarah's been my bed-warmer, and I've been prancing Karen around the estate between the shafts for weeks, excellent little cunt-lickers both of them, but what with trying to re-establish the Gate, my wedding and a whole new culture to learn about, I've just been too busy to get around to all of you. I know! Who would have thought you could ever be too busy to whip a firm little tail?"

Jenny had already seen her fellow students in various restraints, naked and in ball-gags as she was, as she'd approached. But a slave-girl never took her eyes off her Mistress. The glimpse out of the corner of her eye had been quite enough. Mistress Phillips-Webber reached out and scooped up her breasts.

"My, Jenny. What big tits you have."

There was satisfaction in her voice, a hard edge to her tone, and no mercy whatsoever in her eyes. Jenny wondered that she'd ever been dumb enough to consider this woman a cheerful, plump, jolly, frigid source of tweed-wearing amusement. She'd obviously had her vision surgically corrected here, no more peering over silly half-moon spectacles, but it was far more than that. The difference between a shark in an aquarium tank, and a fin in the water off the beach, maybe.

"All the better for you to look at, Mistress," she answered herself in a high, squeaky falsetto.

"My Jenny, what silky, soft, velvet tits you have."

"All the better for you to stroke, Mistress," she answered herself again.

"My Jenny, what heavy tits you have."

"All the better for you to slap, squeeze and rope, Mistress."

Jenny, quietly drooling around her gag, listened in disbelief as her udders were pulled, hefted, kneaded and squeezed, slipping and sliding together, lubricated again by her saliva. What had come over the professor? Was she this desperate to fit into Lord Franklin's lifestyle?

"I'm so glad I let Isobell talk me into making them even bigger. I nearly didn't you know. But then I realised it would be more humiliating for you, and there'd be so much more for me to punish."

She looked up from the ample flesh she handled.

"You do realise that these big, heavy, tits are going to have to be punished, don't you Jenny?"

Jenny nodded obediently.

"Good. I knew you'd understand. You always were the brightest of the bunch. Andrew, Charles, and even Sarah; they all pretended they didn't know why. But you do. I'm going to scald, whip and shock these lovely tits, and then lick them all over, every time I fuck you. And you know why?"

Totally mystified, Jenny nodded subserviently anyway.

"Good slut," her teacher told her absently.

She took hold of Jenny's nipple rings, lifting first one breast and then the other, admiring the weight she held, then idly bounced the heavy globes together. She smiled, a little-girl smile of delight, when her victim moaned softly.

"And now you pay the price for all those months of teasing. And I always liked you. Why did you do it?"

Jenny gasped in delight when her new owner gave her breasts a few playful slaps. Not that hard. Just making her breasts bounce about.

"All those times I looked down your blouse, standing beside your desk, and you pretended not to know! That lovely swell of flesh, a glimpse of your bra when you were being especially cruel. And do you remember my birthday? May the 28th! You didn't wear a bra, and I kept trying to see your nipples, and you wouldn't let me! You don't know how long I've longed to have you on your knees like this, your tits in my hands and you with your hands cuffed behind you."

Jenny, listening dumfounded, would have gaped in amazement, but fortunately the ball strapped into her mouth disguised her expression. What was she saying? Mistress Phillips-Webber was talking too fast, slightly breathlessly.

"All you little teases are the same. Year after year, flaunting your firm little bodies in front of me in your tight clothes, tantalising me with bare stomachs and pierced belly-buttons, taunting me with cleavages and thighs, mocking me with hard muscles, tight butts and cock-bulges and driving me to distraction with your cruelty. Do you realise I cried myself to

193

sleep in frustration that time Sarah flashed me her panties in that too-short skirt, when you pretended to knock my pen off the desk? I bet you all had a good laugh about that one. Why were you so cruel to me Jenny? You always seemed such a nice girl!"

Jenny whimpered in pain, her tutor's fingernails deep in the flesh of her breasts. Phillips-Webber looked down in surprise, and relaxed her grip.

"Now you're sorry of course. But it's too late." She nodded in satisfaction. "Now you pay the price. All of you! You teased me with these tits, so I'm going to punish them. It's only fair. Andrew, flaunting his cute little butt in my face in tight jeans all those times? Well he's going to get his ass thoroughly reamed. Now Karen, you wouldn't believe how often Karen came to my tutorials straight from the gym. No shower. God I lay awake at nights with the musk of her in my nostrils! Well now she's going to get more exercise than she bargained for. Once I've had my fill of her in bed, she's going to be whipped to exhaustion pulling a pony-trap on every racetrack in the Kingdom. Don't they make a sweet couple?"

Jenny obediently looked where she gestured. The big, strong Andrew with his rugby player's physique was quite helpless on his knees, bent forward, arms pulled up behind him to a ceiling winch, ankles chained wide to floor ring-bolts. Karen kneeling behind him was pumping a fat double dildo into his anus, which the ball-gagged slave was taking quite badly. Sobbing, snuffling and trying to beg around the obstruction in his mouth, tears were streaming down his face. Jenny had heard the sounds, but automatically tuned them out. Cellblock conditioning.

Karen, her pussy stretched wide by her end of the shaft, had her arms behind her back, folded elbow to wrist. Her dark skin gleamed from her exertions. A V-shaped plastic frame hung from her nipples, point down, a contact point at the end of the V trailing a red wire. An automated whip swung across her backside at random intervals, causing her hips to jerk forward and ram the dildo into Andrew with each stroke. And then the contact point of the frame would swing and touch her belly, and an electric shock would jerk her back again, withdrawing the dildo three quarters of its fat length.

Neither slave could pull out of the double dildo completely, Karen with a chain looping down between her buttocks from the back of a tight belt secured to a ring in the shaft's centre. And Andrew, sobbing at his rape, couldn't pull away because a length of chain from the Arab-strap buckled tightly around his cock and balls was linked to the same ring. His veined, purple shaft was very swollen indeed, she couldn't help noticing.

Not totally random whip stokes, Jenny guessed. They could probably be set regular, or entirely controlled, by Mistress Phillips-Webber's remote control. She looked back when her owner began talking again.

"Now Charles and Sarah I had to give some thought to punishing. Little tart was always letting him touch her in public, bra undone under her jumper, panties in his pocket. Would you believe I once watched his hand under her skirt an entire lecture, frigging the little slut? And now, when it's time for retribution, they claim they weren't teasing me! She actually said, she didn't think I could see under the desk from the lectern!"

She shook her head in disgust, still absently handling Jenny's breasts.

"Obviously they're a pair, and I don't want to break them up. I may even let them get married. I've definitely decided I'll keep them as pets once I've sold off you other three, and of course I'll use them for sex together, but they're never going to be allowed to make love again, and all punishments will have to be shared. That's only fair I think? I make them tease each other like they teased me!"

Jenny looked back to where the woman toying with her carelessly waved. The blond lovers, inseparable, devoted and fun-loving, were obediently torturing each other. Sarah knelt, bent forward over a low table, arms strapped behind her wrist to elbow like Karen, a large mechanical vibrator-dildo slowly thrusting in and out of her sex on a piston. Like Andrew and Karen, a simple chain prevented her pulling out of the shaft stuffing her pussy, pierced clitoris linked to a ring on the invader's base.

Charles stood behind her, a choke-chain from another of the ubiquitous ceiling winches around his neck holding him in place, one arm pulled up painfully behind him and secured to the back of his collar. The clinic had turned out another supple slave, Jenny thought inconsequentially. One of a bundle of red wires disappeared into his anus, a half-dozen were trailed by sharp-jawed electrodes biting into his scrotum, and the remaining four went to metal bands screwed down at intervals along his throbbing erection. In his free hand he held a whip.

"I don't think it'll take me long to get them hating each other," Phillips-Webber said, the familiar animation of scientific discovery in her tone. "And then, when they can't stand the sight of each other, loathe each other, then I'll have them fuck each other while I watch."

Charles slashed his whip down across Sarah's already well-marked backside, his bound, naked, dildo impaled girlfriend crying out in pain behind her gag. It took Jenny a moment to work out what she was watching. Oh, right! Ingenious.

The sharp metal clamps, trailing taut chains, that bit cruelly into Sarah's nipples; that Jenny had thought were just holding her in position, were in fact the on/off switch to the electrodes attached to Charles's genitals. If the petite blonde didn't keep pulling back on her tortured nipples, head up and back arched, Charles would be delivered a series of agonising jolts.

Charles, having been persuaded he preferred his fellow slave doing the suffering, was using the greater pain of the whip across his former girlfriend's buttocks, to keep her obediently enduring her nipple-torment. And increasingly, Jenny realised, he was using pain to keep her focused in the face of eye-glazing lust. Sarah moaned in pleasure, her juices coating the buzzing piston-driven shaft pumping into her, and slumped down a moment. Charles squealed like a girl, a flurry of whip-slashes bringing Sarah back up into position.

"Aren't they sweet?" the student's teacher asked Jenny.

Jenny again nodded obediently, nipples so hard they ached now, breasts swollen with lust from her professor's manipulations, an uncontrollable heat raging in her loins despite her fear. Her stunned amazement was so great, she was still able to think clearly despite overwhelming arousal. She never, in a million years, would have guessed that her tutor had harboured anything but professional interest in her. That the respected academic would want to see her own students naked in humiliating bonds, mouths filled with identical ball-gags, suffering sexual abuse for her amusement; was almost beyond comprehension.

Her professor must have seen this as an opportunity to put a collar around her neck from the moment the Gate was opened, Jenny belatedly realised. Her own punishment for being the latest in a long line of students who'd unknowingly been the object of Phillips-Webber's desires, and allegedly flaunting herself and sexually teasing the middle-aged woman, was familiar. She'd seen Lady Isobell use the device, now waiting for her, on another unfortunate slave-toy. A dildo that had to be constantly pumped down to jack up a weight and prevent the completion of a punishment electric circuit.

But first, before she could be allowed to take her place with her fellow students, came the promised breast-punishment. Her professor looped two lengths of rope tightly around the base of each of Jenny's heavily enlarged slave-breasts, the white cord digging deep into her flesh, squeezing hard, and then led her over to a wooden framework. Like stocks, but with only two holes between the scissor-arms instead of the usual three; head and two smaller for wrists. Hobbled, arms bound and almost naked, Jenny let herself be led before what she was beginning to suspect was a set of breast-stocks.

She was right. Mistress Phillips-Webber lifted the top bar

197

and pulled Jenny forward by her nipple-rings so that the roped groove in her breasts rested in the two semicircular depressions. Her teacher lowered the top bar; and snapped a lock closed. The holes weren't that big, and when the constricting ropes were removed, Jenny's breasts bulged out through the holes, the wooden jaws gripping her flesh tightly and holding her helplessly in place.

"Pull back," Phillips-Webber ordered.

Jenny obediently swayed back, gradually putting more weight on her trapped, squeezed out, flesh, eventually almost her whole body-weight, but the wooden frame just creaked; holding her tightly. It was obvious to both of them that the large globes were squeezed too tightly, were just simply too big to pull out of the stocks grip. She was trapped!

Jenny's legal owner stroked her stockinged thighs, patted her buttocks and then stroked her wetness up from between her sex-lips into her pubic hair. Her head firmly held up by her collar, mouth filled with gag, perched on her toes and with her elbows touching where her arms were bound behind her, Jenny placidly endured the inspection. The professor seemed especially taken with her tit-clamped property's waist-nipping corset and ball-gag.

"Isobell's right you know," Phillips-Webber whispered. "You really are a quite magnificent animal!"

Jenny watched with heart-pounding, fearful, arousal as her tutor prepared two bowls of water and pulled on a pair of rubber gloves. Her clamped breasts stood out proudly, skin shiny-taut, the tit-stocks' constriction forcing her ringed nipples to protrude. One bowl was almost hidden under a rising cloud of steam, the other full of floating ice.

Jenny whimpered and gasped as her breasts were washed with a cloth from the hot bowl; the heat only just bearable, like easing herself very gingerly into a scalding bath. The trapped globes were soon a uniform shade of scarlet; the sting still burning deeper long after the cloth had been removed.

She squeaked in shock as the iced-water cloth was run over

her bulging breasts, the tit-stocks creaking as she jerked and yanked back against the wooden clamp locked down around the base of each tightly squeezed melon, panting around her ball-gag now. Squealing in pain as the hot cloth was applied again, the scalding heat burning into her flesh worse after the iced water, cuffed hands clenched into tight fists behind her. Then cold. Then hot! The cloth stroking icy water across her flesh was dreadful, a gasping shock that drove the air out of Jenny's lungs each time; but at least the same. The scalding water by contrast, was worse with every application.

"My Jenny! What red tits you have!"

Mistress Phillips-Webber pulled Jenny's head down so that she could lick the first tear that rolled down her cheek. She still had to stand on tiptoe to do it, the lightest touch of her robe on Jenny's trapped, reddened, squeezed-taut, breasts, exquisite torture, her flesh now unbelievably sensitive. Jenny wailed behind her ball-gag in helpless, forced, arousal as her former tutor slowly licked the big, heavy, ring-tipped mounds, her tongue like a rasp. Biting down on the orange ball strapped into her mouth, pussy-juices flowing, the breast-stocks creaked louder as she twisted, but the wooden framework had been solidly constructed.

Gasping helplessly, Jenny watched her Mistress produce a thin-stranded horsehair-like whisk through tear-blurred eyes. She whined plaintively for mercy, but it was no use. The whisk hissed down across Jenny's breasts, scalded flesh more than doubling the pain of the lash's sting. She squealed, yanking and jerking back against her own bound flesh as the whisk licked across the big heavy globes again and again.

Finally, as Jenny sobbed gently, the professor touched a shock baton lightly to first one nipple and then the other, over and over, clearly delighting in Jenny's high-pitched squeals. Each shock was a bolt of agony that filled, engulfed, the trapped melons, Jenny doing a desperate dance in her hobble, but her punished breasts were still held perfectly still.

The burn from whisk and scalding water, melting slowly

into her flesh from the outside, met a deep, throbbing, ache caused by the shocks flowing out from the centre of each abused mound, nipples pulsing as if on fire. Worse still was her former teacher's bland assertion that Jenny would only be released from the stocks so that she could see the large, heavy, globes she'd been punishing quivering as her plaything sobbed. The next round of tit-torture would be more intense and longer! Without looking, Jenny could feel her own flesh wobble as she trembled and snuffled when the top bar of the stocks was unlocked.

Jenny was then taken to her place in the show, made to kneel astride a pussy-filling pole-mounted dildo, electrodes clamped to her nipples, and began docilely fucking herself. If she didn't keep thrusting down on the shaft that impaled her, each stroke of which jacked up a little weight, it would click down and touch a contact pad. An electric circuit would be completed, and a jolt of agony would be delivered to her nipples. Her flesh on fire, Jenny had her first orgasm as Professor Phillips-Webber licked her whipped and scalded breasts again.

Like the ringmaster in some strange circus of pain, robe hanging carelessly open, Phillips-Webber wandered amongst her bound students. Pulling a nipple here, flicking her lash across a buttock there, a pat here, a stroke there, here a squeezed testicle, there a stroked penis. Here and there she would pause to taste tears, sweat and slave-girl's juices, going back and forth amongst them to compare, clearly quite delighted with her little theatre of cruelty. She explained, quite earnestly, as she stoked Jenny's reddened breasts with ice-cubes, before pushing the cubes one by one into Jenny's anus, that the lifetime of abuse stretching out before them was necessary, and quite fair. To make up for all the teases over the years who had escaped her.

Finally, when her toys were too exhausted to amuse her, Charles was tied spread-eagled facedown on her bed, and anally raped with a strap-on-dildo. He was only the first.

200

TEN
NAMED

"Please, please, please! I'll be good!" Jenny squeaked desperately.

The clock's second hand continued its remorseless advance. Ten seconds, five, four, three, two... Jenny squealed, as a bolt of agony was delivered to her body through sharp-jawed electrodes clamped to her nipples, tongue and sex-lips. She blinked away tears, helplessly focusing on the clock's sweeping hand, like a rabbit mesmerised by headlights.

50 seconds!

Her punishment for helping the Master-at-Arm's personal pet to come without permission, Jenny lay face-down on her stomach on a plain wooden surface, her arms, legs and a rope woven into her hair, pulling her limbs up behind her to a pulley above in a suspended hog-tie. Heart pounding and gleaming in sweat, she watched the clock.

30 seconds!

A metal framework had been screwed into place behind her teeth to hold her mouth open. At first, she'd assumed it was so that she didn't involuntarily clench down on the clamp biting into her tongue and injure herself. Now it was obviously so that a desperate slave didn't try to interfere with her punishment by biting through the wire!

20 seconds!

A soldier appeared in the doorway, looking over her tortured, bound, nudity with interest. The slave grapevine said you could win a reprieve from broadcast punishment if one of the soldiers chose to exercise his sexual rights! It was understandably rare, as the uniformed man could, from his point of view, allow the stimulating punishment to continue, and then enjoy her afterwards. But possible! In desperate hope, Jenny focused on the red-uniformed man's sergeant's stripes.

"Please Sir, use me!" Jenny begged.

Her spine and neck were arched hard back by her

suspension, but still her heavy breasts lay on the wooden surface. She reared and twisted up off the table, making the large mounds sway.

"Fuck my tits Master. Squeeze them, whip them! I could take your cock right down my throat," she offered desperately.

It was no longer important that her clamp-distorted pleas were being broadcast around the whole cellblock, only that the uniformed man should be interested. And then she was out of time!

"I'll be..." Jenny started to say, the sentence cut off with a squeal of pain.

"Lost interest in me?" the soldier asked, amused.

"No Master," she panted. 50 seconds! "I want you so much my cunt's dripping wet! Please let me serve you. I want... I want to swallow your come! I want to lick your feet and feel your hands on my body," she invented desperately. "Please let me worship you; show you how hot I am!"

The amused man slid a hand under one breast, hefting its full weight with an approving nod.

"You could slap, squeeze and bite my big, heavy, tits," she coaxed. "Come all over them!"

30 seconds!

The man's free hand slid between her buttocks and then down between the sharp-jawed clamps biting into the plump, sensitive flesh of her pussy-lips, plunging into her wetness. The punishment had been driving Jenny wild with desire; her clitoris swollen fit to burst. She groaned in lust. His fingers stroked in and out of her, penetrating deeply, squeezing her breast in time with his probes.

"Oh thank you Sir! You see what a slut I am? A hot, wet, big titted slut! I promise you'll enjoy using me."

Jenny shrieked in delight, orgasm crashing down on her helpless body and consuming her as fingers found her clitoris and brutally squeezed. The man's hands left her. Four seconds, three, two...

Jenny squealed in pain.

Her senses dulled by pleasure as well as arousal and pain now, the clock had ticked away twenty seconds—forty until the next shock! —before she managed to focus on its sweeping second hand again. The soldier patted a buttock.

"I'll tit-fuck you this evening," he decided. "And you'd better be as good as you say!"

30 seconds! 29. 28...

***

Later that morning Jenny sat astride Master Franklin, impaled on the cock she'd just licked and kissed into swollen stiffness, her arms as usual bound behind her, strapped wrist to elbow today. Mistress Phillips-Webber standing beside the bed was visibly anxious that nothing go wrong on this the first time they'd shared one of her slaves, not his. Her former teacher controlled her with one hand wrapped around the chain linking Jenny's nipples, her breasts lifted high, bobbing together, and in the other hand the crop that stroked Jenny's buttocks.

Jenny groaned in pleasure at the first sting of leather across her behind, obediently thrusting her hips forward, filling herself to the hilt on the penis of her owner's fiancé. The crop hissed through the air again, and again, Jenny mechanically thrusting her hips in time with its loud cracks on her flesh, the painful bite of each stroke slowly fading into a familiar, deep, arousing, heat.

"Oh damn. I forgot to put her gag back in," Phillips-Webber said, sounding forlorn.

Master Franklin chuckled amiably. "Don't worry yourself," he reassured her. "It's got a pretty enough face without a ball-gag, and I'm sure it's intelligent enough to know not to speak without permission. Do I recognise my daughter's hand in the size of those tits?"

Jenny's owner nodded shyly.

"Thought so. Can you whip her a bit faster now?"

Jenny subserviently allowed braided leather and tormented nipples to control her actions, thrusting her hips faster and harder, hearing herself gasping in delight, without shame, as she was used for sexual gratification by a man old enough to be her grandfather. She bit her lip when he reached up for her breasts, as promised, her owner thoroughly punishing and then happily licking the full mounds each time Jenny was expected to perform sexually; knowing she was going to be allowed to come if she was docile enough.

***

That afternoon saw Jenny standing naked in the sunlight, straps digging into her body and constricting her head, a soldier hitching her to the pony-trap she was standing between the shafts of. It was her first taste of the bit, the rubber bar buckled tightly into her mouth. Bells had been hung from her nipples rings. Master Franklin and his fiancé, leant on the fence watching a first-time carriage-pony put through her paces, Charles and Sarah, naked on leads, kneeling at Mistress Phillips-Webber's feet. Lady Isobell and a Lord Jenny didn't recognise, accompanied by another unfamiliar couple, also watched, as well as a scattering of off-duty soldiers on the other side of the paddock. She was almost panting, a mixture of fear and excitement!

"Steady," her driver calmed her, stroking her belly, fingers following her crotch-strap to cup her sex. "Calm down, there's a good pet."

The dildo was going to drive her mad when she was made to prance, Jenny knew, just the walk from the stables had been exquisite torture. Walking in a dildo was very different from being mounted on a pole or having her pussy stuffed in bed, she was belatedly realising. As she moved, her internal dimensions shifted; the effect was as if the plastic invader was shifting, flexing and pumping inside her, stirring her insides to jelly.

She felt his weight through the shafts as her driver climbed into the seat of the pony-trap she was now secured to. Her bells tinkled as she shifted her stance to compensate, breathing heavier, terror and lustful anticipation leaving her almost incapable of rational thought.

"Light whip or heavy whip, My Lady?" the soldier asked.

"Oh, heavy whip," Jenny's owner decided. "I'm sure she can take it."

Jenny gasped as a vicious whip-stroke cracked down on her behind, hard enough for her to feel her own flesh ripple, causing her to bite down on her bit with a distressed cry, lunging forward against the burden of driver and pony-trap.

"Trot on!"

Her breasts swung and bounced uncomfortably despite the tightly criss-crossed straps that bound them, the girth far too tight, Jenny convinced she would be able to keep pace if only she could take a proper deep breath. The driver's lash licked across her hindquarters again, and then again. The little two-wheeled carriage—they were starting her off on a lightweight racing-trap—was surprisingly easy to pull, moving lightly over the grass; but she'd covered nearly 50 metres at a near-sprint already! The bit yanked her head to one side, the pull of her reins impossible to disobey, curving her back around towards her watching owner.

Puffing like a steam-train, eyes wide, her bit already foam-flecked, her nipple-ring bells jingling merrily, the dildo pumping and flexing inside her and the pressure of her crotch-strap on her clitoris driving her wild, Jenny swept past her former teacher, who clapped in delight. The lash licked across her flesh again, and again, allowing no respite. Implacable reins swung her around and back down the railing for another pass past her watching owner.

"Sprint!"

The order was accompanied by a harder whip-stroke, Jenny squealing even as she lunged forward, so wet her juices were already running down her thighs. Sweat gleaming on her flanks and slavering on her breasts now, Jenny knew she was exhausted, couldn't go on! But a steady flurry of lashes from her driver accelerated her smoothly past her watching Mistress, thighs pumping, breasts bouncing and crotch-strap digging ever deeper.

"Faster! Drive her faster!" Professor Phillips-Webber called.

And, Jenny realised, through her haze of lust and exhaustion, the lash cracking across her haunches again, she still had to be tit-fucked by the sergeant from the punishment-room before the day was through!

***

Because she was now being kept hooded and in earplugs in the cellblock as the second part of her punishment, Jenny quickly became disorientated, losing track of time. Blind and deaf now, as well as bound and gagged, when lying in her cell or being exercised, the hood only removed for grooming, there were no longer days, just the occasions she was enjoyed by her Mistress. A toy increasingly grateful to be taken out of its box to be used, this another such occasion. She had no idea what day it was.

Wearing what was now becoming a familiar uniform of ball-gag, collar, hobble, 5" heels and corset, Mistress Phillips-Webber having been persuaded the stockings and suspenders looked very strange to aristocratic eyes, Jenny stood neatly to attention, arms bound behind her. One side of a round-cornered square tray was secured to two rings on the bottom of her corset, there for that purpose, the other two corners of the tray supported by chains from her nipple-rings. On the tray waited a condensation-dewed champagne glass.

Like so many slave-games, Jenny was being set up to fail in her assigned task. Supporting a serving-tray with nipple-rings was usually a task for a small-breasted slave. Large breasts, no matter how firm, simply had too much movement and stretch in them. Being careful to stand perfectly still, even taking small breaths, she'd been treated to the bizarre sight of her plump former professor riding Andrew's cock.

Jenny's former infatuation was hooded and tied down on their Mistress's bed, she astride him, Karen and Sarah set to sucking on her nipples, Charles licking her ride's balls from behind her to keep his attention focused. All three students were encased in head-to-toe latex with only mouths free, hands locked behind them.

Andrew's torso was nicely criss-crossed with whip-stripes and globules of dried wax, Jenny quite envying him. As far as she knew he hadn't blubbered again since his first, obviously traumatic, rape, but he was still a little subdued when not perked up with pain or lust. Jenny no longer had the slightest sexual interest in her fellow student/slave, though she'd been properly enthusiastic on the three occasions they'd been made to perform together, Mistress watching. In fact she resented being jointly punished for his lacklustre performance; but she still felt sympathy for a fellow sex-slave. With a happy sigh, Mistress rolled off the strapped-down slave, pushing the other three aside, and flopped limp.

"Jenny! Champagne," she ordered. Jenny stepped carefully forward, aware of the slightest wobble in her flesh, and breathed a sigh of relief when the glass was finally taken. "Good slut. Now you can lick this come out of me, then we'll torture those tits some more."

***

Karen was the first to go. Mistress Phillips-Webber still owned her, Jenny was to learn, but racing-ponies were placed in the care of professional trainers, owners only enjoying their property's sexual favours out of season and after races they'd attended.

Much later, Jenny would learn from overheard comments, sneaked glances at the 3D TV when she could and the slave grapevine, that the dark-skinned pony-girl became very popular with the crowd. She was fast, and the betting public always liked a pony they could easily pick out of the pack.

***

"See, there's no way the nooses will slip off," Lady Isobell said, carelessly jerking and lifting Jenny's breasts with the two lengths of rope she held. The ropes sank deep into the soft flesh of Jenny's weighty slave-breasts; the usual ball-gag was in her mouth and her wrists in handcuffs behind her back. "I often tie my girls to things by their tits. It's much more personal than a collar."

She passed over the two ropes and Jenny was tied to the back of her owner's chair, the two having a slightly drunken girls-night in, to get to know each other.

"I like that," Mistress Phillips-Webber decided looking down at Jenny. "Humiliating, but totally secure. Good for her attitude?"

"Oh yes."

"What else have you got?"

Lady Isobell rummaged in her toy-box. "Nipple stretchers? Tit harness? Oh, here's a good one; radio controlled shock-dildo. You use it as a pager to bring her to heel when she's running loose. Tell Tits to present her haunches."

At a languid wave from her owner, Jenny obediently faced away and pressed her face and roped breasts into the carpet, tail up and thighs spread. The dildo going in, harness buckled tight around her hips and up between her buttocks, was quite pleasant.

The first shock wasn't too bad, just a gasp-producing sting deep inside her body that made her twitch, not the bolt of agony Jenny had been half-expecting. As Lady Isobell had said, a pager, not a training or punishment device. The question of the pager's range came up.

In the dead of the night Jenny was ordered to walk down the tree-lined front drive until shocked, and then report back with how far she'd got. The first electric-shock deep inside her belly occurred just as she was walking across the broad expanse of the drive. Obediently she turned around and returned to her owner's book-lined study. The next time she managed to get about a hundred metres down the drive before the shock-dildo strapped inside her, pussy stretched wide, called her obediently trotting back. Without being told, Jenny knew to trot. You didn't keep an owner waiting when called. Juices running down her thighs, and not just because she'd had to trot with her pussy stuffed, anticipating the shaft's shock with growing arousal, she got to almost the end of the driveway the next time.

Dawn saw Jenny plodding wearily down a country lane, naked, ropes trailing from her now purple breasts and wrists still cuffed behind her back. Her feet were killing her, stiletto's definitely for looking cute in, not for hiking, the discomfort almost enough to distract her from the gentle pressure of the fat shaft strapped inside her squelching in her juices.

Forgotten, or just out of range of the pager, Jenny didn't know. But her last order had been to walk until shocked, so she had no choice. Besides, she was satellite-tagged. Her owner could find her whenever she wanted. The range wasn't the problem she discovered, when the last shock came it was the strongest and sent her exhausted body staggering to its knees. Then she had to pull herself up and begin the long trot home.

***

Andrew was the next to go. Mistress Phillips-Webber, taking great delight in the act, framing the bill-of-sale and, unusually, taking cash, sold him to Lady Sybill who mostly used him as power for her tandem bicycle. The aristocrat was a cruel owner, and rarely allowed him to come, never forgetting how he'd tried to manipulate her and how she'd had to accept a commoner's proposal of marriage to secure his help in re-establishing the Gate. She had the engagement ring he'd bought her set through his nose.

Jenny couldn't help but be aware that she was next!

***

Some days later, Jenny, standing hobbled beside another pony-girl, panting gently and gleaming with sweat after a hard workout, her first outing in public, stood on the gravel

209

driveway of Franklin House. Unlike the pony-traps where you were harnessed between two shafts, this larger two-person carriage had a single shaft running forward, a T at its end secured to each pony's girth. Even with two of them pulling it was harder work than a pony-trap, and the two miles to the village and then back had been a nightmare, Jenny needing a lot of whip to keep her pace on the return journey, despite nearly two hours rest hitched outside the courtroom. It had been strangely thrilling though, trotting through the village, naked and in harness, and then standing there, a dildo inside her and hitched to a railing by her nipples, while all those people had filed past, pretending not to notice, but looking all the same!

She looked up wearily at the approach of a Lord and Lady, the Lady's shoes tip-tapping as she skipped down the marble steps. She recognised one of Lady Isobell's brothers, the Lady's face new, but known to Jenny through the slave grapevine. She was Franklin's goddaughter.

"Oh, look at that one! Isn't she gorgeous," the young Lady breathed, her eyes wide drinking in Jenny's bound nudity.

Most aristocrats were older than they looked thanks to rejuvenation treatments, but this one looked the age she was. Tomorrow was her eighteenth birthday, and she was being given the pick of the toys on the estate to celebrate that important milestone.

"Nice," the Lord agreed. "You like her?"

"I like it when they drool on their tits like that," the young aristocrat said shyly. "And hasn't she got lovely legs?"

"The blonde you picked was a bit shorter," he agreed, "but I'm sure she could be persuaded to drool."

"This pony's got nicer haunches. And prettier eyes. Look how placid she is, with all those whip marks on her hindquarters?"

"Changing your mind?" he chuckled.

"Can I?"

"Of course! It's your day. Are you sure you don't want an

unmarked backside to whip though?"

"I can whip the rest of her can't I?" she asked.

"You can do absolutely anything you like with her," her guide assured her.

"Then I'll mark her tits," the girl said defiantly. "And her belly and her thighs are hardly marked at all."

"This is the one then," he agreed. "I'll have her put to bed early so she's fresh for you."

"Gosh! I won't be able to sleep a wink tonight thinking about her."

He chuckled. "I know. I didn't. And you punish her for it. It's an eighteenth birthday tradition," he explained earnestly. He looked Jenny up and down. "She can take it if I'm any judge of slave-flesh. Don't be soft."

Lady Isobell's brother chased up a soldier to trot the carriage up and down the long tree-lined drive a couple of times, so that the birthday girl could see her choice in motion. Jenny, under a fresh layer of sweat, strapped breasts bouncing and responding docilely to yanked nipples and a whip licking across her buttocks, obviously didn't disappoint.

"Has she got a dildo in her? A big one?" the teenager piped happily as Jenny and her fellow ponies were pranced past.

Her smile was delighted, eyes wide as saucers when Jenny was pulled up to a gasping halt in front of her, as required, drooling and slavering on her harnessed breasts.

As she was led away, the young Lady cast one longing look back at the bound, naked body she was soon going to be allowed to play with. She obviously couldn't wait. Jenny found she envied the young girl/woman her freedom, and was experiencing some slight trepidation; but not hate or reproach no matter how hard she examined her feelings. Someone who'd admired so many pony-girls in harness, had longed to drive a pair of them and hadn't hesitated when the chance came up to enjoy one, was in no position to judge.

***

Jenny was taken from her cage-like cell bright and early the next morning, naked, wrists chained behind her, the night's ball-gag still in her mouth. For the first time she was one of the first batch of four taken to the shower-block for grooming. Quite used to being groped by the on-duty soldiers by now, she stood placidly with only a little moan of pleasure when a new corporal hefted, stroked and squeezed her large breasts with evident pleasure. The sergeant in charge brusquely told him that you didn't delay a special order on the Franklin estate.

"You can tit-fuck her tomorrow," the Sergeant concluded, with the casual disinterest of a man who'd handled countless, naked, bound, girls over the years, coming in mouths and between breasts as he pleased.

Scrubbed, shampooed, blow-dried and brushed, Jenny was fitted with the standard 4" stiletto heeled pumps, her ball-gag buckled back into her mouth once her teeth had been brushed. She was taken to a playroom adjoining one of the guest-suites; her wrists buckled together in cuffs and then pulled up high above her head, attached to one of the many winches any playroom was equipped with. Her body was pulled taut, her stiletto heels just brushing the carpet, all her weight on her toes; displayed in the approved Franklin estate manner. The young soldier who'd delivered her, concluded by pulling a burgundy, silk hood down over Jenny's head, lacing it tightly up the back. One last pat on her belly, fingers lingering to trail over her pussy, and then she was left in silent darkness.

Most of her weight was on her wrists, but by pushing down hard on her toes, she could relieve the pressure a little. Completely naked, her wrists chained above her, Jenny found herself trembling lightly, longing to be used by the birthday-girl! It felt slightly strange not to have her head held up by a broad, tight, collar; gone also the usual waist-nipping waspie-corset Mistress Phillips-Webber liked on her so much. Just heels, gag, and a tightly laced hood.

The hood pulled her hair back into a ponytail, the tip of the swinging mane thicker and longer than ever after treatments, just brushing the top swell of her buttocks as she shifted position on her toes. Jenny was used to breathing mostly through her nose now, panting around the large orange ball buckled into her mouth only when forced to exert herself sexually. Today she had the added difficulty of having to breath through fine silk pulled taut over her face as well.

The hood was soon sodden in front of her nose and mouth, Jenny gasping for breath, but she felt no panic, knowing her distress would be safe, and quite planned! From her own training as well as her pre-slave experience, she was well aware heavy breathing added to a slave-girl's allure. When the birthday-girl finally entered the playroom, she might find the swell and fall of Jenny's stomach and the deeper rise and fall of her weighty slave-breasts, fractionally more pleasing than if Jenny had been allowed to breath unhindered.

Nipples tight, but not nearly as stiff as they would soon be, gently aroused, Jenny waited. And waited, and waited, for the young Lady who was to be allowed to enjoy her. The birthday-girl would probably wake after a relaxing lie-in, untroubled by an alarm-clock, and then enjoy a leisurely breakfast before sampling her chosen sexual-plaything.

Jenny imagined the teenager's eyes on her, already in the room, watching silently! Feeling herself getting wetter, breasts swelling with lust, she imagined appraising, lust-filled, cruel eyes on her ringed nipples, her enlarged breasts, her clinic-slender waist and long legs; and the whip-marks on her behind from yesterday's workout as a carriage-pony. Blind under her hood, it was easy to imagine eyes trailing down the length of her legs, muscles defined because she was on her toes, and lingering on her defenceless nudity, pussy plump and clean-shaven, only a decorative tuft of pubic hair above her sex remaining, to draw the eye. In the confinement of her hood, after what felt like hours, the first hesitant touch, fingernails indenting and trailing lightly down her stomach, was still a shock. By then Jenny had worked herself into a state of desperate arousal, but she still gasped in fright, twisting away

213

by reflex.

"Bad girl!" the teenager piped, landing a stinging slap on Jenny's backside.

The young aristocrat's cut-glass accent was unmistakable, as was the unconscious, haughty, hint of command in her tone, even though her voice was soft, sweet, almost innocent sounding. Jenny's nipples sprang up at the Lady's barked rebuke as well as the sting of her slap, her breasts now so swollen they ached, and her juices flowing. She'd thought she was hot before, but that was just ordinary lust. Now it was fanned into a raging, uncontrollable heat by surgically implanted aphrodisiacs.

With a sigh of delight Jenny held herself obediently still as a cautious, hesitant, hand stroked down her belly, roughly inexperienced fingers stroking her pussy and then unexpectedly penetrating. The birthday-girl jerked her hand away, obviously surprised at the ease with which Jenny's sex had swallowed her fingers as well as her bound plaything's cry of pleasure. And then slowly, deliberately, she forced all four fingers deep back inside Jenny's sex. Jenny groaned in lust, the aristocrat twisting her fingers deeper, and then withdrawing, wiping Jenny's wetness off her fingers onto her stomach.

Hands stroked Jenny's body, exploring where and as they wished. Down her legs and back up, tracing the lines left by the carriage-driver's whip across her haunches. Up her spine, counting vertebrae, squeezing the ridge of muscle to either side of her backbone, back down. A cruel grip on her pubic-hair pulled her body forward into an arched, trembling, bow, Jenny forced further up onto her toes, forced to offer her sex to the young aristocrat. Bolder now, hands stroked her breasts, weighing the full mounds, lifting and squeezing firm, heavy, flesh together. Jenny wailed in mingled pleasure and pain as her nipples were bitten. This time when Jenny cried out, the birthday-girl, growing more confident, didn't pull away but bit down harder, tonguing the erect nubs and the rings set through her prize's flesh, fingernails sinking deeper into the full breasts she held to her mouth. Jenny felt lips, then teeth, followed by pressure. Then again, and again, the eighteen-year-old scattering love-bites all across both huge globes, sucking deep, taking great big mouthfuls of flesh. Then slowly her kisses trailed down Jenny's stomach, belly and thighs.

Growing bolder with each passing second, the young aristocrat was handling Jenny's naked, bound, body without hesitation now. Marking her territory; establishing a claim, Jenny realised.

After a light breast-slapping, her flesh swinging and bouncing with each stinging, burning, blow, fingers again penetrated her sex. Jenny squeaked in surprise as a thumb was thrust into her anus, twisting in time with the fingers. She felt flesh against hers, realising the birthday-girl was also naked, now bold enough to rub her body up against her hooded, sex-toy. A firm, slender, toned, body, nipples as hard as her own, slid and pressed against Jenny's lushly voluptuous, clinic-formed figure.

"Your skin's like velvet, Pony," the aristocrat murmured, melting against her.

Jenny was panting in lust, dripping wet and desperate to be allowed to come when the birthday-girl at last removed her hood. Finally unencumbered by sodden silk, she dragged in a deep, grateful lungful of cool, fresh air. The naked eighteen year old, hands light on Jenny's hips, her erect nipples and firm pointed breasts pushing into the full, soft, weight of Jenny's slave-breasts, was looking into her chosen slave's eyes with inquisitive delight.

"Aren't you beautiful!" she breathed, pushing up on tip-toe, body hard against Jenny's, to slowly lick Jenny's lips around the orange ball that filled her mouth and parted them. "Such placid eyes."

The young girl stepped back, sliding a hand up Jenny's back again, her free hand toying with pubic curls.

"You're going to be a good pony aren't you?" she asked

215

almost plaintively. "I am going to enjoy you aren't I? You want me to enjoy you? I've waited a long time for this!"

Jenny nodded obediently, emphatically, to each question.

"You're going to be the best birthday present ever," she said with growing enthusiasm, adding, "I knew you were the toy for me, Pony, when I saw how well you took the whip. To take pain so placidly! I just know I couldn't."

Almost hanging naked by her wrists, legal property, a young stranger toying with her ringed nipples, Jenny might have dared to laugh out loud if her customary ball-gag hadn't been buckled into her mouth. The girl's tone was strangely hesitant, wondering; shy almost. Didn't she realise a slave could take whatever the owner chose to give, simply because she had no choice?

Revelation came in a light-bulb flash, and Jenny was suddenly glad she hadn't mocked the eighteen year old slave user, who was soon going to be—sadistically and enthusiastically—sexually abusing her, by laughing at her. The birthday-girl was a virgin!

Of course! Lady Isobell had half-explained it to her. Aristocrat's didn't take each other as physical lovers, and didn't legally get their hands on their first slave until that all-important eighteenth birthday. Probably the majority were virgins when they sampled their first sex-slave. Despite apprehension and raging lust, Jenny had to bite down a giggle. And to think she'd expected to be in control, a teacher and gentle reassuring guide, with her first virgin. Instead, she would be subject to the capricious whims, and completely at the mercy of, a beautiful but spoilt, eighteen year old!

The teenager laid a hand on Jenny's pussy again, dropping to one knee and licking up through her pubic hair, matting the dark curls onto her belly. Her tongue flicked lightly across Jenny's sex, just tasting, Jenny whimpering in frustration at the fleeting touch. Abruptly the young girl stood, in almost one sweeping movement, stepped over to a rack, selected a whip, and swung it in a hissing arc onto Jenny's belly.

Jenny squealed in agony as the lash cracked across her flesh, knees coming up to her breasts in a futile attempt to protect herself, twisting, spinning away on the pulley-chain that dragged up her wrist-cuffs. The next stroke smacked down high across her buttocks.

"Face me Pony!" the beautiful girl demanded, "Or I'll whip your ass to ribbons!"

Quaking, gasping, Jenny forced her toes to the floor and swung herself back. The eighteen year old had a look of stunned surprise on her pretty face, becoming a slow, blossoming, smile as she realised the full extent of the power she had. Jenny whimpered as braided leather was laid lightly across her skin again.

"Face me," she repeated more firmly. "I want to whip unmarked flesh."

The cruel lash was swung again and again, Jenny able to see raised welts across her belly in the playroom's full-length mirror, until tears blurred her eyes. Each time she shrieked, twisting away. And each time her young torturer forced her back, lightly laying the whip ready on her flesh for the next stroke.

"Pony? Is it true a wet whip hurts more," the now clearly entranced Lady asked.

Snuffling, Jenny nodded reluctantly.

The aristocrat stroked her whip between Jenny's sex-lips, pushing and twisting it deeply into her wetness. Forced by pain to new heights of arousal, Jenny moaned in pleasure, hips twitching. Wet leather left a blaze of agony across her belly, Jenny squealing around her gag, jerking on her winch-chain like a hooked fish.

Her stomach and the fronts of her thighs were whipped, the birthday-girl stroking the whip into her juices between swings, Jenny's breasts quivering as she sobbed. Even as tears splashed onto the heavy mounds, the whip stroking into her pussy would make her groan in pleasure around the orange ball strapped into her mouth. And each time the lash smacked onto flesh with a crack, her knees would jerk up, she would twist away with a squeal, and then have to force herself to face her abuser again.

The birthday-girl put the whip under her breasts, trying to lift the large globes, but the long lash just bent under the weight of Jenny's flesh.

"Please no!" Jenny tried to beg around her gag.

The young aristocrat torturing her looked up, clearly surprised that her plaything might voice the slightest, or any, objections to any activity that was giving her so much pleasure.

"Oops! Almost forgot," she said, turning away.

Tears running down her cheeks, Jenny sagged in relief when the naked girl left the room; unable to suppress a whimper of fear when she reappeared, whip still in hand. The aristocrat tossed a small belt-worn computer end over end in one hand, flicking it on and scanning the bar-code tattooed on the underside of Jenny's left breast.

"Comp; monitor. Until further notice I want to know if this slave comes," she instructed the device.

The teenager set aside her computer, and swung an unexpected backhand stroke across Jenny's breasts. Caught by surprise again, Jenny screamed. The blow, an explosion of pain, landed across both breasts just below the nipples. Without thinking she kicked out, narrowly missing the eighteen-year-old aristocrat.

"Bad pony!" the teenager scolded with a wide grin.

She quickly buckled bands snug around Jenny's ankles, and pulled her legs wide, securing the cuffs to ringbolts set in the floor. Almost hanging from her wrists now, only the tips of her toes able to brush the floor, Jenny wailed in wordless, terrified, protest as the birthday-girl again lightly laid the whip on her quaking breasts, resting on her ringed nipples.

Jenny thrashed and squealed as her breasts were whipped, the big globes quivering each time the whip slashed down, too heavy to swing as when slapped, but bouncing, dancing and wobbling as she sobbed and desperately tried to twist away from her tormentor. In the tear-blurred mirror, raised welts criss-crossed the heaving, creamy mounds, saliva and tears splashing down on her marked flesh.

And again, each time the girl laid the whip lightly on the throbbing melons, waiting with cruel patience, for Jenny to compose herself and hold still. And then the whip would again hiss through the air; and land on flesh with an agonising crack. Jenny cried out, a mark left down the side of her right breast, and then after a breathless wait, the left. The beautiful young virgin exploring the exciting new world of sadism she'd discovered, with relish, and without mercy.

Although Jenny now had quite a lot of experience of being tit-tortured, by her owner, her gag-muffled pleas and shrieks were still totally uninhibited, the pain quite unbearable. Torment that only a bound and gagged girl, who had no choice, could endure. She was sweat-slick, crying for mercy and no longer able to see in the mirror past tears, when the young sadist who'd been torturing her finally dropped her lash and buried her face between the throbbing, burning, pulsing, mounds she'd been whipping.

Hands trailing down Jenny's body, the aristocrat dropped to her knees, her tongue darting inside Jenny's pussy without hesitation now. Desperately hot from her whipping, dripping wet, Jenny came almost instantly, throwing back her head and shrieking ecstasy into her mouth-filling gag. The Lady's belt-computer probably announced Jenny's orgasm, but her victim was too overwhelmed by sensation to notice.

As she hung panting in her bonds, she was barely aware of the teenager rearranging her restraints to start with. Jenny squealed, a long, drawn-out, rising wail of distress as fingers sank painfully deep into her abused breasts, and twisted. Her legs had been pulled up behind her on two separate winches, spread wide, and now she hung facedown in her bonds.

"I love your udders," the proud apprentice-sadist said gaily, all hesitation gone now. "All my girls are going to have huge, heavy tits, just like these, for me to torture."

She used the electric winches to pull Jenny's legs higher and higher still, and then Jenny's arms were lowered and her wrists unhooked from the original pulley, so that she was now hanging totally upside-down. Jenny groaned in pained delight as an unfamiliar device selected from a display-case was pushed into her anus. The usual elongated, pear-shaped, butt-plug seemed to be mounted on one end of a U-shaped hook, a ring at the other end. An anal-hook?

It was! Jenny's still cuffed wrists were pulled back behind her head and tightly secured between her shoulder-blades to the hook's ring with a short length of rope. No matter how hard she pulled against the restraint, she just tugged the device deeper into her own back-passage.

Jenny couldn't help a little shiver of anticipation when she saw the candle, trained to enjoy the stinging bite of hot wax by Lady Isobell and her owner. The birthday-girl pushed the fat shaft deep into her defencelessly spread pussy, the candle, soft and warm, sliding inside her easily. She heard a match flare, then there was the unmistakable smell of sulphur.

Having the insides of her thighs whipped was new, and excruciatingly painful, but the added spice of hot wax dripping down onto her sex as she jerked, twisted and gasped, hanging upside-down from her ankles, only fanned the raging heat in her belly. Jenny shrieked, twisting away and up, as molten wax ran inside her pussy, the familiar sting, burning painfully hotter for just that one delicious second, further intensified on delicate flesh.

Again and again. Crack! A new mark on her flesh, a gag-muffled squeal, helplessly twisting this way and that in her bonds and yanking the anal-plug deeper into her ass as she squirmed; and then the delicious agony burning into her sex. Jenny wailed in mingled pain, animal-lust and humiliated despair as the whip hissed through the air again.

Not just a budding sadist, but an inventive one, she was belatedly discovering.

The girl dropped down to her knees again, licking Jenny's

whip-tender breasts, sucking and biting on her swollen, throbbing, nipples. Pleasure overwhelmed Jenny; consuming her, earthing in groin and chewed nipples, her sex clenching tight around the candle tormenting her. Her orgasm left her panting, shattered, leaving her passive, waiting with blank-minded acceptance of what was to come. This time she recovered quickly enough to hear the metallic voice of the computer monitoring the surgically implanted sensors at her temples, telling the teenager that her plaything had come again.

The candle removed, Jenny was lowered back to the floor and her ankles released. At a snap of the birthday-girl's fingers, she struggled back to her feet and stood where the teenager pointed. Presenting her naked, whip-marked, sweat-gleaming body for inspection; her shoes' padlocked ankle-straps touching, arms still pulled back over her head, wrists between her shoulder-blades, still secured to the anal-hook.

"Cunt!" the girl ordered, having obviously been advised by someone the normal method of obedience-testing a sex-toy.

Jenny stepped forward and pressed her wax-covered pussy into a waiting palm.

"Tits!"

Without hesitation she dropped to her knees and pushed the heavy globes into waiting hands.

"Good toy. Stand!"

Jenny scrambled back to her feet, eager to be used further, she realised.

"I want a massage now. You know how to do that?"

Jenny nodded subserviently. A slave-massage was quite simple in theory. A slave-girl, with her arms bound behind her in some way, had to squirm on her belly in a tray of aromatic massage-oil, and then use her body instead of hands to massage the owner. Sometimes astride the owner, sometimes kneeling beside her, dipping herself back in the tray for a fresh coat of oil as necessary. But she'd only ever done it once before.

The beautiful young aristocrat completed a delighted inspection of the welts she'd left on her plaything's skin, eyes sparkling bright. Ordering Jenny to turn in place with a leisurely turn of one finger, so that she could see the end of the anal-hook pulled up hard between Jenny's buttocks, the eighteen year old finally nodded to herself, and removed Jenny's stiletto heels.

Jenny knelt, and then squirmed herself into the tray of massage-oil. Getting herself back upright on the slippery oil with her wrists pulled back between her shoulder-blades, was almost impossible, the birthday-girl watching her desperate struggles with a faint smile. Jenny eventually just had to roll out of the tray onto the carpet to get her knees under her, knowing she'd be punished for staining the deep pile.

The young Lady lay face-up or face-down, as she wished, on a low table, Jenny squirming, sliding and pushing her body up against her. Sometimes sitting astride her, rubbing her crotch up and down her body, sometimes kneeling beside the aristocrat, trailing her breasts up and down the girl's naked body. Though her boobs were still sore from the whipping, Jenny was still careful to push her flesh hard against the girl, the heavy mounds slipping and sliding in oil, flattened and squeezed. As she'd been told by her legal owner, she'd been given huge tits for a reason, and it had nothing to do with her own comfort.

"Oh that's nice. Keep rubbing your nipple-rings on my clit. Harder! Ooooh, that's nice! Good pony."

Kneeling beside the sweet-voiced virgin, Jenny docilely pushed down harder, her anal-hook dragging deeper into her back-passage every time she leant forward, her breasts gliding across the girl's stomach and thighs on a layer of aromatic oil.

"Now astride me again!"

Awkward with her arms pulled back behind her head, her whole body slippery, Jenny swung a thigh over the girl's body again. Feeling one of her knees slipping under her, there was nothing she could do. She came down heavily on the teenager's stomach!

"Ooof! Clumsy bitch!"

Sitting astride the naked aristocrat, the spoilt well-bred young Miss now totally at ease in control of an older sexual-slave, Jenny held herself obediently still as her breasts were slapped again, the whip-marked, love-bite covered melons swinging and quivering with each blow. The birthday-girl's palm cracking on her flesh was louder than before, stinging far worse, her breasts already sore. Jenny gasped behind her gag with each slap.

"Good pony! You really enjoy being disciplined, don't you?" the eighteen year old said in tones of pleased, but smug, surprise.

Jenny belatedly realised she'd been rubbing her crotch against the naked aristocrat's in time with her slaps. The girl held up Jenny's reddened breasts by the nipple rings for inspection, their tips cruelly stretched with the full weight of both large globes hanging from the small rings set through her flesh.

"Carry on," the teenager decided.

Jenny lay full length down on her young tormentor, sliding her whip-tender belly across hers and gripping with whip-burned thighs, as well as squeezing and rubbing her tortured breasts between their bodies. Deliberately she yanked the anal-hook her bound wrists were secured to deeper inside herself now. The birthday-girl was clearly sexually aroused by her slave-massage; but Jenny was being driven mad with lust, desperate to be allowed to come again.

"Oooh, nice!" the aristocrat breathed softly.

She abruptly reached up behind Jenny's neck and under her chin, to unbuckle the large orange ball filling her plaything's mouth.

"Lick me!"

Jenny slipped back, sitting between the aristocrat's thighs on her heels, but her anal-hook didn't let her bend that far forward. Hurriedly, seeing a petulant frown marring the

223

birthday-girl's lovely face, Jenny squirmed back off the table and pushed her face between firm thighs, her upper body lying on the table.

As she lightly licked, all she could taste to start with was the aromatic massage-oil, slightly bitter, the teenage virgin jerking as if shocked at the first touch of Jenny's lips; and then ramming Jenny's head down with two handfuls of hair. When her tongue delicately probed deeper into the eighteen year old's tight sex, Jenny found sweetness, the young sadist sighing in contentment.

"I think I'm going to come!" she called.

Jenny, far more experienced, didn't think so, but obligingly licked up between her sex-lips in a long, slow, broad, stroke to her clitoris, and then nibbled, tongued and sucked the tender nub.

"Yes, yes, yes!" the aristocrat squeaked.

Jenny closed her lips over the girl's pussy, breathing hot on her flesh, tongue probing deeper. Applying all the, expertise she'd gained wearing a collar to the task of giving her torturer pleasure.

"Oh yes..."

The girl's pussy spasmed, her juices jetting into Jenny's mouth. Surprised, but too well-trained to pull away, Jenny swallowed, breathing hot onto the teenager's pussy, tonguing her clitoris. She'd heard of female ejaculation, knew from her own experience that dripping-wet could be an accurate description, but it was still a first.

For both of them apparently. The birthday-girl yanked Jenny's head aside with a handful of hair and lay panting, her breathing gradually slowing, for what seemed like ages. Jenny lay half on the table beside her, apparently forgotten. Finally she sat up, pulling Jenny to her knees on the floor and straddling her to force her ball-gag back into Jenny's mouth from behind. The familiar orange ball was buckled back into place, cruelly tight.

"Oh Pony, I'm never going to forget you. People tell you;

you read books, but you just can't imagine how good your first slave is going to be. I'm never going to masturbate again!"

All inhibitions long gone now, the birthday-girl fucked Jenny doggie-style and then spread-eagled across a bed using a strap-on-dildo. For a revitalising break, she had Jenny harnessed, bridled and hitched to a pony-trap, and then trotted and pranced her to exhaustion touring the estate. In the afternoon, Jenny, bound and mostly gagged, was again screwed and made to lick the aristocrat's pussy. In between sex, there was humiliation, experiments with bondage, and pain; Jenny forced to beg and squeal while the young sadist investigated the results of electric shocks applied to various points on her voluptuous, helplessly bound, anatomy.

Finally, at the end of an exhausting day, Jenny was butt-fucked with the aristocrat's strap-on one last time, tied face-down on the bed with her breasts in a tight cat's-cradle of rope. Her teenage torturer, finally satisfied, flopped down limp on top of Jenny's body one last time.

"Computer? How many times did Pony come?"

"Please clarify," the machine said in its soft metallic tone.

"How many time did the monitored slave come?" the birthday-girl asked in exasperation.

"Slave 673 has achieved 37 orgasms since monitoring began," the machine responded.

"Good pony," Franklin's goddaughter said, rolling off Jenny's tightly tied-down body and patting a buttock.

She lifted Jenny's head with a handful of thick, now-tangled, hair.

"Are you for sale?" the eighteen year old asked.

Still gagged, but knowing Mistress Phillips-Webber didn't plan to keep her, Jenny could only nod obediently one last time. Cruel, hungry, calculating eyes, regarded her speculatively.

***

Jenny stood upright in the display case, forced by the straps that bound her to a rigid attention. The first strap was around her forehead, the next around her neck, dozens around her body and arms and legs. Slaves, servants, soldiers and Lords and Ladies passed, some without appearing to notice her, the more unhurried aristocrats often pausing to admire the displayed sexual playthings. If she took a really deep breath, she could just get her much-abused nipples to touch the glass. That provided amusement for about five seconds.

She was bored!

Say what you liked about being a sex-toy and undergoing sexual torture, at least it wasn't dull. Lady Isobell gave the marks on her body a faint approving smile about mid-morning, but it was after lunch before anyone took a real interest in her.

Franklin's god-daughter taking her leave while two soldiers stacked a mountain of luggage into a waiting limousine, saw Jenny, who had been put there specifically for her, and pulled her unresisting mother over to the display case. Once again transformed from cruel, sadistic, Mistress to bubbly teenager, she ebulliently pulled open the display-case door, babbling happily. Her indulgent parent, wearing a fond but proud smile and handling Jenny as her daughter directed, agreed, that yes, the naked plaything on display had velvet skin, pretty eyes, very nice tits, and obviously loved sex.

"...and then I hung her upside-down to whip the insides of her thighs, and when she jerked, the candle I put in her snatch dribbled hot wax all over her! She was crying and begging, but she liked it really, because the computer said she came when I was chewing on her nipples! See how fat they are? You can get three electrodes on them at once, and she just comes and comes again, even when I wired up her clit. Have you ever spanked a toy until your hand was sore, Mummy?"

"Once or twice, darling."

"I did it just like Daddy said. Sex only after I'd tortured her hot and docile, and I never let her out of her restraints once!"

"You've marked her up nicely. My little girl all grown up! Did you let her lick you, or did you just use dildos on her?"

"Both! I think she really liked being ridden by me actually. She kept rubbing herself up against me, putting her tits in my hands, and kissing my feet and licking her juices off the strap-on-dildo whenever her gag wasn't in. Do you think she loves me?"

"Oh, I expect she's just well-trained, darling. Remember, we call them toys for a reason. Slave-sluts like this don't feel love like real people. She just wants to be kept in chains, fucked, and have her tits slapped occasionally. Like any rutting animal, she's controlled by her instincts, not reason like you and I."

"But Uncle Samuel has a pet?"

"I'm not saying they can't be trained to be affectionate," the girl's mother said, closing the display-case door, "But it takes more than a single...."

Jenny was once again left in the quiet of her glass box. She still didn't know the inventive and enthusiastic young sadist's name, but did know that she had a strawberry birthmark on her thigh. She was quite familiar with the taste of her pussy, and knew that she liked the gagged slave she was playing with to be loud. She was also quite keen on electricity as a means of obedience-training and foreplay. Jenny was a little hurt that the girl had never bothered to use her name once, only wanting to know it for her diary, Jenny responding to "Pony" throughout her sexual trial.

Strangely enough, her feelings for the eighteen-year-old Lady still hadn't changed in the slightest. She couldn't even imagine hating her; just envied the lovely girl her freedom, was jealous that she could exercise sexual choice, and coveted her legal right to pick this or that sex-slave to use for her pleasure.

***

The bride looked radiant in white, her four-wheeled carriage pulled by four now-identical, frisky, prancing, show-ponies. The heavy-breasted, dildo-stuffed slave-girls had gold rings set in their flesh and white plumes on their bridles. The Master-at-Arms in ornate dress uniform drove the carriage himself, his whip cracking in the air, but leaving the well-trained team's hindquarters unmarked. Jenny had been one of the carriage-slaves for the rehearsal. A trembler switch in the base of the whip-handle delivered a remote-controlled shock to the ponies' battery filled dildos each time he swung it.

The wedding was of course a major social event, the Franklins being an old, established family, and the guest-list was huge, the ceremonies conducted under awnings outside. In the evening the reception spread through most of the lower floors of Franklin House and out onto the lawns. The happy couple received a total of seventeen slaves as wedding presents, twelve girls and five boys, which were hung naked from their wrists from the balcony above the great hall for all to admire. Scattered throughout the party, household slaves chained on their knees in curtained alcoves, provided oral-sex for guests in need of a little light relief.

Jenny had been pressed into service as a serving-slave, wearing her now-familiar and comfortable uniform of ball-gag, high collar, tight waspie-corset and 5" heels. Just the way her owner liked her best. Her arms were folded neatly behind her wrist to elbow, held there by gently swinging chains running around her body from wrist-cuffs to nipple-rings. She pulled a small serving-trolley loaded down with drinks and canapés with a dildo-prong.

The trolley ran on four silent wheels, the front two turning by means of the T-bar that ran forward and curved up into Jenny's prong, a pressure-pad built into its surface. All she had to do was walk slowly along, pause when somebody wanted to help themselves or examine her nudity, and the trolley would follow along behind. When there was no longer enough weight on the trolley's pressure-sensor her dildo would deliver a shock deep inside her dripping pussy, and she knew to go to the kitchens for a reload.

Jenny's freedom to roam through the reception at will was

of course a privilege, the Master-at-Arms had explained to her, and she would be punished if she abused it. Pulling a serving trolley was usually a job for a more experienced slave—the docile Pretty was on the other side of the hall having her breasts squeezed—but the Master of the cellblock had been impressed with Jenny's endurance and enthusiasm when he'd finally got around to sampling her sexually for himself. She'd walked the garden paths in the cool night air, watched couples dance in the ballroom, and pulled her trolley in and out of most of the open ground-floor rooms, being groped, stroked and admired as she went.

The Master-at-Arms had been right. It was a privilege, the most freedom of choice she'd had since being enslaved, and more than many girls in her position saw in years. In many ways it was like a normal party. People were chatting, gossiping, telling tales and exchanging scandal; making new friends, meeting old ones and trying to pick each other up. And then she would turn a corner and see naked, bound, slaves having sex on a stage, while aristocrats sipped drinks, nibbled snacks and mocked their technique.

"Stand, slut!" she was ordered, a hand landing on her backside with a crack.

Jenny obediently put her ankles together and looked directly forward.

Unseen guests helping themselves to the choice on her trolley discussed her, every aristocrat considering themselves an expert on slave-flesh. Not dainty enough to be a show-pony, tits too big to hunt. Obviously a pillow-slave, but powerful enough to be a carriage-pony. Nice and juicy though, wasn't she? Obviously liked her dildo.

"Carry on," she was ordered, making a half-dozen metres before she was stopped again.

"Now see these are excellent tits," a hundred year old Lord announced, his fingers sinking into the heavy globes he was squeezing together. Jenny moaned softly. "This is what that little redhead of yours should look like. Don't see enough tits this heavy these days."

"Oh Granddad," a young Lord protested. "Huge tits just aren't fashionable, and Silky's a hunter!"

"Never slowed my hunters down. Feel that. Go on, give them a squeeze. You tell me that isn't heavenly?"

Jenny bit hard into the gag filling her mouth, drooling helplessly, nipples rigid as the young noble lifted her breasts out of his grandfather's hands, a fire raging in her loins. God, the kid was younger than she was, Jenny realised! The birthday-girl had been bad enough, but that had been a special occasion, and as well, she'd been beautiful. A free woman could be attracted to her, the old Jenny might have, but she wouldn't have given this spotty kid the time of day! She had a sudden vision of her future; a mature woman, another year older, catching the eye of a succession of new birthday-girls and boys! From her point of view, her users were only going to get younger!

"I don't know," the young Lord said dubiously, hefting Jenny's breasts. "I really prefer slave-boys. I really just bought Silky so I'd have a girl to share with Marie."

Mistress Phillips-Webber; Franklin now, danced most of the night away, but found time in the midnight hours to have a soldier lead Jenny before her. She stroked, probed and squeezed, Jenny dildo-impaled and with her wrist-cuffs chained to her nipples, standing unresisting, told by her owner, this was the way she always wanted to remember her.

She had the soldier tie a pink ribbon tightly around each breast, a bow resting on the top of each now-bulging mound, another ribbon tied around her neck, bow at her throat, and a broader ribbon and bow tied around her waist. She gave Jenny's dildo-stuffed belly one last pat, and then led her by a nipple ring through the party in search of Lady Isobell.

"Isobell. I know you like her. I want you to have her. A present from me for making me feel so welcome and helping to arrange the wedding."

"Really?"

"Yes. I hope you enjoy her as much as I have."

"Thank you, I will," Jenny's new owner said, clearly delighted. "This is really very kind of you."

Mistress Franklin smiled shyly, the small gathering around them clapping politely at her generous gesture, and mostly wandering off with her. Lady Isobell was left contentedly stroking her prize's behind with a few friends remaining.

"Carriage-pony or pillow-slave?" asked a friend.

"Maybe neither," Jenny's owner grinned. "We'll have to see what she can do."

Her free hand stroked Jenny's belly, toying with her pubic curls, head impulsively ducking forward to plant a kiss on one of the over-large breasts she liked so much.

"First she needs a tan. A nice light gold. And a much longer fringe as well. Perhaps a pierced tongue?" The aristocrat was speaking softly, more to herself than her friends, Jenny realised. "And I'll have to think about a pussy-lock. I wonder how big a dildo you can really take," she said speculatively, looking from the trolley's prong to Jenny's eyes "Oh, we're going to have such fun, you and I."

Jenny wasn't as delighted to be the aristocrat's property as the woman who now owned her clearly was, but she wasn't exactly in tears about it either, she was quite shocked to discover.

Unbidden, the image came to mind. The broken-in, trained, horse, pricking up its ears, eager to be ridden, seeing its owner approaching with saddle and bridle, crop in hand and spurs on boots. Jenny gave a little whinny of pleasure as her Mistress stroked her.

The aristocrat ducked into a study and reappeared with a tag which she fastened to Jenny's collar. She of course couldn't see it, but assumed, hoped, it was something along the lines of PRIVATE PROPERTY—NOT TO BE SCREWED WITHOUT OWNER'S PERMISSION.

Guests still continued to grope her as she continued on her rounds through house and grounds.

A couple of hours or so later, the happy-couple set off on their honeymoon, Jenny just able to see the travel-cages containing Pretty, Sarah and Charles strapped onto the limousine's roof over the heads of the crowd of well-wishers. The party was definitely winding down by the time the happy-couple left, less dancing now, some guests preparing to leave themselves, others scattered in chairs, glasses and cigars in hand. Jenny was roped into a party-game.

A kindly looking older Lady grabbed her as she passed and used a thick, black marker-pen to draw target-circles on Jenny's buttocks and belly, then two more around the areola on her breasts, finally pulling a prey-slave's visor over her eyes. Jenny was sent to the kitchen for a reload and told to remain within the house from now on.

She squeaked at the first sharp pinprick, unexpected as well as painful, another then another, quickly following. Jenny didn't realise what was happening, stung several more times, until she saw a pearl-wearing matron raise a small blow-pipe, aim it at her chest and then send a dart speeding on its way with a huff of air. Another pin stuck itself in her flesh. The game was mostly played by older aristocrats, but a few youngsters not feeling up to the exertion of moonlight pony-racing joined in. Jenny moaned in pleasure when she saw herself in a hall mirror, her juices running down thighs again, two more darts stinging her breasts even as she admired herself. A half dozen or so red and blue tufted darts were already decorating the heavy globes, three red tufts on the firm swell of her belly, ten or so of both colours decorating her backside.

Jenny pulled her dildo-trolley slowly, not having to pause, because as a human-target, the delicacies on her trolley were being given a wide birth by guests. An audible puff from behind was accompanied by another small dart burying itself in her flesh—she'd always hated injections as well—she whimpered in fearful lust as she saw a young Lady raise a blowpipe to her lips. The dart was actually deflected by a nipple-ring with an audible click.

Arms still neatly folded behind her, the chains linking her nipple-rings to her wrist-cuffs swinging harder against her sides, huge breasts quivering as she gasped, Jenny's hands clenched into tight fists as another dart drove home. Panting around her ball-gag was making her drool more than ever, and she still had to lean into the weight of the trolley with her dildo-prong. Jenny wailed in mingled delight and pain as a dart embedded itself in one of her pussy-lips.

Most of the shots were at least in the outer target circles, but a few went astray, Jenny taking occasional pinpricks to thighs, body and arms. But most of the aristocrats, perhaps through long practice, were relentlessly accurate, her areola looking like red and blue tufted pincushions in the next mirror. Erect, swollen nipples, aching with excitement, rose up through the darts' coloured flights, as yet, unpierced.

Speak of the devil and he appears!

Jenny squeaked in anguished delight as a dart drove its short pin directly into one rigid nipple. A grey-haired ancient lowered his blowpipe with a pleased grin, as fellow drink or cigar-holding players congratulated him.

After completing a circuit of the house's lower floors, in the central hall, a gasping, trembling, desperately hot, Jenny was examined by the Master-at-Arms. Red darts were the Lords, blue, their Ladies. Target centre or areola, was 10 points, inner circle 5, outer circle 2 points.

"My Lords and Ladies," the Master-at-Arm's finally announced after the count. "The Lords, 207 points. The Ladies, 191. First match to the gentlemen."

A full breasted blonde, target-circles already drawn ready on her flesh, looked with wide eyes at the coloured tufts of the darts' flights decorating Jenny's body, steel pins embedded in flesh. She was sent on her way with a slap on the behind, the next game-piece!

A familiar bound slave-boy was set to pulling out the thin, tufted, pins from Jenny's body with his teeth so that she could be used again. His lips lingered deliciously on her dildo-stuffed pussy, tongue brushing her clitoris as he pulled out the dart that had strayed. Jenny couldn't help a wail of ecstasy as she came, probably getting the slave-boy into trouble, but the Master-at-Arms' pet owed her one anyway.

Her new owner returned to collect her before she could be made to walk the course again, Lady Isobell ordering another girl mounted on the trolley and leading Jenny upstairs to one of her studies. Jenny was bent forward over a desk, a chain looped through her nipple-rings to hold her down, and her ball-gag removed. Jenny absently licked her lips as the aristocrat placed a wire-trailing headband on her head, sticking sensors to either side of her throat.

"Private party, lover?" asked a cultured, male voice from behind her.

Jenny's owner nodded agreement, settling herself in the chair in front of the desk, placing a box in front of her and sliding her hands under heavy breasts. A hand slid lightly over Jenny's behind, but properly, her eyes never left her owner.

"This is a lie-detector, Jenny," Lady Isobell told her nodding to the box between them. It was plain, black plastic, a single light on top of it glowing red then green when tested. "I'm going to ask you some questions. Reply instantly, understood?"

"Yes Mistress," Jenny breathed, her voice sounding strained, hoarse, after so long without speaking except in whispers to other slaves.

"Is this the one you've had your eye on?" the man asked. "Got hold of her at last?"

"Yes, all mine! Isn't she gorgeous?" Lady Isobell said with glowing pride.

"Quite nice, I suppose," the unseen man agreed.

"My fiancé, Lord Percy," the aristocrat told Jenny. "He fucks you whenever he likes, understood?"

"Yes Mistress," Jenny agreed, a green light glowing on the lie detector.

"Actually, do you mind?" the man asked.

Jenny's owner nodded agreement, and immediately a meat shaft was plunged into her sex, Jenny crying out in pleasure as she was penetrated. The man settled his hands onto her hips and began to pump into her with a slow, steady rhythm.

"Concentrate on me, Jenny!" Lady Isobell demanded.

"Yes Mistress," Jenny gasped.

"Do you find me attractive?"

"Oh...Oh! Yes Mistress!"

"Do you love me?"

"I...I..." the light flickered red for a second, "...I hope to learn to Mistress. I want to please you more than anything."

Green. The aristocrat gave her breasts an approving squeeze, Jenny lying on her belly now, legs widespread, the heavy mounds flattened in Lady Isobell's hands. Behind, the unseen man continued to remorselessly fuck her.

"You like having big, huge tits for me to play with, don't you?"

"Ah, ah...oh God yes...Mistress!" Jenny gasped.

"And the other improvements I made to you?"

"Yes Mistress!" Jenny shrieked, lust and pleasure driving her to distraction.

The light glowed red.

"Jenny!" the aristocrat warned in a low snarl, "You don't ever lie to me. Not even if you think you're sparing my feelings or pleasing me. Never! Now I want you to tell me, and mean it, that you are never going to lie to me again!"

"I'll...I'll never lie to you again as long as I live, Mistress," she moaned in pleasure.

Meaning every word of it, the light glowed green again! The man shafting her gave her a few encouraging slaps, Jenny's hips bucking and twisting, thrusting back against his thrusts.

"Now what don't you like about the improvements I made to you?" her owner coaxed.

"The drugs scare me," she gasped, "I worry about becoming

a mindless robot. Losing my individuality."

Lady Isobell nodded. "Now truthfully mind, you hung about the lab on your side after you'd shut down the Gate, hoping there'd be some way back, didn't you?"

"Yes Mistress," Jenny groaned, the man behind her, cock deep inside her, reaching under her to yank pubic hair in time with his thrusts, his free hand in her hair now.

"And you wanted to be a slave right from the start?"

"Almost the start, Mistress. I was afraid," Jenny whimpered, rammed down harder on the desk by faster, body-rocking thrusts.

Squeaking helplessly with each thrust now, her owner's fingernails sinking deeper into her breasts forced Jenny to stay focused on the aristocrat's eyes.

"You know, my new step-mother—a quite brilliant woman—thinks it may be possible to force a Gate from just one side, not two having to link. Theoretically. I might be able to send you home."

"Please don't send me back, Mistress!" Jenny blurted out, without thought.

The light glowed green, Lady Isobell laughing in delight.

"Good puppy! You can come now," the aristocrat told her, stroking breasts now, having heard all that she needed to.

No longer required to focus on her Mistress, Jenny let sensation overwhelm her. She came again, and again, and again.

***

She woke slowly, sleepy and relaxed, in her owner's bed. Facedown, wrists chained to the headboard above her. Lady Isobell lay snuggled up against her, one thigh over Jenny's leg, a small hand under one of her breasts. She held herself carefully still, breathing deliberately slowly and deeply, enjoying the moment of tranquillity and comfort, no gag, not even a collar around her neck, her naked body totally and luxuriantly unadorned. Besides, the penalty for a slavegirl bed-warmer waking her Mistress was twelve of the best, and her backside was already on intimate terms with a wide variety of canes, crops, paddles, tawses, cats and floggers.

Jenny didn't kid herself that a lie-in was going to make any difference to the day's exertions; she was just enjoying the moment. Today, she'd been told, she would be driven as a pony-girl by an owner for the first time; and would notice the difference, Lady Isobell had promised ominously. And having already seen her owner drive pony-girls, knowing the aristocrat's exacting standards, she was very afraid she wouldn't be capable of the total surrender, loyal resilience and frisky sex-appeal required. But she didn't just exist for sex, and knew she would have to learn. A faint throbbing pain in her earlobe reminded her of last night's excesses.

Moving very carefully so as not to disturb the woman who'd tired herself enjoying Jenny's bound body until the early hours, she turned her head to look at the bedside mirror. Her new owner had used a punch to painfully pierce her earlobe, and had snapped into place a pet's nametag, now hanging like an earring. No, the mirror was too far away to make out the back-to-front letters.

It wasn't until the day after that Jenny discovered her new name was Treasure.

THE END

THE SLAVEWORLD SERIES
ROYAL SLAVE
STEPHEN DOUGLAS

The deliciously beautiful 'Treasure' is a slave to the royal family that rules over and alternative England where a slave-owning aristocracy has held sway for two thousand years. As the story opens she is the property of Prince Samuel, but his mother, the Queen, has designs on her; and there are others who appreciate Treasure's unique qualities. Rivalry within the family looms and even Treasure dreams of escape, despite her love of Slavery. But when Treasure's true identity becomes known to the Queen, the Slaveworld's attention turns to this world, where there could be many more Treasures!

'Royal Slave' will delight readers new to Stephen Douglas as well as the many who enjoyed 'Slaveworld'

SLAVE SCHOOL
STEPHEN DOUGLAS

In a secret government department girls are trained in submissiveness so they can accompany agents to The Slaveworld. But once there, will they be able to blend into the ancient slave-owning aristocracy which holds sway over that alternative reality? The price of discovery is terrifyingly high - a lifetime as the legally owned sexual plaything of a dominant class that has been steeped in the ways of cruelty and arrogance for generations.

Once again Stephen Douglas successfully combines superb eroticism with an unforgettable story. 'Slave School' will further enhance his reputation as a brilliant exponent of SM erotica.

SLAVEWORLD EMBASSY
STEPHEN DOUGLAS

Clandestine diplomatic relations have been established between this world and the Slaveworld - a world where the Roman legions never left England and a slave-owning aristocracy has held sway ever since.

Now the Slaveworld nobles are becoming aware that girls from this reality react very favourably to their surgically implanted aphrodisiac, and they want more of them! The captured agents from our world are proving to be enthusiastic and compliant toys but the nobles' appetites are insatiable.

Meanwhile, the ambassador to the Slaveworld is enjoying every second of his new posting and is keen to help in any way he can.......

The Slaveworld saga continues with all the style and ingenuity Stephen Douglas's many fans have come to expect.